A MAID OF MANY MOODS

BY
VIRNA SHEARD

A Maid Of Many Moods

I

It was Christmas Eve, and all the small diamond window panes of One Tree Inn, the half-way house upon the road from Stratford to Shottery, were aglitter with light from the great fire in the front room chimney-place and from the many candles Mistress Debora had set in their brass candlesticks and started a-burning herself. The place, usually so dark and quiet at this time of night, seemed to have gone off in a whirligig of gaiety to celebrate the Noel-tide.

In vain had old Marjorie, the housekeeper, scolded. In vain had Master Thornbury, who was of a thrifty and saving nature, followed his daughter about and expostulated. She only laughed and waved the lighted end of the long spill around his broad red face and bright flowered jerkin.

"Nay, Dad!" she had cried, teasing him thus, "I'll help thee save thy pennies to-morrow, but to-night I'm of another mind, and will have such a lighting up in One Tree Inn the rustics will come running from Coventry to see if it be really ablaze. There'll not be a candle in any room whatever without its own little feather of fire, not a dip in the kitchen left dark! So just save thy breath to blow them out later."

"Come, mend thy saucy speech, thou'lt light no more, I tell thee," blustered the old fellow, trying to reach the spill which the girl held high above her head. "Give over thy foolishness; thou'lt light no more!"

"Ay, but I will, then," said she wilfully, "an' 'tis but just to welcome Darby, Dad dear. Nay, then," waving the light and laughing, "don't thou dare catch it. An' I touch thy fringe o' pretty hair, dad—thy only ornament, remember—'twould be a fearsome calamity! I' faith! it must be most time for the coach, an' the clusters in the long room not yet lit. Hinder me no more, but go enjoy thyself with old Saddler and John Sevenoakes. I warrant the posset is o'erdone, though I cautioned thee not to leave it."

"Thou art a wench to break a man's heart," said Thornbury, backing away and shaking a finger at the pretty figure winding fiery ribbons and criss-crosses with her bright-tipped wand. "Thou art a provoking wench, who doth need locking up and feeding on bread and water. Marry, there'll be naught for thee on Christmas, and thou canst whistle for the ruff and silver buckles I meant to have given thee. Aye, an' for the shoes with red heels." Then with dignity, "I'll snuff out some o' the candles soon as I go below."

"An' thou do, dad, I'll make thee a day o' trouble on the morrow!" she called after him. And well he knew she would. Therefore, it was with a disturbed mind that he entered the sitting-room and went towards the hearth to stir the simmering contents of the copper pot on the crane.

John Sevenoakes and old Ned Saddler, his nearest neighbours and friends, sat one each side of the fire in their deep rush-bottomed chairs, as they sat at least five nights out of the week, come what weather would. Sevenoakes held a small child, whose yellow, curly head nodded with sleep. The hot wine bubbled up as the inn-keeper stirred it and the little spiced apples, brown with cloves, bobbed madly on top.

"It hath a savoury smell, Thornbury," remarked Saddler. "Methinks 'tis most ready to be lifted."

"'Twill not be lifted till Deb hears the coach," answered Sevenoakes. "'Twas so she timed it. 'On it goes at nine,' quoth she, 'an' off it comes at ten, Cousin John. Just when Darby will be jumping from the coach an' running in. Oh! I can't wait for the hour to come!' she says."

"She's a headstrong, contrary wench as ever heaven sent a man," put in Thornbury, straightening himself. "'Twere trouble saved an' I'd broken her in long ago."

"'Twas she broke thee in long ago," said Saddler, rubbing his knotty hands. "She hath led thee by the ear since she was three years old. An' I had married now, an' had such a lass, I'd a brought her up different, I warrant. Zounds! 'tis a show to see. She coaxes thee, she bullies thee, she comes it over thee with cajolery and blandishments an' leads thee a pretty dance."

"Thou art an old fool," returned Thornbury, mopping his face, which was sorely scorched, "What should thou know of the bringing up of wenches? Thou—a crabbed bachelor o' three score an' odd. Thou hast no way with children;—i' truth I've heard Will Shakespeare say the tartness of that face o' thine would sour ripe grapes."

Sevenoakes trotted the baby gently up and down, a look of troubled apprehension disturbing his usually placid features. His was ever the office of peace-maker between these two ancient cronies, and he knew to a nicety the moment when it was wisest to try and adjust matters.

"'Tis well I mind the night this baby came," he began retrospectively, looking up as the door opened and a tall young fellow entered, stamping the snow off his long boots. "Marry, Nick! thou dost bring a lot o' cold in with thee," he ended briskly, shifting his chair. "Any news o' the coach?"

"None that I've heard," replied the man, going to the hearth and turning his broad back to the fire. "'Tis a still night, still and frosty, but no sound of the horn or wheels reached me though I stood a-listening at the cross-roads. Then I turned down here an' saw how grandly thou had'st lit the house up to welcome Darby. My faith! I'll be glad to see him, for 'tis an age since he was home, Master Thornbury, an' he comes now in high feather. Not every lad hath wit and good looks enough to turn the head o' London after him. The stage is a great place for bringing a man out. Egad! I'm half minded to try it myself."

"I doubt not thou wilt, Nick, sooner or later; thou art a jack-o'-all-trades," answered Thornbury, in surly tones.

Nicholas Berwick laughed and shrugged his well-set shoulders, as he bent over and touched the child sleeping sweetly in old Sevenoakes' arms.

"What was't I heard thee saying o' the baby as I came in; he is not ailing, surely?"

"Not he!" answered Sevenoakes, stroking the moist yellow curls. "He's lusty as a year-old robin, an' as chirpy when he's awake; but he's in the land o' nod now, though his will was good to wait up for Darby like the rest of us."

"He's a rarely beautiful little lad," said Berwick. "I've asked Deb about him often, but she will tell me naught."

"I warrant she will na," piped up old Ned Saddler, in his reedy voice. "I warrant she will na; 'tis no tale for a young maid's repeating. Beshrew me! but the coach be late," he wound up irrelevantly.

"How came the child here?" persisted the young fellow, knocking back a red log with his foot. "An' it be such a tale as you hint, Saddler, I doubt not it's hard to keep it from slipping off thy tongue."

"'Tis a tale that slips off some tongue whenever this time o' year comes," answered Thornbury. "I desire no more Christmas Eves like that one four years back—please God! We were around the hearth as it might be now, and a grand yule log we had burning, I mind me; the room was trimmed gay an' fine with holly an' mistletoe as 'tis to-night. Saddler was there, Sevenoaks just where he be now, an' Deb sitting a-dreaming on the black oak settle yonder, the way she often sits, her chin on her hand—you mind, Nick!"

"Ay!" said the man, smiling.

"She wore her hair down then," went on Thornbury, "an' a sight it were to see."

"'Twere red as fox-fire," interrupted Saddler, aggrieved that the tale-telling had been taken from him. "When thou start'st off on Deb, Thornbury, thou know'st not where to bring up."

"An' Deb was sitting yonder on the oak settle," continued the innkeeper calmly.

"An' she had not lit the house up scandalously that year as 'tis now—for Darby was home," put in Saddler again.

"Ay! Darby was home—an' thou away, Nick—but the lad was worriting to try his luck on the stage in London, an' all on account o' a play little Judith Shakespeare lent him. I mind me 'twas rightly named, 'The Pleasant History o' the Taming o' a Shrew,' for most of it he read aloud to us. Ay, Darby was home, an' we were sitting here as it might be now, when the door burst open an' in come my lad carrying a bit of a baby muffled top an' toe in a shepherd's plaid. 'Twas crying pitiful and hoarse, as it had been long in the night wind."

"'Quick, Dad!' called Darby, 'Quick,' handing the bundle to Deb, 'there be a woman perished of cold not thirty yards from the house.'

"I tramped out after him saying naught. 'Twas a bitter night an' the road rang like metal under our feet. The country was silver-white with snow, an' the sky was sown thick with stars. Darby'd hastened on ahead an' lifted the wench in his arms, but I just took her from him an' carried her in myself. Marry! she were not much more weight than a child.

"We laid her near the fire and forced her to drink some hot sherry sack. Then she opened her eyes wild, raised herself and looked around in a sort o' terror, while she cried out for the baby. Deb brought it, an' the lass seemed content, for she smiled an' fell back on the pillow holding a bit of the shepherd's plaid tight in her small fingers.

"She was dressed in fashion of the Puritans, with kirtle of sad-coloured homespun. The only bright thing about her was her hair, and that curled out of the white coif she wore, golden as ripe corn.

"Well-a-day! I sent quickly for Mother Durley, she who only comes to a house when there be a birth or a death. I knew how 'twould end, for there was a look on the little wench's face that comes but once. She lived till break o' day and part o' the time she raved, an' then 'twas all o' London an' one she would go to find there; but, again she just lay quiet, staring open-eyed. At the last she came to herself, so said Mother Durley, an' there was the light of reason on her face. 'Twas then she beckoned Deb, who was sitting by, to bend down close, and she whispered something to her, though what 'twas we never knew, for my girl said naught—and even as she spoke the end came.

"Soul o' me! but we were at our wits' end to know what to do. Where she came from and who she was there was no telling, an' Deb raised such a storm when I spoke o' her being buried by the parish, that 'twas not to be thought of. One an' another came in to gaze at the little creature till the inn was nigh full. I bethought me 'twould mayhap serve to discover whom she might be. And so it fell. A lumbering yeoman passing through to Oxford stood looking at her a moment as she lay dressed the way we found her in the sad-coloured gown an' white coif.

"'Why! Od's pitikins!' he cried. 'Marry an' Amen! This be none but Nell Quinten! Old Makepeace Quinten's daughter from near Kenilworth. I'd a known her anywhere!'

"Then I bid Darby ride out to bring the Puritan in all haste, but he had the devil's work to get the man to come. He said the lass had shamed him, and he had turned her out months before. She was no daughter o' his he swore—with much quoting o' Scripture to prove he was justified in disowning her.

"Darby argued with him gently to no purpose; so my lad let his temper have way an' told the fellow he'd come to take him to One Tree Inn, an' would take him there dead or alive. The upshot was, they came in together before nightfall. The wench was in truth the old Puritan's daughter, and he took her home an' buried her. But for the child, he'd not touch it.

""Tis a living lie!' he cried. "Tis branded by Satan as his own! Give it to the Parish or to them that wants it, or marry, let it bide here! 'Tis a proper place for it in good sooth, for this be a public house where sinful drinking goeth on an' all worldly conversation. Moreover I saw one Master William Shakespeare pass out the door but now—a play actor, an' the maker o' ungodly plays.'Twas such a one who wrought my Nell's ruin!'

"So he went on an' moore o' the sort. Gra'mercy! I had the will to horsewhip him, an' but for the little dead maid I would. I clenched my hands hard and watched him away; he sitting stiff atop o' Stratford hearse by the driver. Thus he took his leave, calling back at me bits o' Holy Writ," finished Thornbury grimly.

"And Debora told naught of what the girl said at the last?" asked Nicholas Berwick. "That doth seem strange."

"Never a word, lad, beyond this much—she prayed her to care for the child till his father be found."

"By St. George! but that was no modest request. What had'st thou to say in the matter? Did'st take the heaven-sent Christmas box in good part, Master Thornbury?"

"Nay, Nick! thou should know him some better than to ask that," said Saddler. "Gadzooks, there were scenes! 'Twas like Thornbury to grandfather a stray infant now, was't not?" rubbing his knees and chuckling. "Marry! I think I see the face he wore for a full month. 'Twill go to the Parish!' he would cry, stamping around and speaking words 'twould pass me to repeat. 'A plague on't! Here be a kettle of fish! Why should the wench fall at my door in heaven's name? Egad! I am a much-put-upon man.' Ay, Nick, 'twas a marvellous rare treat to hear him."

"How came you to keep the child, sir?" asked Berwick, gravely.

The innkeeper shrugged his shoulders. "'Twas Deb would have it so," he answered. "She was fair bewitched by the little one. Thou knowest her way, Nick, when her heart is set on anything. Peradventure, I have humoured the lass too much, as Saddler maintains. But she coaxed and she cried, an' never did I see her cry so before, such a storm o' tears—save for rage," reflectively.

"Well put!" said Saddler. "Well put, Thornbury!"

"Ever had she wished for just such a one to pet, she pleaded, an' well I knew no small child came in sight o' the inn but Deb was after it for a plaything. Nay, there never was a stray beast about the place, that it did not find her and follow her close, knowing 'twould be best off so.

"Well do I mind her cuffing a big lad she found drowning some day-old kittens in the stable—and he minds it yet I'll gainsay! She fished out the blind wet things, an' gathering them in her quilted petticoat brought them in here a-dripping. I' fecks! she made such a moan over them as never was."

"Ay, Deb always has a following o' ugly, ill-begotten beasts that nobody wants but she," said Sevenoakes. "There be old Tramp for one now—did'st ever see such an ill-favoured beast? An' nowhere will he sit but fair on the edge o' her gown."

"He is a dog of rare discernment—and a lucky dog to boot," said Berwick.

"So, the outcome of it, Master Thornbury, was that the little lad is here."

"What could a man do?" answered Thornbury, ruefully. "Hark!" starting up as the old housekeeper entered the room, "Where be the lass, Marjorie? An' the candles—are they burning safe?"

"Safe, but growing to the half length," she answered, peering out of the window. "The coach must a-got overtipped, Maister."

"Where be Deb—I asked thee?"

"Soul o' me! then if thou must know, Mistress Debora hath just taken the great stable lantern and gone along the road to meet the coach. 'An' thou dost tell my father I'll pinch thee, Marjorie!' she cried back to me. 'When I love thee—I love thee; an' when I pinch—I pinch! So tell him not.' But 'tis over late an' I would have it off my mind, Maister."

"Did Tramp go with her?" asked Berwick, buttoning on his great cape and starting for the door.

"Odso! yes! an' she be safe enow. Thou'lt see the lantern bobbing long before thou com'st up with her."

"'Tis a wench to break a man's heart!" Thornbury muttered, standing at the door and watching the tall figure of Berwick swing along the road.

The innkeeper waited there though a light snow was powdering his scanty fringe of hair—white already—and lying in sparkles on his bald pate and holiday jerkin. He was a hardy old Englishman and a little cold was nought to him.

The night was frosty, and the "star-bitten" sky of a fathomless purple. About the inn the snow was tinted rosily from the many twinkling lights within.

The great oak, standing opposite the open door and stretching out its kindly arms on either side as far as the house reached, made a network of shadows that carpeted the ground like fine lace.

Thornbury bent his head to listen. Far off sounded the ripple of a girl's laugh. A little wind caught it up and it echoed—fainter—fainter. Then did his old heart take to thumping hard, and his breath came quick.

"Ay! they be coming!" he said half aloud. "My lad—an' lass. My lad—an' lass." He strained his eyes to see afar down the road if a light might not be swaying from side to side. Presently he spied it, a merry will-o'-the-wisp, and the sound of voices came to him.

So he waited tremblingly.

Darby it was who saw him first.

"'Tis Dad at the door!" he called, breaking away from Debora and Berwick.

The girl took a step to follow, then stopped and glanced up at the man beside her. "Let him go on alone, Nick," she said. "He hath not seen Dad close onto two years, an' this play-acting of his hath been a bitter dose for my father to swallow. In good sooth I have small patience with Dad, yet more am I sorry for him. I' faith! I would that maidens might also be in the play. Judith Shakespeare says some day they may be—but 'twill serve me little. One of us at that business is all Dad could bear with—an' my work is at home."

"Ay, Deb!" he answered; "thy work is at home, for now."

"For always," she answered, quickly; then, her tone changing, "think'st thou not, Nick, that my Darby is taller? An' did'st note how handsome?"

"He is a handsome fellow," answered Berwick. "Still, I cannot see that he hath grown. He will not be of large pattern."

"Marry!" cried the girl, "Darby is a good head taller than I. Where dost thou keep thine eyes, Nick?"

"Nay, verily, then, he is not," answered the other; "thou art almost shoulder to shoulder, an' still as much alike—I saw by the lantern—as of old, when save for thy dress 'twas a puzzle to say which was which. 'Tis a reasonable likeness, as thou art twins."

Debora pursed up her lips. "He is much taller than I," she said, determinedly. "Thou art no friend o' mine, Nicholas Berwick, an' thou dost cut three full inches off my brother's height. He is a head taller, an' mayhap more—so."

They were drawing up to the inn now, and through the window saw the little group about the fire, Darby with the baby, who was fully awake, perched high on his shoulder.

Berwick caught Deb gently, swinging her close to him, as they stood in the shadow of the oak.

"Ah, Deb!" he said, bending his face to hers, "thou could'st make me swear that black was white. As for Darby, the lad is as tall as thou dost desire. Thou hast my word for't."

"'Tis well thou dost own it," she said, frowning; "though I like not the manner o' it. Let me go, Nick."

"Nay, I will not," he said, passionately. "Be kind; give me one kiss for Christmas. I know thou hast no love for me; thou hast told me so often enough. I will not tarry here, Sweet; 'twould madden me—but give me one kiss to remember when I be gone."

She turned away and shook her head.

"Thou know'st me better than to ask it," she said, softly. "Kisses are not things to give because 'tis Christmas."

The man let go his hold of her, his handsome face darkening.

"Dost hate me?" he asked.

"Nay, then, I hate thee not," with a little toss of her head. "Neither do I love thee."

"Dost love any other? Come, tell me for love's sake, sweetheart. An' I thought so!"

"Marry, no!" she said. Then with a short, half-checked laugh, "Well—Prithee but one!"

"Ah!" cried Berwick, "is't so?"

"Verily," she answered mockingly. "It is so in truth, an' 'tis just Dad. As for Darby, I cannot tell what I feel for him. 'Twould be full as easy to say were I to put it to myself, 'Dost love Debora Thornbury?' 'Yea' or 'Nay,' for, Heaven knows, sometimes I love her mightily—and sometimes I don't; an' then 'tis a fearsome 'don't,' Nick. But come thee in."

"No!" answered Berwick, bitterly. "I am not one of you." Catching her little hands he held them a moment against his coat, and the girl felt the heavy beating of his heart before he let them fall, and strode away.

She stood on the step looking after the solitary figure. Her cheeks burned, and she tapped her foot impatiently on the threshold.

"Ever it doth end thus," she said. "I am not one of you," echoing his tone. "In good sooth no. Neither is old Ned Saddler or dear John Sevenoaks. We be but three; just Dad, an' Darby, an' Deb." Then, another thought coming to her. "Nay four when I count little Dorian. Little Dorian, sweet lamb,—an' so I will count him till I find his father."

A shade went over her face but vanished as she entered the room.

"I have given thee time to take a long look at Darby, Dad," she cried. "Is't not good to have him at home?" slipping one arm around her brother's throat and leaning her head against him.

"Where be the coach, truant?" asked Saddler.

"It went round by the Bidford road—there was no other traveller for us. Marry, I care not for coaches nor travellers now I have Darby safe here! See, Dad, he hath become a fine gentleman. Did'st note how grand he is in his manner, an' what a rare tone his voice hath taken?"

The handsome boy flushed a little and gave a half embarrassed laugh.

"Nay, Debora, I have not changed; 'tis thy fancy. My doublet hath a less rustical cut and is of different stuff from any seen hereabout, and my hose and boots fit—which could not be said of them in olden times. This fashion of ruff moreover," touching it with dainty complacency, "this fashion of ruff is such as the Queen's Players themselves wear."

Old Thornbury's brows contracted darkly and the girl turned to him with a laugh.

"Oh—Dad! Dad! thou must e'en learn to hear of the playhouses, an' actors with a better grace than that. Note the wry face he doth make, Darby!"

"I have little stomach for their follies and buffooneries—albeit my son be one of them," the innkeeper answered, in sharp tone. Then struggling with some intense inward feeling, "Still I am not a man to go half-way, Darby. Thou hast chosen for thyself, an' the blame will not be mine if thy road be the wrong one. Thou canst walk upright on any highway, lad."

"Ay!" put in old Saddler, "Ay, neighbour, but a wilful lad must have his way."

Soon old Marjorie came in and clattered about the supper table, after having made a great to-do over the young master.

Thornbury poured the hot spiced wine into an ancient punch-bowl, and set it in the centre of the simple feast, and they all drew their chairs up to the table as the bells in Stratford rang Christmas in.

Never had the inn echoed to more joyous laughing and talking, for Thornbury and his two old friends mellowed in temper as they refilled their flagons, and they even added to the occasion by each rendering a song. Saddler bringing one forth from the dim recesses of his memory that related, in seventeen verses and much monotonous chorus, the love affairs of a certain Dinah Linn.

The child slumbered again on the oak settle in the inglenook. The firelight danced over his yellow hair and pretty dimpled hands. The candles burned low. Then Darby sang in flute-like voice a carol, that was, as he told them, "the rage in London," and, afterwards, just to please Deb, the old song that will never wear out its welcome at Christmas-tide, "When shepherds watched their flocks."

The girl would have joined him, but there came a tightness in her throat, and the hot stinging of tears to her eyes, and when the last note of it went into silence she said good night, lifted the sleeping child and carried him away.

"Deb grows more beautiful, Dad," said the young fellow, looking after her. "Egad! what a carriage she hath! She steps like a very princess of the blood. Hark! then," going to the latticed window and throwing it open. "Here come the waits, Dad, as motley a crowd as ever."

The innkeeper was trimming the lantern and seeing his neighbours to the door.

"Keep well hold of each other," called Darby after them. "I trow 'tis a timely proverb—'United we stand, divided we fall.'"

Saddler turned with a chuckle and shook his fist at the lad, but lurched dangerously in the operation.

"The apples were too highly spiced for such as thee," said Thornbury, laughing. "Thou had'st best stick to caudles an' small beer."

"Nay, then, neighbour," called back Sevenoakes, with much solemnity, "Christmas comes but once a year, when it comes it brings good cheer—'tis no time for caudles, or small beer!"

At this Darby went into such a peal of laughter—in which the waits who were discordantly tuning up joined him—that the sound of it must have awakened the very echoes in Stratford town.

II

During the days following Christmas, One Tree Inn was given over to festivity. It had always been a favoured spot with the young people from Stratford and Shottery. In spring they came trooping to Master Thornbury's meadow, bringing their flower-crowned queen and ribbon-decked May-pole. It was there they had their games of barley-break, blindman's buff and the merry cushion dance during the long summer evenings; and when dusk fell they would stroll homeward through the lanes sweet with flowering hedges, each one of them all carrying a posy from Deb Thornbury's garden—for where else grew such wondrous clove-pinks, ragged lady, lad's love, sweet-william and Queen Anne's lace, as there? So now these old playmates of Darby's came one by one to welcome him home and gaze at him in unembarrassed admiration.

Judith Shakespeare, who was a friend and gossip of Debora's, spent many evenings with them, and those who knew the little maid best alone could say what that meant, for never was there a gayer lass, or one who had a prettier wit. To hear Judith enlarging upon her daily experiences with people and things, was to listen to thrilling tales, garnished and gilded in fanciful manner, till the commonplace became delightful, and life in Stratford town a thing to be desired above the simple passing of days in other places.

No trivial occurrence went by this little daughter of the great poet without making some vivid impression upon her mind, for she viewed the every-day world lying beside the peaceful Avon through the wonderful rose-coloured glasses of youth, and an imagination bequeathed to her direct from her father.

It was on an evening when Judith Shakespeare was with them and Deb was roasting chestnuts by the hearth, that they fell to talking of London, and the marvellous way people had of living there.

A sudden storm had blown up, flakes of frozen snow came whirling against the windows, beating a fairy rataplan on the frosted glass, while the heavy boughs of the old oak creaked and groaned in the wind. Darby and the two girls listened to the sounds without and drew their chairs nearer the fire with a sense of the warm comfort of the long cheery room. They chatted about the city and the pleasures and pastimes that held sway there, doings that seemed so extravagant to country-bred folk, and that often turned night into day—a day moreover not akin to any spent elsewhere on top of the earth.

"Dost sometimes act in the same play with my father, Darby, at the Globe Theatre?" asked Judith, after a pause in the conversation, and at a moment when the innkeeper had just left the room.

The girl was sitting in a chair whose oaken frame was black with age. Now she grasped the arms of it tightly, and Darby noted the beautiful form of her hands and the tapering delicate fingers; he saw also a nervous tremor go through them as she spoke.

"Oh! I would know somewhat of my father's life in London," continued Judith, "and of the people he meets there. He hath acquaintance with many gentlemen of the Queen's Court and Parliament, for he hath twice been bidden to play in Her Majesty's theatre in the palace at

Greenwich. Yet of all those doings of his and of the nobles who make much of him he doth say so little, Darby."

Debora, who was standing by the high mantel, turned towards her brother expectantly. She said nothing, but her eyes—shadowy eyes of a blue that was not all blue, but had a glint of green about it—her eyes burned as though they held imprisoned a bit of living light, like the fire in an opal.

The young player smiled; he was looking intently into the glowing coals and for the instant his thoughts seemed far away from the tranquil home scene.

There was no pose of Darby's figure which was not graceful; he was always a picture even to those who knew him best, and it was to this unconscious grace probably more than actual talent that his measure of success upon the stage was due. Now as he leant forward, his elbow on his knee, his chin on his white, almost girlish hand, the burnished auburn love-locks shading his oval face, and matching in colour the outward sweeping lashes of his eyes, Judith could not look away from him the while she waited his tardy answer.

After a moment he came out of his brown study with a little start, and glanced over at her.

"Ah, Judith, an' the master will give you but scant information on those points, why should I give more? As for the playhouses where he is constantly, now peradventure he is fore-wearied of them when once at home, or," with a slight uplifting of his brows, "or else he think'th them no topics for a young maid," he ended somewhat priggishly.

"'Tis ever so!" Judith answered with impatience. "Thou wilt give a body no satisfaction either. Soul o' me! but men be all alike. If ever I have a husband—which heaven forbid!—I shall fare to London four times o' the year an' see for myself what it be like."

"I am going to London with Darby when he doth go back again," said Debora, speaking with quiet deliberation. Thornbury entered the room at the moment and heard what his daughter said. The man caught at the edge of the heavy table by which he stood, as though needing to hold by it. He waited there, unheeded by the three around the hearth.

"Thou art joking, Deb," answered her brother after an astonished pause. "Egad! how could'st thou fare to London?"

"I' faith, how could I fare to London?" she said with spirit, mimicking his tone. "An' are there no maids in London then? An' there be not, my faith, t'were time they saw what one is like! Prithee, I have reason to believe I could pass a marvellous pleasant month there if all I hear be true. What say'th thou, Judith, to coming with me?"

"Why, sweetheart," answered the girl, rising, "for all I have protested, I would not go save my father took me. His word is my will always, know'st thou not so? An' if it be his pleasure that I go not to London—well then, I have no mind to go. That is just my thought of it. But," sighing a little, "thou art wiser than I, for thou can'st read books, an' did'st keep pace with Darby page for page, when he went to Stratford grammar school. Furthermore, thou art given thy own way more than I, and art so different—so vastly different—Deb."

"Truly, yes," Debora answered. Then, flinging out her arms, and tossing her head up with a quick, petulant gesture, "Oh, I wish, I wish ten thousand-fold that I were a man and could be with thee, Darby. 'Tis so tame and tantalizing to be but a maid with this one to say 'Gra'mercy! Thou can'st not go there,' an' that one to add 'Alack! an' alack! however cam'st thou to fancy thou could'st do so? Art void o' wit? Beshrew me but ladies never deport themselves in such unmannerly fashion—no, nor even think on't. There is thy little beaten track all bordered with box—'tis precise, yet pleasant—walk thou in it thankfully. Marry, an' thou must not gaze over the hedges neither!'"

A deep, sweet laugh followed her words as an echo, and a man tall and finely built came striding over from the door where he had been standing in shadow, an amused listener. He put his two hands on the girl's shoulders and looked down into the beautiful, rebellious face.

"Heigho, and heigho!" he said. "Just listen to this mutinous one, good Master Thornbury! Here is a whirlwind in petticoats equal to my pretty shrew who was so well tamed at the last. Marry, an' I could show them such a brilliant bit of acting at the new Globe—such tone! such intensity! 'twould surely inspire the Company and so lighten my work by a hundred-fold. But, alas! while we have but lads to play the parts that maidens should take, acting is oft a very weariness and giveth one an ache o' the heart!"

"Thou would'st not have me upon the stage, father?" said Judith, looking at him.

The man smiled down at her, then his face grew suddenly grave and his hazel eyes narrowed.

"By all the gods—No!—not thee sweetheart. But," his voice changing, "but there are those I would. We must away, neighbour Thornbury. I am due in London shortly, and need the night's rest."

They pressed him to stay longer, but he would not tarry. So Judith tied on her hooded cloak, and many a warm good-bye was spoken.

The innkeeper, with Darby and Debora, stood on the threshold and watched the two take the road to Stratford; and the sky was pranked out with many a golden star, for the storm had blown over, and the night winds were at peace.

After they entered the house a silence settled over the little group. The child Dorian slept on the cushioned settle, for he was sorely spoilt by Debora, who would not have him go above stairs till she carried him up herself. The girl sat down beside him now and watched Darby, who was carving a strange head upon a stout bit of wood cut from the tree before the door.

"What art so busy over, lad?" asked Thornbury. His voice trembled, and there was an unusual pallor on his face.

"'Tis but a bit of home I will take away with me, Dad. In an act of 'Romeo and Juliet,' the new play we are but rehearsing, I carry a little cane. I am a dashing fellow, one Mercutio. I would thou could'st see me. Well-a-day! I have just an odd fancy for this bit o' the old tree."

Debora rose and went over to her father. She laid one hand on his arm and patted it gently.

"I would go to London, Dad," she said coaxingly. "Nay, I must go to London, Dad. I pray thee put no stumbling blocks in the way o' it—but be kind as thou art always. See! an' thou dost let me away I will stay but a month, a short month—but four weeks—it doth seem shorter to say it so—an' then I'll fare home again swiftly an' bide in content. Oh! think of it, Dad! to go to London! It is to go where one can hear the heart of the whole world beat!"

The old man shook his head in feeble remonstrance.

"Thou wilt fare there an' thou hast the mind, Deb, but thou wilt never come back an' bide in peace at One Tree Inn."

The girl suddenly wound her arms about his neck and laid her cool sweet face against his. When she raised it, it glistened with tears.

"I will, Dad! I will, I will," she cried softly, then bent and caught little Dorian up and went swiftly out of the room.

III

The house in London where Darby Thornbury lodged was on the southern side of the Thames in the neighbourhood of the theatres, a part of the city known as Bankside. The mistress of the house was one Dame Blossom, a wholesome-looking woman who had passed her girlhood at Shottery, and remembered Darby and Debora when they were but babies. It was on this account, probably, that she gave to the young actor an amount of consideration and comfort he could not have found elsewhere in the whole of Southwark. When he returned from his holiday, bringing his sister with him, she welcomed them with a heartiness that lacked no tone of absolute sincerity.

The winter had broken when the two reached London; there was even a hint of Spring in the air, though it was but February, and the whole world seemed to be waking after a sleep. At least that was the way it felt to Debora Thornbury. For then began a life so rich in enjoyment, so varied and full of new delights that she sometimes, when brushing that heavy hair of hers before the little copper mirror in the high room that looked away to the river, paused as in a half dream, vaguely wondering if she were in reality the very maid who had lived so long and quietly at the old Inn away there in the pleasant Warwickshire country.

Her impulsive nature responded eagerly to the rapid flow of life in the city, and she received each fresh impression with vivid interest and pleasure. There was a new sparkle in her changeful blue eyes, and the colour drifted in and out of her face with every passing emotion.

Darby also, it struck the girl, was quite different here in London. There was an undefined something about him, a certain assurance both of himself and the situation that she had never noticed before. Truly they had not seen anything of each other for the past two years, but he appeared unchanged when he came home at Christmas. A trifle more manly looking perchance, and with a somewhat greater elegance of manner and speech, yet in verity the same Darby as of old; here in the city it was not so, there was a dashing way about him now, a foppishness, an elaborate attention to every detail of fashion and custom that he had not burdened himself with at the little half-way house. The hours he kept moreover were very late and uncertain, and this sorely troubled his sister. Still each morning he spoke so freely of the many gentlemen he had been with the evening before—at the Tabard—or the Falcon—or even the Devil's Tavern near Temple Bar—where Debora had gazed open-eyed at the flaunting sign of St. Dunstan tweaking the devil by the nose—indeed, all these places he mentioned so entirely as a matter of course, that she soon ceased to worry over the hour he returned. The names of Marlowe and Richard Burbage, Beaumont, Fletcher, Lodge, Greene and even Dick Tarleton, became very familiar to her, beside those of many a lesser light who was wont to shine upon the boards. It seemed reasonable and fair that Darby should wish to pass as much time with reputable players as possible, and moreover he was often, he said, with Ned Shakespeare—who was playing at Blackfriars—and the girl knew that where he was, the master himself was most likely to be for shorter or longer time, for he ever shadowed his brother's life with loving care.

Through the day, when he was not at the theatre, Darby took his sister abroad to see the sights. The young actor was proud to be seen with her, and though he loved her for her own sweet sake, perhaps there was more than a trifle of vanity mixed with the pleasure he obtained from showing the city to one so easily charmed and entertained.

The whispered words of admiration that caught his ear as Debora stood beside him here and there in the public gardens and places of amusement, were as honey to his taste. And it may be because they were acknowledged to be so strikingly alike that it pleased his fancy to have my lord this—and the French Count of that—the beaus and young bloods of the town who haunted the playhouses and therefore knew the actors well—plead with him, after having seen Debora once, to be allowed to pay her at least some slight attention and courtesy.

But Darby Thornbury knew his time and the men of it, and where his little sister was concerned his actions were cool and calculating to a degree.

He was careful to keep her away from those places where she would chance to meet and become acquainted with any of the players whom she knew so well by name, and this the girl thought passing strange. Further, he would not take her to the theatres, though in truth she pleaded, argued, and finally lost her temper over it.

"Nay, Deb," said her brother loftily, "let me be the best judge of where I take thee and whom thou dost meet. I have not lived in London more than twice twelve months for naught. Thou, sweeting, art as fresh and dew-washed as the lilac bushes under Dad's window—and as green. Therefore, I pray thee allow me to decide these matters. Did I not take thee to Greenwich but yesterday to view the Queen's Plaisance, as the place is rightly named?—Methinks I can smell yet that faint scent of roses that so pervaded the place. Egad! 'tis not every lass hath luck enow to see the very rooms Her Majesty hath graced. Marry no! Such tapestries and draperies laced with Spanish gold-thread! Such ancient portraits and miniatures set on ivory! Such chairs and tables inlaid thick with mother o' pearl and beaten silver! That feast of the eye should last thee awhile and save thy temper from going off at a tangent."

Debora lifted her straight brows by way of answer, and her red curved mouth set itself in a dangerously firm line; but Darby appeared not to notice these warning signals and continued in more masterful tone:—

"Moreover, I took thee to the Paris Gardens on a day when there was a passable show, and one 'twas possible for a maid to view, yet even then much against my will and better judgment. I have taken thee to the notable churches and famous tombs. Thou hast seen the pike ponds and the park and palace of the Lord Bishop of Winchester! And further, thou hast walked with me again and again through Pimlico Garden when the very fashion of the city was abroad. Ah! and Nonsuch House! Hast forgotten Nonsuch House on London Bridge, and how we climbed the gilded stairway and went up into the cupola for a fair outlook at the river? 'Tis a place to be remembered. Why, they brought it over from France piecemeal, so 'tis said, and put it together with great wooden pegs instead of nails. The city was sorely taxed for it all, doubtless." He waited half a moment, apparently for some response, but as none came, went on again:

"As for the shops and streets, thou know'st them by heart, for there has not been a day o' fog since we came to keep us in. Art not satisfied, sweet?"

"Nay then I am not!" she answered, with an impatient gesture. "Thou dost know mightily well 'tis the playhouses, the playhouses I would see!"

"'Fore Heaven now! Did a man ever listen to such childishness!" cried Darby. "And hast not seen them then?"

"Marry, no!" she exclaimed, her lovely face reddening.

"Now, by St. George! Then 'twas for naught I let thee gaze so long on 'The Swan,' and I would thou could'st just have seen thine eyes when they ran up the red flag with the swan broidered upon it. Ay! and also when their trumpeter blew that ear-splitting blast which is their barbarous unmannerly fashion of calling the masses in and announcing the play hath opened."

The girl made no reply, but beat a soft, quick tattoo with her little foot on the sanded floor.

After watching her in amused silence Darby again returned to his tantalising recital.

"And I pointed out, as we passed it, the 'Rose Theatre' where the Lord High Admiral's men have the boards. Fine gentlemen all, and hail-fellow-well-met with the Earl of Pembroke's players, though they care little for our Company. Since we have been giving Will Shakespeare's comedies, the run of luck hath been too much with us to make us vastly popular. Anon, I showed thee 'The Hope,' dost not remember the red-tiled roof of it? 'Tis a private theatre, an' marvellous comfortable, they tell me. An' thou has forgotten all those; thou surely canst bring to mind the morning we were in Shoreditch, how I stopped before 'The Fortune' and 'The Curtain' with thee? 'Tis an antiquated place 'The Curtain,' but the playhouse where Master Shakespeare first appeared, and even now well patronised, for Ben Jonson's new comedy 'Every Man in his Humour' is running there to full houses, an' Dick Burbage himself hath the leading part."

He paused again, a merry light in his eyes and his lips twitching a little.

"Thou didst see 'The Globe' an' my memory fails me not, Deb? 'Tis our summer theatre—where I fain we could play all year round—but that is so far impossible as 'tis open to the sky, and a shower o' cold rain or an impromptu sprinkling of sleet on one, in critical moments of the play, hath disastrous effect. Come, thou surely hast not forgotten 'The Globe,' where we of the Lord High Chamberlain's Company have so oft disported ourselves. Above the entrance there is the huge sign of Atlas carrying his load and beneath, the words in Latin, 'All the world acts a play.'"

Debora tossed her head and caught her breath quickly. "My patience is gone with thee, since thou art minded to take me for a very fool, Darby Thornbury," she said with short cutting inflection. "Hearts mercy! 'Tis not the outside o' the playhouses I desire to see, as thou dost understand—'tis the inside—where Master Shakespeare is and the great Burbage, an' Kemp, an' all o' them. Be not so unkind to thy little sister. I would go in an' see the play—Marry an' amen! I am beside myself to go in with thee, Darby!"

The young actor frowned. "Nay then, Deb," he answered, "those ladies (an' I strain a point to call them so) who enter, are usually masked. I would not have thee of them. The play is but for men, like the bear-baiting and bull-baiting places."

"How can'st thou tell me such things," she cried, "an' so belittle the stage? Listen now! this did I hear thee saying over and over last night. So wonderful it was—and rarely, strangely beautiful—yet fearful—it chilled the blood o' my heart! Still I remembered."

Rising the girl walked to the far end of the room with slow, pretty movement, then lifted her face, so like Darby's own—pausing as though she listened.

Her brother could only gaze at her as she stood thus, her plain grey gown lying in folds about her, the sun burnishing the red-gold of her hair; but when she began to speak he forgot all else and only for the moment heard Juliet—the very Juliet the world's poet must have dreamed of.

On and on she spoke with thrilling intensity. Her voice, in its full sweetness, never once failed or lost the words. It was the long soliloquy of the maid of Capulet in the potion scene. After she finished she stood quite still for a moment, then swayed a little and covered her face with her hands.

"It taketh my very life to speak the words so," she said slowly, "yet the wonder of them doth carry me away from myself. But," going over to Darby, "but, dear heart, how dost come thou art studying such a part? 'Tis just for the love of it surely!"

The player rose and walked to the small window. He stood there quite still and answered nothing.

Debora laid one firm, soft hand upon his and spoke, half coaxingly, half diffidently, altogether as though touching some difficult question.

"Dost take the part o' Juliet, dear heart?"

"Ay!" he answered, with a short, hard laugh. "They have cast me for it, without my consent. At first I was given the lines of Mercutio, then, after all my labour over the character—an' I did not spare myself—was called on to give it up. There has been difficulty in finding a Juliet, for Cecil Davenant, who hath the sweetest voice for a girl's part of any o' us, fell suddenly ill. In an evil moment 'twas decided I might make shift to take the character, for none other in the Company com'th so near it in voice, they say, though Ned Shakespeare hath a pink and white face, comely enow for any girl. Beshrew me, sweetheart—but I loathe the taking of such parts. To succeed doth certainly bespeak some womanish beauty in one—to fail doth mar the play. At best I must be as the Master says, 'too young to be a man, too old to be a boy.' 'Tis but the third time I have essayed such a role, an 't shall be the last, I swear."

"I would I could take the part o' Juliet for thee, Darby," said the girl, softly patting the sleeve of his velvet tabard.

"Thou art a pretty comforter," he answered, pinching her ear lightly and trying to recover himself.

"'Twould suit thee bravely, Deb, yet I'd rather see thee busy over a love affair of thine own at home in Shottery. Ah, well! I'd best whistle 'Begone dull care,' for 'twill be a good week before we give the people the new play, though they clamour for it now. We are but rehearsing as yet, and 'Two Gentlemen of Verona' hath the boards."

"I would I could see the play if but for once," said Debora, clasping her hands about his arm. "Indeed," coaxingly, "thou could'st manage to take me an' thou did'st have the will."

Darby knit his brows and answered nothing, yet the girl fancied he was turning something in his mind. With a fair measure of wisdom for one so eager she forebore questioning him further, but glanced up in his face, which was grave and unreadable.

Perchance when she had given up all hope of any favourable answer, he spoke.

"There is a way—though it pleases me not, Deb—whereby thou might be able to see the rehearsals at least. The Company assembles at eight of the morning, thou dost know; now I could take thee in earlier by an entrance I wot of, at Blackfriars, a little half-hidden doorway but seldom used—thence through my tiring-room—and so—and so—where dost think?"

"Nay! I know not," she exclaimed. "Where then, Darby?"

"To the Royal Box!" he answered. "'Tis fair above the stage, yet a little to the right. The curtains are always drawn closely there to save the tinselled velvet and cloth o' gold hangings with which 't hath lately been fitted. Now I will part these drapings ever so little, yet enough to give thee a full sweeping view o' the stage, an' if thou keep'st well to the back o' the box, Deb, thou wilt be as invisible to us as though Queen Mab had cast her charmed cloak about thee. Egad! there be men amongst the High Chamberlain's Players I would not have discover thee for many reasons, my little sister," he ended, watching her face.

For half a moment the girl's lips quivered, then her eyes gathered two great tears which rolled heavily down and lay glittering on her grey kirtle.

"'Tis ever like this with me!" she exclaimed, dashing her hand across her eyes, "whenever I get what I have longed and longed for. First com'th a ball i' my throat, then a queer trembling, an' I all but cry. 'Tis vastly silly is't not, but 'tis just by reason o' being a girl one doth act so." Then eagerly, "Thou would'st not fool me, Darby, or change thy mind? Thou art in earnest? Swear it! Cross thy heart!"

"Ay! I am in earnest," he replied, smiling; "in very truth thou shalt see thy brother turn love-sick maid and mince giddily about in petticoats. I warrant thou'lt be poppy-red, though thou art hidden behind the gold curtains, just to hear the noble Romeo vow me such desperate lover's vows."

"By St. George, Deb! we have a Romeo who might turn any maid's heart and head. He is a handsome, admirable fellow, Sherwood, and hath a way with him most fascinating. He doth act even at rehearsals as though 'twere all most deadly passionate reality, and this with only me for inspiration. I oft' fancy what 'twould be—his love-making—an' he had a proper Juliet—one such as thou would'st make, for instance."

"I will have eyes only for thee, Darby," answered Debora, softly, "but for thee, an', yes, for Master Will Shakespeare, should he be by."

"He is often about the theatre, sweet, but hath no part in this new play. No sooner hath he one written, than another is under his pen; and I am told that even now he hath been reading lines from a wonderful strange history concerning a Jew of Venice, to a party of his friends—Ben

Jonson and Dick Burbage, and more than likely Lord Brooke—who gather nightly at 'The Mermaid,' where, thou dost remember, Master Shakespeare usually stays."

"I forget nothing thou dost tell me of him," said the girl, as she turned to leave the room. "O wilt take me with thee on the morrow, Darby? Wilt really take me?——"

"On the morrow," he answered, watching her away.

IV

Thus it fell that each morning for one heavenly week Debora Thornbury found herself safely hidden away in what was called by courtesy "The Royal Box." In truth her Majesty had never honoured it, but commanded the players to journey down to Greenwich when it was her whim to see their performances. Now, in 1597, the Queen had grown too world-weary to care much for such pastimes, and rarely had any London entertainment at Court, save a concert by her choir boys from St. Paul's—for these lads with their ofttimes beautiful faces, and their fine voices, she loved and indulged in many ways.

At first Debora felt strangely alone after Darby left her in the little compartment above the stage at Blackfriars. Lingering about it was a passing sweet odour, for the silken cushions were stuffed with fragrant grasses from the West Indies, and the hand-railings and footstools were of carven sandalwood. Mingled with these heavy perfumes was the scent of tobacco, since the young nobles who usually filled the box indulged much in the new weed.

The girl would lean back against the seat in this dim, richly coloured place, and give her mind up to a perfect enjoyment of the moment.

From her tiny aperture in the curtains, skilfully arranged by Darby, she could easily see the stage—all but the east wing—and, furthermore, had a fair view of the two-story circular building.

How gay it must be, she thought, when filled in gallery and pit with a merry company! How bright and glittering when all the great cressets and clusters of candles were alight! How charming to feel free to come and go here as one would, and not have to be conveyed in by private doorways like a bale of smuggled goods!

Then she would dream of olden times, when the sable friars went in and out of the old Dominican friary that stood upon the very place where the theatre was now built.

"'Twas marvellous strange," she thought, "that it should be a playhouse that was erected on this ground that used to be a place of prayer."

So the time would pass till the actors assembled. They were a jovial, swaggering, happy-go-lucky lot, and it took all their Master-player's patience to bring them into straight and steady work. But when the play once began each one followed his part with keen enthusiasm, for there was no half-hearted man amongst the number.

Debora watched each actor, listened for each word and cue the prompter gave them with an absorbed intensity she was scarcely conscious of.

She soon discovered that play-goers were not greatly beguiled through the eye, for the stage-settings changed but little, and the details of a scene were simplified by leaving them to the imagination. Neither did the music furnished by a few sad-looking musicians who appeared to have been entrapped in a small balcony above the stage appeal to her, for it was a thing the least said about the soonest mended.

The actors wore no especial dress or makeup during these rehearsals, save Darby, and he to grow better accustomed to such garments as befitted the maid of Capulet, disported himself throughout in a cumbersome flowing gown of white corduroy that at times clung about him as might a winding sheet, and again dragged behind like a melancholy flag of truce. Yet with the auburn love-locks shading his fair oval face, now clean shaven and tinted like a girl's, and his clear-toned voice, even Debora admitted, he was not so far amiss in the role.

What struck her most from the moment he came upon the stage was his wonderful likeness to herself.

"I' faith," she half whispered, "did I not know that Deb Thornbury were here—an' I have to pinch my arm to make that real—I should have no shadow of a doubt but that Deb Thornbury were there, a player with the rest, though I never could make so sad a tangle of any gown however bad its cut—an' no woman e'er cut that one. Darby doth lose himself in it as if 'twere a maze, and yet withal doth, so far, the part fair justice."

When Don Sherwood came upon the boards the girl's eyes grew brilliant and dark. Darby had but spoken truth regarding this man's fascinating personality. He was a strong, straight-limbed fellow, and his face was such as it pleased the people to watch, though it was not of perfect cast nor strictly beautiful; but he was happy in possessing a certain magnetism which was the one thing needful.

Yet it was not to manner or stage presence that Sherwood owed his success, but rather to his voice, for there was no other could compare to it in the Lord Chamberlain's Company. Truly the gods had been good to this player—for first of all their gifts is such a golden-toned voice as he had brought into this world of sorry discords. Never had Debora listened to anything like it as it thrilled the stillness of the empty house with the passionate words of Romeo.

She followed the tragedy intensely from one scene to another till the ending that stirs all tender hearts to tears.

The lines of the different characters seemed branded upon her brain, and she remembered them without effort and knew them quite by heart. Sometimes Darby, struggling with the distressing complications of his detested dress, would hesitate over some word or break a sentence, thereby marring the perfect beauty of it, and while Sherwood would smile and shrug his shoulders lightly as though as to say, "Have I not enough to put up with, that thou art what thou art, but thou must need'st bungle the words!" Then would Debora clench her hands and tap her little foot against the soft rugs.

"Oh! I would I had but the chance to speak his lines," she said to herself at such times. "Prithee 'twould be in different fashion! 'Tis not his fault, in sooth, for no living man could quite understand or say the words as they should be said, but none the less it doth sorely try my patience."

So the enchanted hours passed and none came to disturb the girl, or discover her till the last morning, which was Saturday. The rehearsal had ended, and Debora was waiting for Darby. The theatre looked gray and deserted. At the back of the stage the great velvet traverses through which the actors made their exits and entrances, hung in dark folds, sombre as the folds of a pall. A chill struck to her heart, for she seemed to be the only living thing in the building, and Darby did not come.

She grew at last undecided whether to wait longer or risk going across the river, and so home alone, when a quick step came echoing along the passage that led to the box. In a moment a man had gathered back the hangings and entered. He started when he saw the slight figure standing in the uncertain light, then took a step towards her.

The girl did not move but looked up into his face with an expression of quick, glad recognition, then she leaned a little towards him and smiled. "Romeo!" she exclaimed softly. "Romeo!" and as though compelled to it by some strange impulse, followed his name with the question that has so much of pathos, "Wherefore," she said, "Wherefore art thou Romeo?"

The man laughed a little as he let the curtains drop behind him.

"Why, an' I be Romeo," he answered in that rare voice of his, full and sweet as a golden bell, "then who art thou? Art not Juliet? Nay, pardon me, mademoiselle," his tone changing, "I know whom thou art beyond question, by thy likeness to Thornbury. 'Fore Heaven! 'tis a very singular likeness, and thou must be, in truth, his sister. I would ask your grace for coming in with such scant announcement. I thought the box empty. The young Duke of Nottingham lost a jewelled pin here yestere'en—or fancied so—and sent word to me to have the place searched. Ah! there it is glittering above you in the tassel to the right."

"I have seen naught but the stage," she said, "and now await my brother. Peradventure he did wrong to bring me here, but I so desired to see the play that I persuaded and teased him withal till he could no longer deny me. 'Twas not over-pleasant being hidden i' the box, but 'twas the only way Darby would hear of. Moreover," with a little proud gesture, "I have the greater interest in this new tragedy that I be well acquainted with Master William Shakespeare himself."

"That is to be fortunate indeed," Sherwood answered, looking into her eyes, "and I fancy thou could'st have but little difficulty in persuading a man to anything. I hold small blame for Thornbury."

Debora laughed merrily. "'Tis a pretty speech," she said, "an' of a fine London flavour." Then uneasily, "I would my brother came; 'tis marvellous unlike him to leave me so."

"I will tell thee somewhat," said Sherwood, after a moment's thought. "A party o' the players went off to 'The Castle Inn'—'tis hard by—an' I believe their intention was to drink success to the play. Possibly they will make short work and drink it in one bumper, but I cannot be sure—they may drink it in more."

"'Tis not like my brother to tarry thus," the girl answered. "I wonder at him greatly."

"Trouble nothing over it," said Sherwood; "indeed, he went against his will; they were an uproarious lot o' roisterers, and carried him off willy-nilly, fairly by main force, now I think on't. Perchance thou would'st rather I left thee alone, mademoiselle?" he ended, as by afterthought.

"'Twould be more seemly," she answered, the colour rising in her face.

"I do protest to that," said the man quickly. "And I found thee out—here alone—why, marry, so might another."

"An' why not another as well?" Debora replied, lifting her brows; "an' why not another full as well as thee, good Sir Romeo? There is no harm in a maid being here. But I would that Darby came," she added.

"We will give him license of five minutes longer," he returned. "Come tell me, what dost think o' the play?"

"'Tis a very wonder," said Debora; "more beautiful each time I see it." Then irrelevantly, "Dost really fancy in me so great a likeness to my brother?"

"Thou art like him truly, and yet no more like him than I am like—well, say the apothecary, though 'tis not a good instance."

"Oh! the poor apothecary!" she cried, laughing. "Prithee, hath he been starved to fit the part? Surely never before saw I one so altogether made of bones."

"Ay!" said Sherwood. "He is a very herring. I wot heaven forecasted we should need such a man, an' made him so."

"Think'st thou that?" she said absently. "O heart o' me! Why doth Darby tarry. Perchance some accident may have happened him or he hath fallen ill! Dost think so?"

The player gave a short laugh, but looked as suddenly grave.

"Do not vex thyself with such imaginings, sweet mistress Thornbury. He hath not come to grief, I give thee my word for it. There is no youth that know'th London better than that same brother o' thine, an' I do not fear that he is ill."

"Why, then, I will not wait here longer," she returned, starting. "I can take care o' myself an' it be London ten times over. 'Tis a simple matter to cross in the ferry to Southwark on the one we so oft have taken; the ferry-man knoweth me already, an' I fear nothing. Moreover, many maids go to and fro alone."

"Thou shalt not," he said. "Wait till I see if the coast be clear. By the Saints! 'twill do Thornbury no harm to find thee gone. He doth need a lesson," ended the man in a lower tone, striding down the narrow passage-way that led to the green-room.

"Come," he said, returning after a few moments, "we have the place to ourselves, and there is not a soul between Blackfriars an' the river house, I believe, save an old stage carpenter, a fellow short o' wit, but so over-fond of the theatre he scarce ever leaves it. Come!"

As the girl stepped eagerly forward to join him, Sherwood entered the box again.

"Nay," on second thought—"wait. Before we go, I pray thee, tell me thy name."

"'Tis Debora," she said softly; "just Debora."

"Ah!" he answered, in a tone she had heard him use in the play—passing tender and passionate. "Well, it suiteth me not; the rest may call thee Debora, an' they will—but I, I have a fancy to think of thee by another title, one sweeter a thousand-fold!" So leaning towards her and looking into her face with compelling eyes that brought hers up to them, "Dost not see, an' my name be Romeo, thine must be——?"

"Nay then," she cried, "I will not hear, I will not hear; let me pass, I pray thee."

"Pardon, mademoiselle," returned the player with grave, quick courtesy, and holding back the curtain, "I would not risk thy displeasure."

They went out together down the little twisted hall into the green-room where the dried rushes that strewed the floor crackled beneath their feet; through the empty tiring rooms, past the old half-mad stage carpenter, who smiled and nodded at them, and so by the hidden door out into the pale early spring sunshine. Then down the steep stairs to Blackfriars Landing where the ferryman took them over the river. They did not say a word to each other, and the girl watched with unfathomable eyes the little curling line of flashing water the boat left behind, though it may be she did not see it. As for Sherwood, he watched only her face with the crisp rings of gold-red hair blown about it from out the border of her fur-edged hood. He had forgotten altogether a promise given to dine with some good fellows at Dick Tarleton's ordinary, and only knew that there was a velvety sea-scented wind blowing up the river wild and free; that the sky was of such a wondrous blue as he had never seen before; that across from him in the old weather-worn ferry was a maid whose face was the one thing worth looking at in all the world.

When the boat bumped against the slippery landing, the player sprang ashore and gave Debora his hand that she might not miss the step. There was a little amused smile in his eyes at her long silence, but he would not help her break it.

Together they went up and through the park where buds on tree and bush were showing creamy white through the brown, and underfoot the grass hinted of coming green. Then along the Southwark common past the theatres. Upon all the road Sherwood was watchful lest they should run across some of his company.

To be seen alone and at mid-day with a new beauty was to court endless questions and much bantering.

For some reason Thornbury had been silent regarding his sister, and the man felt no more willing to publish his chance meeting with Debora.

He glanced often at her as though eager for some word or look, but she gave him neither. Her lips were pressed firmly together, for she was struggling with many feelings, one of which was anger against Darby. So she held her lovely head high and went along with feverish haste.

When they came to the house, which was home now out of all the others in London, she gave a sweeping glance at the high windows lest at one might be discovered the round, good-tempered, yet curious face of Dame Blossom. But the tiny panes winked down quite blankly and her return seemed to be unnoticed.

Running up the steps she lifted her hand to the quaint knocker of the door, turned, and looked down at the man standing on the walk.

"I give thee many thanks, Sir Romeo," said the girl; "thou hast in verity been a most chivalrous knight to a maiden in distress. I give thee thanks, an' if thou art ever minded to travel to Shottery my father will be glad to have thee stop at One Tree Inn." Then she raised the knocker, a rap of which would bring the bustling Dame.

Quickly the man sprang up the steps and laid his hand beneath it, so that, though it fell, there should be no sound.

"Nay, wait," he said, in a low, intense voice. "London is wide and the times are busy; therefore I have no will to leave it to chance when I shall see thee again. Fate has been marvellous kind to-day, but 'tis not always so with fate, as peradventure thou hast some time discovered."

"Ay!" she answered, gently, "Ay! Sir Romeo. Thou art right, fate is not always kind. Yet 'tis best to leave most things to its disposal—at least so it doth seem to me."

"Egad!" said Sherwood, with a short laugh, "'tis a way that may serve well enow for maids but not for men. Tell me, when may I see thee? To-night?"

"A thousand times no!" Debora cried, quickly. "To-night," with a little nod of her head, "to-night I have somewhat to settle with Darby."

"He hath my sympathy," said Sherwood. "Then on the morrow?——"

"Nay, nay, I know not. That is the Sabbath; players be but for week-days."

"Then Monday? I beseech thee, make it no later than Monday, and thou dost wish to keep me in fairly reasonable mind."

"Well, Monday, an' it please the fate thou has maligned," she answered, smiling. Noticing that the firm, brown hand was withdrawn a few inches from the place it had held on the panelling of the door, the girl gave a mischievous little smile and let the knocker fall. It made a loud echoing through the empty hall, and the player raised his laced black-velvet cap, gave Debora so low a bow that the silver-gray plume in it swept the ground, and, before the heavy-footed Mistress Blossom made her appearance, was on his way swiftly towards London Bridge.

Debora went up the narrow stairs with eyes ashine, and a smile curving her lips. For the moment Darby was forgotten. When she closed the chamber door she remembered.

It was past high noon, and Dame Blossom had been waiting in impatience since eleven to serve dinner. Yet the girl would not now dine alone, but stood by the gabled window which looked down on the road, watching, watching, and thinking, till it almost seemed that another morning had passed.

Along Southwark thoroughfare through the day went people from all classes, groups of richly-dressed gentlemen, beruffled and befeathered; their laces and their hair perfuming the wind. Officers of the Queen booted and spurred; sober Puritans, long-jowled and over-sallow, living protests against frivolity and light-heartedness. Portly aldermen, jealous of their dignity. Swarthy foreigners with silver rings swinging in their ears. Sun-browned sailors. Tankard-bearers carrying along with their supply of fresh drinking water the cream of the hour's gossip. Keepers of the watch with lanterns trimmed for the night's burning adangle from oaken poles braced across their shoulders. Little maidens whose long gowns cut after the fashion of their mothers, fretted their dancing feet. Ruddy-hued little lads, turning

Catherine wheels for the very joy of being alive, and because the winter time was over and the wine of spring had gone to the young heads.

Debora stood and watched the passing of the people till she wearied of them, and her ears ached with sounds of the street.

Something had gone away from the girl, some carelessness, some content of the heart, and in its place had come a restlessness, as deep, as impossible to quiet, as the restlessness of the sea.

After a time Mistress Blossom knocked at the door, and coaxed her to go below.

"There is no sight o' the young Master, Mistress Debora. Marry, but he be over late, an' the jugged hare I made ready for his pleasuring is fair wasted. Dost think he'll return here to dine or hast gone to the Tabard?"

"I know not," answered Debora, shortly, following the woman down stairs. "He gave me no hint of his intentions, good Mistress Blossom."

"Ods fish!" returned the other, "but that be not mannerly. Still thou need'st not spoil a sweet appetite by tarrying for him. Take thee a taste o' the cowslip cordial, an' a bit o' devilled ham. 'Tis a toothsome dish, an' piping hot."

"I give thee thanks," said Debora, absently. Some question turned itself over in her mind and gave her no peace. Looking up at the busy Dame she spoke in a sudden impulsive fashion.

"Hath my brother—hath my brother been oft so late? Hath he always kept such uncertain hours by night—and day also—I mean?" she ended falteringly.

"Why, sometimes. Now and again as 'twere—but not often. There be gay young gentlemen about London-town, and Master Darby hath with him a ready wit an' a charm o' manner that maketh him rare good company. I doubt his friends be not overwilling to let him away home early," said the woman in troubled tones.

"Hath——he ever come in not—not—quite himself, Mistress Blossom? 'Tis but a passing fancy an' I hate to question thee, yet I must know," said the girl, her face whitening.

"Why then, nothing to speak of," Mistress Blossom replied, bustling about the table, with eyes averted. "See then, Miss Debora, take some o' the Devonshire cream an' one o' the little Banbury cakes with it—there be caraways through them. No? Marry, where be thy appetite? Thou hast no fancy for aught. Try a taste of the conserved cherries, they be white hearts from a Shottery orchard. Trouble not thy pretty self. Men be all alike, sweet, an' not worth a salt tear. Even Blossom cometh home now an' again in a manner not to be spoken of! Ods pitikins! I be thankful to have him make the house in any form, an' not fall i' the clutch o' the watch! They be right glad of the chance to clap a man i' the stocks where he can make a finish o' the day as a target for all the stale jests an' unsavoury missiles of every scurvy rascal o' the streets. But, Heaven be praised!—'tis not often Blossom breaks out—just once in a blue moon—after a bit of rare good or bad luck."

Debora took no heed but stared ahead with wide, unhappy eyes. The old blue plates on the table, the pewter jugs and platters grew strangely indistinct. Then 'twas true! So had she fancied it might be. He had been drinking—drinking. Carousing with the fast, unmannerly youths who haunted the club-houses and inns. Dicing, without doubt, and gambling at cards also peradventure, when she thought he was passing the time in good fellowship with the worthy players from the Lord Chamberlain's Company.

"He hath never come home so by day, surely, good Mistress Blossom? Not by day?" she asked desperately.

"Well—truly—not many times, dearie. But hark'e. Master Darby is one who cannot touch a glass o' any liquor but it flies straightway to his brains; oft hath he told me so, ay! often and over often; 'I am not to blame for this, Blossom,' hath he said to my goodman when he worked over him—cold water and rubbing, Mistress Debora—no more, no less. 'Nay, verily—'tis just my luck, one draught an' I be under the table, leaving the other men bolt upright till they've swallowed full three bottles apiece!"

Debora dropped her face in her hands and rocked a little back an' forth. "'Tis worse than I thought!" she cried, looking up drawn and white. "Oh! I have a fear that 'tis worse—far, far worse. I have little doubt half his money comes from play an' betting, ay! an' at stakes on the bear-baiting, an'—an'—anything else o' wickedness there be left in London—while we at home have thought 'twas earned honestly." As she spoke a heavy rapping sounded down the hall, loud, uneven, yet prolonged.

Mistress Blossom went to answer it quickly, and Debora followed, her limbs trembling and all strength seeming to slip away from her. Lifting the latch the woman flung the outer door open and Darby Thornbury lurched in, falling clumsily against his sister, who straightened her slight figure and hardly wavered with the shock, for her strength had come swiftly back with the sight of him.

The man who lay in the hall in such a miserable heap, had scarce any reminder in him of Darby Thornbury, the dainty young gallant whose laces were always the freshest, and whose ruffs and doublets never bore a mark of wear. Now his long cordovan boots were mud-stained and crumpled about the ankles. His broidered cuffs and collar were wrenched out of all shape. But worse and far more terrible was his face, for its beauty was gone as though a blight had passed across it. He was flushed a purplish red, and his eyes were bloodshot, while above one was a bruised swelling that fairly closed the lid. He tried to get on his feet, and in a manner succeeded.

"By St. George, Deb!" he exclaimed in wrath, "I swear thou 'r a fine sister to take f' outing. I was a double-dyed fool e'er to bring thee t' London. Why couldn't y' wait f' fellow? When I go f' y'—y' not there."

Then he smiled in maudlin fashion and altered his tone. "Egad! I'm proud o' thee, Deb, thou art a very beauty. All the bloods i' town ar' mad to meet thee—th' give me no peace."

"Oh! Mistress Blossom," cried Debora, clasping her hands, "can we not take him above stairs and so to bed? Dear, dear Mistress Blossom, silence him, I pray thee, or my heart will break."

"Be thee quiet, Master Darby, lad," said the woman, persuasively. "Wait, then, an' talk no more. I'll fetch Blossom; he'll fix thee into proper shape, I warrant. 'Tis more thy misfortune than thy fault. Yes, yes, I know thou be sore upset—but why did'st not steer clear o' temptation?"

"Temp-ation, Odso! 'tis a marvellous good word," put in Thornbury. "Any man'd walk a chalk—line—if he could steer clear o' temptation." So, in a state of verbose contrition, was he borne away to his chamber by the sympathetic Blossom, who had a fellow-feeling for the lad that made him wondrous kind.

V

All Saturday night Debora waited by her window—the one that looked across the commonland to the Thames. The girl could not face what might be ahead. Darby—her Darby—her father's delight. Their handsome boy come to such a pass. "'Twas nothing more than being a common drunkard. One whom the watch might have arrested in the Queen's name for breaking the peace," she said to herself. "Oh! the horror of it, the shame!" In the dark of her room her face burned.

Never had such a fear come to her for Darby till to-day. When was it? Who raised the doubt of him in her mind? Yes, she remembered; 'twas a look—a strange look—a half smile, satirical, pitying, that passed over the player Sherwood's face when he spoke of Darby's being persuaded to drink with the others. In a flash at that moment the fear had come, though she would not give it room then. It was a dangerous life, this life in the city, and she knew now what that expression in the actor's eyes had meant; realised now the full import of it. So. It was all summed up in what she had witnessed to-day. But if they knew—if Master Shakespeare and James Burbage knew—these responsible men of the Company—how did they come to trust Darby with such parts as he had long played. What reliance could be placed upon him?

"Nay, then, 'twas a thing not known save by the few. He had not yet become common gossip. Oh! he must be saved from himself—he must be saved from himself," she said, wildly, and then fell to crying. Resting her face, blanched and tear-washed, on the window ledge, she gazed across the peaceful openland that was silvered by the late moon. Truly such a landscape might one see in a dream. Away yonder over the river was the city, its minarets and domes pointing to the purple, shadowless sky, where a few scattered stars made golden twinkling. "In London," she had said to her father, "one could hear the world's heart beat." It seemed to come to her—that sound—far off—muffled—mysterious—on the wings of the night wind. Away in Stratford it would be dark and quiet now, save where the Avon dappled with moonlight hurried high between its banks on its way to the sea—and it would be dark and quiet in Shottery. The lights all out at One Tree Inn, all but the great stable lantern, that swayed to and fro till morning, as a beacon for belated travellers. How long—how very, very long ago it seemed since she had unhooked it and gone off down the snowy road to meet the coach. Ah! yes, Nicholas Berwick had caught up with her, and they came home together. Nicholas Berwick! He was a rarely good friend, Nick Berwick, and 'twas sweet and peaceful away there in Shottery. She had not known this pain in her heart for Darby when she was at home, no, nor this restless craving for the morrow, this unhappy waiting that had stolen all joy away. Nay then, 'twas not so. There in the little room a gladness came over the girl such as had never touched her short, happy life before. A long, fluttering sigh crossed her lips, and they smiled. The troubled thoughts for Darby drifted away, and a voice came to her passing in sweetness all voices that ever she had heard or dreamt of.

"To-morrow?" it said. "Nay, I will not leave it to Fate." And again with steady insistence—"Then Monday?" The words sung themselves over and over till her white eyelids drooped and she slept. And the gray dawn came creeping up the world, while in the eastern sky it was as though an angel of God had plucked a red rose of heaven and scattered its leaves abroad.

VI

When Debora awoke, the sunlight was flooding the chilly room, and on the frosty air sounded a chiming of church bells. A confusion of thoughts stormed her mind as she sprang up and found herself dressed and by the window. Her eyes ached as eyes will that have wept overnight, and her heart was heavy. Still it was not her way to think long; so she bathed in fair water till her face got back its shell-pink tints. She put on the white taffeta kirtle and farthingale that was always kept for Sunday, and fastened a fluted ruff about her throat. When all was finished, her hair coiled freshly and puffed at the sides as Darby would have it dressed to follow the new fashion; when her shoes, with their great silver buckles and red heels, were laced and tied, and when the frills at her wrist were settled, she looked in the mirror and felt better. It was not possible to view such a vision, knowing that it was one's self, without taking comfort.

"Things be past their worst surely," she said. "An' I have no heart in me this morning to give Darby a harsh word. Marry! men take not kindly to upbraiding, and hate a shrew at best o' times. So will I talk to him in sweeter fashion, but in a tone that will be harder to endure than any scolding."

She went down the hall and stopped at her brother's door. No faintest sound came from the room, so she entered and looked about. On the huge four-post bed, from which the funereal-looking curtains were drawn back, lay Darby, in a slumber deep and unrefreshing. Now and again a heavy sigh broke from his lips. His bright locks were tossed and ruffled about his face, and that was dead white, save for the violet rings beneath the eyes and the unabated swelling on his forehead.

"He is a doleful sight," said Debora, gazing down at him, her spirits sinking, "a woful, doleful sight! Ods pitikins! 'tis worse than I thought. What a pass 't has come to that this should be Darby Thornbury. Heart o' me!" a flickering sarcastic little smile going over her face, "Heart o' me, but here be a pretty Juliet!" Then she grew grave.

"Juliet!" verily it would not be possible! That part was out of the question for Darby, at least on the morrow. The bruise on his brow settled it, for the eye beneath was fairly closed.

Alack! alack! she thought, how ever would things fall out at Blackfriars? What of the new play that had already been put off some months and had cost the Company heavily in new dresses, new scenery, even new actors? Oh! was ever such a coil? 'Twould be the lad's undoing upon the London stage. No Master-player would e'er trust him with part or place again.

Debora stood by the bed foot, still and sad, a thousand wild thoughts and questions tangling themselves in her brain. Should she away to Master Shakespeare, who had but just returned to London for the opening day? He was at the Mermaid Inn, and peradventure 'twas best to tell him all. She grew faint at the thought. Had not Judith told her what a very fever of unrest possessed her father before one of these new plays was shown! Debora fancied she could see his sensitive face, with the eyes so wise and kindly, change and grow cold and forbidding as the tale was unfolded.

"Then what is left to do?" she said, desperately. "What is left to do? The play must be saved, Darby must be saved, his reputation, his standing among the players cannot be lost thus." Oh! for some one to turn to—to advise. Oh! for Nick Berwick and his fair cool judgment. Should she report at the theatre that her brother was ill? No, for he had been seen with a merry party drinking at the Castle Tavern on Saturday. If this outbreak could be tided over 'twould be his last, she thought, passionately, her woman's faith coming to the rescue. Some way she must find to save him.

Slowly an idea took possession of the girl and it faded the colour from her cheeks, and set a light in her eyes.

"Debora Thornbury! Ay! there was one could play the part of Juliet." The very life seemed to go out of her at the thought, and she slipped down to the floor and buried her face in the coverlet. Slowly the cold room, the great four-poster, the uneasy sleeper all faded away, and she was alone upon a high balcony in the stillness of a moonlit garden. The tree tops were silver-frosted by the light, and the night was sweet with a perfume from the roses below. She was not Debora Thornbury, but Juliet, the little daughter of the Capulets. The name of her lover was on her lips and a strange happiness filled her soul.

Suddenly rising she went to a heavy press that stood against the wall, swung back the door, and sought out a suit of her brother's. It was of Kendal green cloth, faced about the doublet with tan-coloured leather. The long, soft boots were of the same, and the wide-brimmed hat bore a cluster of white plumes and a buckle of brilliants, while a small lace handkerchief was tucked into the band, after a fashion followed by gentlemen of the court. Opening the door beneath the press the girl selected cuffs and collar wrought in pointed lace.

"In very truth," she said, with a little bitter smile. "Darby Thornbury hath a pretty taste, an' must have coined many rose-nobles in London—or won them. He hath certainly spent them, for never saw I such store o' finery! Here be two velvet tabards slashed and puffed with satin; and a short cloak o' russet silk laid upon with Flemish lace fit for a prince! 'Truth what with his clocked hose, an' scented gloves with stitchery o' silver thread on the backs methinks he hath turned to a very dandy."

Gathering the garments she desired together across her arm, she went again to the bed, and looked down, her eyes growing tender. "I fear me 'tis an unmaidenly thing to even dream o' doing, but if 'tis done, 'tis done for thee, dear heart, albeit without thy consent or Dad's. There will be scant risk o' discovery—we be too much alike. People have wearied us both prating of the likeness. Now 'twill serve; just two or three nights' masquerade for me an' thou wilt be thyself again." Stooping, she kissed the bruised face and went away.

In her own room Debora made quick work of changing her dress. It was an awkward business, for the doublet and green tabard seemed fairly possessed to go contrariwise; the hose were unmanageable, and the cordovan long boots needed stuffing at the toes. Here and there upon the suit was broidered the Lord Chamberlain's coat of arms in gold thread, and when all was finished Deb looked at herself and felt she was a gorgeous and satisfying sight. "Marry! but men be fond o' fine feathers," she thought, studying her reflection.

Then, letting down the coils of auburn hair, she drew the glittering strands through her fingers. "I would it might just be tucked up—it pleasures one little to cut it off. Beshrew me! If I so resemble Darby with such a cloud o' hair about me, what will I be like when 'tis trimmed to match his?" Taking the shears she deliberately severed it to the very length of her brother's. The love-locks curled around her oval face in the self-same charming way.

"My heart! 'tis all most vastly becoming," she exclaimed, fastening the pointed collar. "I liked thee as a girl, Deb, but I love thee, nay, I dote on thee as a lad! Now must I stride an' speak in mannish fashion ('tis well there go'th a long cloak with the suit, for on that I rely to hearten my courage); also I bethink me 'twould be wise to use some strong flavoursome words to garnish my plain speech. By Saint George! now, or Gad Zooks! Heart's mercy! stay'th the hat so? or so? Alack! my courage seem'th to ooze from my boot-heels. Steady, true heart, steady! Nay then, I cannot do it. I will not do it—it look'th a very horror to me. Oh! my poor, pretty hair; my poor, pretty hair!"

On a sudden the girl was down on the floor, and the long locks were caught together and passionately held against her lips. But it was only for a moment. When the storm was over she rose and dashed the mist of it from her eyes.

"What must be, must be! I cannot think on any other plan. I would there were an understudy, but there be none. So must I take the part for Darby—and for Master William Shakespeare."

So saying, Debora went below to the room where the table was laid for breakfast, walking along the hall with a firm step, for her mind was made up and she was never one to do things by halves.

Taking her brother's place she knocked briskly on the little gong and waited. Master Blossom started to answer the summons in a slow-footed, ponderous way peculiar to him, yawning audibly at intervals upon the way.

The Sabbath morn was one whereon good folk should sleep long, and not look to be waited on early, according to him. Dame Blossom herself was but just astir, and lodgers were at best but an inconsiderate lot. Cogitating on these things he entered the room, then stood stock still as though petrified, his light blue eyes vacant with astonishment.

The dainty figure at the table swinging one arm idly over its chair back made no sign, unless the impatient tapping of a fashionable boot-toe upon the sanded floor might be taken for one.

"Ods fish!" exclaimed Blossom, moving heavily a few steps nearer. "I' fecks! but thee art a very dai-asy, young Maister! Dost mind how 'A put 'e to bed? Thou'st pulled tha' self together marvellous, all things considered!

"Marry, where be tha' black eye? 'twere swelled big as a ribstone pippin!"

"Beefsteak," answered Deb, laconically. "Beefsteak, my lively Blossom. Tie a piece on tight next time thou hast an eye like mine—an' see what thou shalt see."

"But where gottest thou the beefsteak?"

"Egad! where does any one get it? Don't stand there chattering like a magpie, but bring me my breakfast. This head I have doth not feel like the head o' Darby Thornbury. 'Tis nigh to breaking. Fetch me my breakfast and give over staring at a man. See'st aught odd enough about me to make thee go daft?"

"I' fecks! 'tis the first time 'A ever heard thee call so loud for breakfast after such a bout as thine o' yestere'en! I wonder thou hast stomach for 't. Howbeit, 'tis thine own affair."

The girl bit her lip. "Nay," she said with cool accent, "I may have small appetite for it—but, as thou say'st, 'tis mine own affair."

"Thou need'st good advice more than breakfast, young Maister," said Blossom, solemnly. "Thy sister was in a way, 'A tell thee. Thou art become a roisterer, a drinker an' a gambler that lives but to hear the clink o' gold against the table. Ay! Such a devil-may-care gambler, an' thou had'st a beard an' no money thou would'st stake that o'er the dice. Being these things, an' a player o' plays, marry! 'A see no fair end ahead o' thee."

"Oh! get thee away an' send thy good wife—thou dost make my nerves spin with thy prating. Get thee away," said Deb, petulantly.

"Zounds! but thou art full like thyself in speech. Too much wine i' thy stomach one day makes a monstrous uncivil tongue i' thy head next."

"Nay then! I ask thy pardon, Blossom," cried the girl, laughing, and holding out a crown piece she had discovered in a pocket of the doublet, "thou art a friend I have no will to offend. Now send thy good Dame."

Shortly Mistress Blossom came bustling in, rosy in the face from bending over an open fire. She carried high in one hand a platter from which drifted a savoury smell, and a steaming flagon was in the other. Setting these down she smoothed her voluminous skirt and stood waiting, an expression of severe displeasure hardening her face.

"A goodly day to you, and a fresh morning, mistress," Deb said shortly—"I pray thee shut the door—an' see it be latched."

The woman did so without speaking.

"Now look at me well. Come"—smiling—"did'st ever see me more like myself?"

"Nay," replied the Dame, after a slow scrutiny of the charming figure. "In looks thou art well enow. An' thy manners matched, 'twere cause for rejoicing. Thou wer't a disgrace yestere'en to thy sister, ay! an' to the hamlet o' Shottery that saw thee raised."

"Make a finish, good Dame," answered Deb, mockingly; "say a disgrace to myself an' the company o' players I have the honour of belonging to."

"Hoity-toity! Play actors!" quoth the other. "Little care I for what disgrace thou be'st to them! But what o' thy broken head, lad? Hath it sore pained thee? Why, my faith, the swelling be quite gone!"

The girl gave way to a short peal of laughter.

"Marry! I laugh," she said, struggling for composure, "yet feel little like it. Look well again, Mistress Blossom. Look well. Surely there be small triumph in befooling thee, for thou art too easy hoodwinked withal. Gaze steady now. Dost still say 'tis Darby Thornbury?"

The woman stared while her complexion went from peony red to pale pink. "Thou giv'st me a turn, an' I be like to swoon," she gasped. "What prank has't afoot, lad?"

"Thou wilt go a bit farther before thou dost faint. Hark then, an' prythee hold by the table an' thou turn'st giddy. Now doth it come. See then, this handsome, well-favoured youth thou art breakfasting," rising and making a pretty bow, "is—is none other than Deb Thornbury!"

"Ods pitikins!" cried the woman.

"Sit down," answered Deb, growing sober. "I would talk with thee, for I need thy good-will and, peradventure, thy help. Things with my brother are in a very coil. He will not be able to take his part i' the new play on the morrow. His face is too sorely marred. Beshrew me, he looks not one half as much like himself as I look like him. Now there be no understudy i' the cast for the character Darby hath taken—further, 'tis an all important one. To have him away would mean confusion and trouble to Blackfriars and I gainsay nothing rejoicing to the Admiral's Company and Lord Pembroke's men. 'Tis not to be contemplated. By the Saints! I would not have trouble come to Master Will Shakespeare through my brother, no, not for the crown jewels! Dost follow me?"

"Nay, that I do not nor what thou'rt coming at," was the dazed response.

Debora shrugged her shoulders. "I hoped 't would have dawned on thee. Why, 'tis just this, I will play the part myself."

"Thou?" cried Dame Blossom, agape. "Thou, Mistress Debora?"

"Yes! yes! Nay, ply me not with questions. My mind is set. There be not one in London who will discover me, an' thou dost not break faith, or let thy good man scent aught on the wind. But I wanted to tell thee, dear Mistress Blossom, and have thy good word. Pray thee say I am not doing wrong, or making any error. I have been so bewildered."

"I will not say thou art i' the right, for I know not. Has't asked Master Darby's consent?"

The girl turned impatiently. "Heart o' me! but thou art able to provoke one. His consent!" with a short laugh. "Nay then—but I will show him his face i' the mirror, an' on sight of it he will leave things for me to settle."

"Ay!" the dame returned, blankly, "I warrant he will. But art not afeared o' the people? What if they should discover thou art a woman!"

"I'll say they are of quicker wit than one I could name," returned Debora. "As for the play—well, I know the play by heart. Now one thing more. I would have thee go with me to Blackfriars. The theatre opens at four o'clock. Say thou wilt bear me company dear, dear Mistress Blossom. Say thou wilt."

"Nay then, I will not. Ods fish! Thou hast gotten thyself in this an' thou can'st get out alone. I will keep a quiet tongue, but ask me to do naught beside."

"Well-a-day! 'Tis as I thought. Now I will go and dress in maidenly clothes. These fearsome things be not needed till the morrow."

VII

By Monday noon Darby Thornbury was unable to lift his head from the pillow by reason of its aching. He remembered nothing about receiving the blow over his eye, and talked little. Dame Blossom and Debora tended him faithfully, keeping Master Blossom away from a true knowledge of affairs. Debora would have had a physician, but Darby would not listen to it.

"I will have no leeching, blood-letting nor evil-smelling draughts," he cried, irritably; "no poultices nor plasters neither! I have misery enough without adding to it, Egad!"

Being brought to this pass and having seen his face in the mirror, he bade Debora find the Master-player of the Company and make what excuse she could for him.

"I be a thrice-dyed fool, Deb," he said with a groan. "Work is over for me in London. I'll ship to the Indies, or America, an' make an ending." Then starting up—"Oh! Deb, could naught be done with me so that I could play this evening?"

"I know not, dear heart," she answered gently, "perchance thy looks might not count an' thou wer't able to act. Art better?"

"Nay, worse!" he said, falling back. "My head maddens me! An' not a word o' the lines sticks i' my memory." So he raved on, fiercely upbraiding himself and wearying Debora. After a time she slipped on her hooded cloak, bade him good-bye, and went out. Returning, she told Darby that he could take courage, for a substitute had been found in his place.

"Ask no questions, dear heart. Nay—an' trouble no more, but rest. Thou wilt be on the boards by Wednesday, an' thy luck is good."

"Dost think so, sweet?" he asked, weakly. "An' will the mark be gone?"

"Why, nearly," she answered; "an' if it still be a little blue, we will paint it. In any case, thine eye will be open, which it is not now."

"Thou art a very angel, Deb, an' I am a brute. I know not where they got one to take my part—an' Marry! I seem not to care. Never will I drink aught but water. Nay, then, thou shalt not go. Stay by me till I sleep, for there be queer lights before my eyes, an' I see thee through them. Thou art so beautiful, Deb, so beautiful."

She waited till he slept, sometimes smiling to herself in a wise way. What children men were when they were ill, she thought. Even Dad would not let her out of his sight when the rheumatism crippled him all last winter. Why, once Nick Berwick came in with a sprained wrist, and naught would be but Deb must bathe and bind it. Nick Berwick! he was so strong and tall and straight. A sigh broke over her lips as she rose and went away to her room.

Half an hour later Debora came down the stairs dressed in the suit of Kendal green. Dame Blossom met her in the hallway.

"Dost keep to thy mad plan, Mistress Deb?"

"Truly," answered the girl. "See, I will be back by sundown. Have no fear for me, the tiring-room hath a latch, an' none know me for myself. Keep thy counsel an' take care o' Darby."

Blackfriars was filled that March afternoon. The narrow windows in the upper gallery had all been darkened, and the house was lit by a thousand lights that twinkled down on eager faces turned towards the stage. Even then at the edge of the rush-strewn boards was a line of stools, which had been taken at a rose-noble apiece by some score of young gallants.

Those who watched the passing of the Master's new romance remembered it while life was in them. Many told their children's children of the marvel of it in the years that followed.

"There was a maid i' the play that day," said a man, long after, "whom they told me was no maid, but a lad. The name was written so on the great coloured bill i' the play-house entrance. 'Marry! an' he be not a maid,' said I, "tis little matter.' He played the part o' Juliet, not as play-acting, but reality. After the curtain was rung down the people stole away in quiet, but their tongues loosened when they got beyond the theatre, for by night the lad was the talk o' London.

"So it went the next day, an' the next, I being there to see, an' fair fascinated by it. Master Will Shakespeare was noticed i' the house the third evening for the first time, though peradventure he had been with the Company behind the scenes, or overhead in the musicians' balcony. Howbeit, when he was discovered there was such a thunder o' voices calling his name that the walls o' the play-house fairly rocked.

"So he came out before the curtain and bowed in the courtly way he hath ever had. His dress was all of black, the doublet o' black satin shining with silver thread, an' the little cloak from his shoulders o' black velvet. He wore, moreover, a mighty ruff fastened with a great pearl, which, I heard whispered, was one the Queen herself had sent him. Report doth says he wears black always, black or sober grays, in memory o' a little lad of his—who died. Well-a-day; I know not if 't be true, but I do know that as he stood there alone upon the stage a quiet fell over the theatre till one could hear one's own heart beat. He spoke with a voice not over-steady, yet far-reaching and sweet and clear, an', if my memory hath not played me false, 'twas this he said:—

"'Good citizens, you who are friendly to all true players of whatever Company they be, I give you thanks, and as a full heart hath ever few words, perchance 'tis left me but to say again and again, I give you thanks. Yet to the gentlemen of my Lord Chamberlain's Company I owe much, for they have played so rarely well, the story hath indeed so gained at their hands, I have dared to hope it will live on.

"'Tis but a beautiful dream crystallised, but may it not, peradventure, be seen again by other people of other times, when we, the players of this little hour, have long grown weary and gone to rest; and when England is kindlier to her actors and reads better the lessons of the stage than now. When England—friends of mine—is older and wiser, for older and wiser she will surely grow, though no dearer—no dearer, God wots—than to-day.'

"Ay!" said he who told of this, "in such manner—though perchance I have garbled the words—he spoke—Will Shakespeare—in the old theatre of Blackfriars, and for us who listened 'twas enough to see him and know he was of ourselves."

Behind the scenes there was much wonderment over the strangely clever acting of Darby Thornbury. Two players guessed the truth; another knew also. This was a man, one Nicholas Berwick.

He stood down by the leathern screenings of the entrance, and three afternoons he was there, his face white as the face of the dead, his eyes burning with an inward fire. He watched the stage with mask-like face, and his great form gave no way though the throng pressed and jostled him. Now and again it would be whispered that he was a little mad. If he heard, he heeded nothing. To him it was as though the end of all things had been reached.

He saw Debora, only Debora. She was there for all those curious eyes to gaze upon, an' this in absolute defiance of every manner and custom of the times. Slowly it came to Berwick's mind, distraught and tortured, that she was playing in Darby's stead, and with some good reason. "That matters not," he thought. "If it be discovered there will be no stilling o' wicked tongues, nor quieting o' Shottery gossip." As for himself, he had no doubt of her. She was his sovereign lady, who could do no wrong, even masquerading thus. But a very terror for her possessed him. Seeming not to listen, he yet heard what the people said in intervals of the play. They were quick to discover the genius of the young actor they called Thornbury, and commented freely upon his wonderful interpretation of lines; but, well as he was known by sight, not a word—a hint, nor an innuendo was spoken to throw a doubt on his identity. Debora's resemblance to him was too perfect, the flowing, heavy garments too completely hid the girlish figure. Further, her accent was Darby's own, even the trick of gesture and smile were his; only the marvel of genius was in one and not in the other.

What the girl's reasons could be for such desperate violation of custom Berwick could not divine, yet while groping blindly for them, with stifled pain in his heart and wild longing to take her away from it all, he gave her his good faith.

Just after sundown, when the play was ended, the man would watch the small side door the actors alone used. Well he knew the figure in the Kendal green suit. Debora must have changed her costume swiftly, for she was among the first to leave the theatre, and twice escaped without being detained by any. On the third evening Berwick saw her followed by two actors.

"Well met, Thornbury!" they called. "Thou hast given us the slip often enough, and further, Master Shakespeare himself was looking for thee as we came out. Hold up, we be going by the ferry also and are bound to have thee for company. 'Fore Heaven, thou art a man o' parts!"

Debora halted, swinging half round toward them with a little laugh.

"Hasten, then," she said. "I have an appointment. Your lines be lighter than mine, in good sooth, or your voices would need resting."

"Thou hast been a very wonder, Thornbury," cried the first. "Talking of voices, what syrup doth use, lad? Never heard I tones more smooth than thine. Thou an' Sherwood together! Egad! 'Twas most singular an' beautiful in effect. Thy modulation was perfect, no wretched cracking nor breaking i' the pathetic portions as we be trained to expect. My voice, now! it hath a fashion of splitting into a thousand fragments an' I try to bridle it."

"'Tis all i' the training," responded Debora, shortly.

"Beshrew me!" said the other; "if 'tis not pity to turn thee back into these clothes, Thornbury. By Saint George! yes—thou dost make too fine a woman."

Berwick clenched his hands as he followed hard behind. The players decided to cross by London Bridge, as the ferries were over-crowded, and still the man kept his watch. Reaching Southwark, the three separated, Debora going on alone. As she came toward Master Blossom's house a man passed Berwick, whom he knew at a glance to be the actor Sherwood. He was not one to be easily forgotten, and upon Nicholas Berwick's memory his features were fixed indelibly; the remembrance of his voice was a torture. Fragments of the passionate, immortal lines, as this man had spoken them at Blackfriars, went through his mind endlessly.

Now Sherwood caught up to the boyish figure as it ran up the steps of the house.

Berwick waited in shadow near by, but they gave him no heed. He saw the girl turn with a smile that illumined her face. The actor lifted his hat and stood bareheaded looking upward. He spoke with eager intensity. Berwick caught the expression of his eyes, and in fancy heard the very words.

Debora shook her head in a wilful fashion of her own, but, bending down, held out her hand. Sherwood raised it to his lips—and—but the lonely watcher saw no more, for he turned away through the twilight.

"The play is ended for thee, Nick Berwick," he said, half aloud. "The play is ended; the curtain dropped. Ay—an' the lights be out." He paced toward the heart of the city, and in the eastern sky, that was of that rare colour that is neither blue nor green, but both blended, a golden star swung, while in the west a line of rose touched the gray above. A benediction seemed to have fallen over the world at the end of the turbulent day. But to Nicholas Berwick there was peace neither in the heavens nor the earth.

VIII

Debora went to her own room swiftly that third evening, and, turning the key, stood with her two hands pressed tight above her heart. "'Tis over," she said—"'tis over, an' well over. Now to tell Darby. I' faith, I know not rightly who I am. Nay, then, I am just Deb Thornbury, not Darby, nor Juliet, for evermore. Oh! what said he at the steps? 'I know thee, I have known thee from the first. See, thou art mine, thou art mine, I tell thee, Juliet, Juliet!'"

Then the girl laughed, a happy little laugh. "Was ever man so imperative? Nay, was ever such a one in the wide, wide world?"

Remembering her dress, she unfastened it with haste and put on the kirtle of white taffeta.

The thought of Sherwood possessed her; his face, the wonderful golden voice of him. The words he had said to her—to her only—in the play.

Of the theatre crowded to the doors, of the stage where the Lord Chamberlain's Company made their exits and entrances, of herself—chief amongst them—she thought nothing. Those things had gone like a dream. She saw only a man standing bareheaded before the little house of Dame Blossom. "I know thee," he had said, looking into her eyes. "Thou art mine."

"Verily, yes—or will be no other's," she had answered him; "and as for Fate, it hath been over-kind." So, with her mind on these thoughts, she went to Darby's room.

He was standing idly by the window, and wheeled about as the girl knocked and entered.

"How look I now, Deb?" he cried. "Come to the light. Nay, 'tis hardly enough to see by, but dost think I will pass muster on the morrow? I am weary o' being mewed up like a cat in a bag."

Debora fixed her eyes on him soberly, not speaking.

"What is't now?" he said, impatiently. "What art staring at? Thine eyes be like saucers."

"I be wondering what thou wilt say an' I tell thee somewhat," she answered, softly.

"Out with it then. Thou hast seen Berwick, I wager. I heard he was to be in town; he hath followed thee, Deb, an'—well, pretty one—things are settled between thee at last?"

"Verily, no!" she cried, her face colouring, "an' thou canst not better that guessing, thou hadst best not try again."

"No? Then what's to do, little sister?"

"Dost remember I told thee they had found one to take thy part at Blackfriars?"

"Egad, yes, that thought has been i' my head ever since. 'Fore Heaven, I would some one sent me word who 'twas. I ache for news. Hast heard who 'twas, Deb?"

"'Twas I," she answered, the pink going from her face. "'Twas I, Debora!"

The young fellow caught at the window ledge and looked at her steadily without a word. Then he broke into a strange laugh. Taking the girl by the shoulder he swung her to the fading light.

"What dost mean?" he said, hoarsely. "Tell me the truth."

"I' faith, that is the truth," she answered, quietly. "The only truth. There was no other way I could think of—and I had the lines by heart. None knew me. All thought 'twas thee, Darby. See, see! when I was fair encased in that Kendal green suit o' thine, why even Dad could not have told 'twas not thy very self! We must be strangely alike o' face, dear heart—though mayhap our souls be different."

"Nay!" he exclaimed, "'tis past belief that thou should'st take my part! My brain whirls to think on't. I saw thee yesternight—the day before—this noon-day—an' thou wert as unruffled as a fresh-blown rose. Naught was wrong with thy colour, and neither by word or sign did'st give me an inkling of such mad doings! 'Gad!—if 'tis true it goes far to prove that a woman can seem most simple when she is most subtle. An' yet—though I like it not, Deb—I know not what to say to thee. 'Twas a venturous, mettlesome thing to do—an' worse—'twas vastly risky. We be not so alike—I cannot see it."

"Nor I, always," she said, with a shrug, "but others do. Have no fear of discovery, one only knows beside Dame Blossom, and they will keep faith. Neither fear for thy reputation. The people gave me much applause, though I played not for that."

Darby threw himself into a chair and dropped his face in his hands.

"Who is't that knows?" he asked, half-roughly, after a pause. "Who is't, Deb?"

"He who played Romeo," she said, in low tone.

"Sherwood?" exclaimed Darby. "Don Sherwood! I might have guessed."

"Ay!" replied the girl. "He only, I have reason to believe." A silence fell between them, while the young fellow restlessly crossed to the window again. Debora went to him and laid her hand upon his shoulder, as was her way.

"Thou wilt not go thy own road again, Darby?" she said, coaxingly. "Perchance 'tis hard to live straightly here in London—still promise me thou wilt not let the ways o' the city warp thy true heart. See, then, what I did was done for thee; mayhap 'twas wrong—thou know'st 'twas fearsome, an' can ne'er be done again."

"'Twill not be needed again, Deb," he answered, and his voice trembled. "Nay, I will go no more my own way, but thy way, and Dad's. Dost believe me?"

"Ay!" she said, smiling, though her lashes were wet, "Dad's way, for 'tis a good way, a far better one than any thy wilful, wayward little sister could show thee."

Out of doors the velvety darkness deepened. Somewhere, up above, a night-hawk called now and again its harsh, yet plaintive, note. A light wind, bearing the smell of coming rain and fresh breaking earth, blew in, spring-like and sweet, yet sharp.

Presently Debora spoke, half hesitatingly.

"I would thou wert minded to tell me somewhat," she started, "somewhat o' Sherwood, the player. Hath he—hath he the good opinion o' Master Will Shakespeare—now?"

"In truth, yes," returned the actor. "And of the whole profession. It seems," smiling a little, "it seems thou dost take Master Shakespeare's word o' a man as final. He stand'th in thy good graces or fall'th out o' them by that, eh!"

"Well, peradventure, 'tis so," she admitted, pursing up her lips. "But Master Don Sherwood—tell me——"

"Oh! as for him," broke in Darby, welcoming any subject that turned thought from himself, "he is a rare good fellow, is Sherwood, though that be not his real name, sweet. 'Tis not often a man makes change of his name on the handbills, but 'tis done now and again."

"It doth seem an over-strange fashion," said Debora, "an' one that must surely have a reason back o' it. What, then, is Master Sherwood called when he be rightly named?"

"Now let me think," returned Darby, frowning, "the sound of it hath slipped me. Nay, I have it—Don—Don, ah! Dorien North. There 'tis, and the fore part is the same as the little lad's at home, an uncommon title, yet smooth to the tongue. Don Sherwood is probably one Dorien Sherwood North, an' that too sounds well. He hath a rare voice. It play'th upon a man strangely, and there be tones in it that bring tears when one would not have them. Thou should'st hear him sing Ben Jonson's song! 'Rare Ben Jonson,' as some fellow hath written him below a verse o' his, carved over the blackwood mantel at the Devil's tavern. Thou should'st hear Sherwood sing, 'Drink to me only with thine eyes.' I' faith! he carries one's soul away! Ah! Deb," he ended, "I am having a struggle to keep my mind free from that escapade o' thine. Jove! an' I thought any other recognised thee!"

"None other did, I'll gainsay," Debora answered, in a strangely quiet way; "an' he only because he found me that day i' the Royal Box—so long ago. What was't thou did'st call him, Darby? Don Sherwood? Nay, Dorien North. Dorien North!"

Her hand, which had been holding Darby's sleeve, slipped away from it, and with a little cry she fell against the window ledge and so to the floor.

Darby hardly realised for a moment that she had fainted. When she did not move he stooped and lifted her quickly, his heart beating fast with fear.

"Why, Deb!" he cried. "What is't? Heaven's mercy! She hath swooned. Nay, then, not quite; there, then, open thine eyes again. Thou hast been forewearied, an' with reason. Art thyself now?" as his sister looked up and strove to rise.

"Whatever came over thee, sweet? Try not to walk. I will lift thee to the bed an' call Dame Blossom. Marry! what queer things women be."

"Ay! truly," she answered, faintly, steadying herself against him. "Ay! vastly queer. Nay, I will not go to the bed, but will sit in your chair."

"Thou art white as linen," anxiously. "May I leave thee to call the Dame? I fear me lest thou go off again."

"Fear naught o' that," said Deb, with a little curl of her lips. "An' call Mistress Blossom an' thou wilt, but 'tis nothing; there—dear heart, I will be well anon. Hast not some jaunt for to-night? I would not keep thee, Darby."

"'Tis naught but the players' meeting-night at The Mermaid. It hath no great charm for me, and I will cry it off on thy account."

"That thou wilt not," she said, with spirit, a bit of pink coming to her face with the effort. "I can trust thee, an' thou must go. 'Twill ne'er do to have one an' another say,—'Now, where be Darby Thornbury?' There might be some suspicions fly about an' they met thee not."

"Thou hast a wise head. 'Twould not do,—and I have a game o' bluff to carry on that thou hast started. Thou little heroine!" kissing her hand. "What pluck thou did'st have! What cool pluck. Egad!" ruefully, "I almost wish thou had'st not had so much. 'Twas a desperate game, and I pray the saints make me equal to the finish."

"'Twas desperate need to play it," she answered, wearily. "Go, then, I would see Mistress Blossom."

Thornbury stood, half hesitating, turned, and went out.

"'Twill ever be so with him," said the girl. "He lov'th me—but he lov'th Darby Thornbury better."

Then she hid her face. "Oh! heart o' me! I cannot bear it, I cannot bear it—'tis too much. I will go away to Shottery to-morrow. I mind me what Dad said, an' 't has come to be truth. 'Thou wilt never bide in peace at One Tree Inn again.' Peace!" she said, with bitter accent. "Peace! I think there be no peace in the world; or else 't hath passed me by."

Resting her chin on her hand, she sat thinking in the shadowy room. Darby had lit a candle on the high mantel, and her sombre eyes rested on the yellow circle of light.

"Who was't I saw 'n the road as I came out o' Blackfriars? Who was't—now let me think. I paid no more heed than though I had seen him in a dream, yet 'twas some one from home— Now I mind me! 'Twas Nicholas Berwick. His eyes burned in his white face. He stared straightway at me an' made no sign. An' so he was in the theatre also. Then he knew! Poor Nick! poor Nick!" she said, with a heavy sigh. "He loved me, or he hath belied himself many times; an' I! I thought little on't."

"Oh! Mistress Blossom," as the door opened. "Is't thou? Come over beside me." As the good Dame came close, the girl threw her arms about her neck.

"Why, sweet lamb!" exclaimed the woman. "What hath happened thee? Whatever hath happened thee?"

"What is one to do when the whole world go'th wrong?" cried Debora. "Oh! gaze not so at me, I be not dazed or distraught. Oh! dear Mistress Blossom, I care not to live to be as old as thou art. I am forewearied o' life."

"Weary o' life! an' at thy time! My faith, thou hast not turned one-and-twenty! Why, then, Mistress Debora, I be eight-an'-forty, yet count that not old by many a year."

Deb gave a tired little gesture. "Every one to their fancy—to me the world and all in it is a twice-told tale. I would not have more o' it—by choice." She rose and turned her face down toward the good Dame. "An' one come to ask for me—a—a player, one Master Sherwood of the Lord Chamberlain's Company—could'st thou—would'st thou bid him wait below i' the small parlour till I come?"

"Ay, truly," answered the woman, brightening. "Thou art heartily welcome to receive him there, Mistress Debora."

"Thank thee kindly. He hath business with me, but will not tarry long."

"I warrant many a grand gentleman would envy him that business," said the Dame, smiling.

Debora gave a little laugh—short and hard. Her eyes, of a blue that was almost black, shone like stars.

"Dost think so?" she said. "Nay, then, thou art a flatterer. I will to my room. My hair is roughened, is't not?"

"Thou art rarely beautiful as thou art; there be little rings o' curls about thy ears. I would not do aught to them. Thy face hath no colour, yet ne'er saw I thee more comely."

"Now, that is well," she answered. "That giveth my faint heart courage, an' marry! 'tis what I need. I would not look woe-begone, or of a cast-down countenance, not I! but would bear me bravely, an' there be cause. Go thou now, good Mistress Blossom; the faintness hath quite passed."

It seemed but a moment before Debora heard the Dame's voice again at the door.

"He hath come," she said, in far-reaching whisper fraught with burden of unrelieved curiosity.

"He doth wait below, Mistress Deb. Beshrew me! but he is as goodly a gentleman as any i' London! His doublet is brocaded an' o'er brave with silver lacings, an' he wear'th a fluted ruff like the quality at Court. Moreover, he hold'th himself like a very Prince."

"Doth he now?" said Debora, going down the hallway. "Why, then he hath fair captivated thee. Thou, at thy age! Well-a-day! What think'st o' his voice," she asked, pausing at the head of the stairs. "What think'st o' his voice, Mistress Blossom?"

"Why, that 'twould be fine an' easy for him to persuade one to his way o' thinking with it—even against their will," answered the woman, smiling.

"Ah! good Dame, I agree not with thee in that," said Debora. "I think he hath bewitched thee, i' faith." So saying, she went below, opened the little parlour door, and entered.

Sherwood was standing in the centre of the room, which was but dimly lit by the high candles. Deb did not speak till she had gone to a window facing the deserted common-land, pulled back the curtains and caught them fast. A flood of white moonlight washed through the place and made it bright.

The player seemed to realise there was something strange about the girl, for he stood quite still, watching her quick yet deliberate movement anxiously.

As she came toward him from the window he held out his hands. "Sweetheart!" he said, unsteadily. "Sweetheart!"

"Nay," she answered, with a little shake of her head and clasping her hands behind. "Not thine."

"Ay!" he cried, passionately, "thou art—all mine. Thine eyes, so truthful, so wondrous; the gold-flecked waves of thine hair; the white o' thy throat that doth dazzle me; the sweetness of thy lips; the little hands behind thee."

"So," said the girl, with a catch of the breath, "so thou dost say, but 'tis not true. As for my body, such as it is, it is my own."

Sherwood leaned toward her, his eyes dark and luminous. "'Fore Heaven, thou art wrong," he said. "Thou dost belong to me."

"What o' my soul?" she asked, softly. "What o' my soul, Sir Romeo? Is that thine, too?"

"Nay," he answered, looking into her face, white from some inward rebellion. "Nay, then, sweetheart, for I think that is God's."

"Then, thou hast left me nothing," she cried, moving away. "Oh!"—throwing out her hands—"hark thee, Master Sherwood. 'Tis a far cry since thou did'st leave me by the steps at sundown. A far, far cry. The world hath had time to change. I did not know thee then. Now I do."

"Why, I love thee," he answered, not understanding. "I love thee, thou dost know that surely. Come, tell me. What else dost know, sweetheart? See! I am but what thou would'st have—bid me by what thou wilt. I will serve thee in any way thou dost desire. I have given my life to thee—and by it I swear again thou art mine."

"That I am not," she said, standing before him still and unyielding. "Look at me—look well!"

The man bent down and looked steadfastly into the girl's tragic face. It was coldly inflexible, and wore the faint shadow of a smile—a smile such as the lips of the dead sometimes wear, as though they knew all things, having unriddled life's problem.

"Debora!" he cried. "Debora! What is it? What hath come to thee?"

She laughed, a little rippling laugh that broke and ended. "Nay, thou traitor—that I will not tell thee—but go—go!"

The player stood a moment irresolute, then caught her wrists and held them. His face had turned hard and coldly grave as her own. Some look in his eyes frightened her.

"'Tis a coil," he said, "and Fate doth work against me. Yet verily 'tis a coil I will unravel. I am not easily worsted, but in the end bend things to my will. An' thou wilt not tell me what stands i' my road, I will discover it for myself. As for the Judas name thou hast called me—it fits me not. Should'st thou desire to tell me so thyself at any time—to take it back—send me but a word. So I go."

The long, swift steps sounded down the hall; there was the opening and shutting of a door, and afterward silence.

IX

The night wore on and the moonlight faded. The stars shone large and bright; the sound of people passing on the street grew less and less. Now and then a party of belated students or merry-makers came by, singing a round or madrigal. A melancholy night-jar called incessantly over the house-tops. As the clocks tolled one, there was a sound of rapid wheels along the road and a coach stopped before goodman Blossom's.

Young Thornbury leaped from it, and with his heavy knocking roused the man, who came stumbling sleepily down the hallway.

"Oh! pray thee, make haste, Blossom," called the young fellow; "keep me not waiting." Then, as the door flew open, "My sister!" he said, pushing by, "is she still up?"

"Gra'mercy! Thou dost worrit sober folk till they be like to lose their wits! Thy sister should be long abed—an' thou too. Thou art become a pranked-out coxcomb with all thy foppery—a coxcomb an' a devil-may-care roysterer with thy blackened eyes—thy dice-playing an' thy coming in o' midnight i' coaches!"

Darby strode past, unheeding; at the stairs Debora met him.

"Thou art dressed," he said, hoarsely. "Well, fetch thy furred cloak; the night turns cold. Lose no moment—but hasten!"

"Where?" she cried. "Oh! what now hath gone amiss?"

"I will tell thee i' the road; tarry not to question me."

It was scarcely a moment before the coach rolled away again. Nothing was said till they came to London Bridge. The flickering links flashed by them as they passed. A sea-scented wind blew freshly over the river and the tide was rising fast.

"I have no heart for more trouble," said the girl, tremulously. "Oh! tell me, Darby, an' keep me not waiting. Where go'th the coach? What hath happened? Whatever hath happened?"

"Just this," he said, shortly. "Nicholas Berwick hath been stabbed by one he differed with at 'The Mermaid.' He is at the point o' death, an' would not die easy till he saw thee."

"Nick Berwick? Say'th thou so—at the point o' death? Nay, dear heart, it cannot be. I will not believe it—he will not die,—he is too great and strong—'tis not so grievous as that," cried Deb.

"'Tis worse, we think. He will be gone by daybreak. He may be gone now. See! the horses have turned into Cheapside. We will soon be there."

"What was the cause?" the girl asked, faintly. "Tell me how he came by the blow."

There was no sound for a while but the whirling of wheels and the ringing of the horses' feet over cobble-stones.

"I will tell thee, though 'tis not easy for either thou nor I.

"'Twas the players' night at 'The Mermaid,' and there was a lot of us gathered. Marry! Ben Jonson and Master Shakespeare, Beaumont and Keene. I need not give thee names, for there were men from 'The Rose' playhouse and 'The Swan.' 'Twas a gay company and a rare. Ay! Sherwood was there for half an hour, though he was overgrave and distraught, it seemed to me. They would have him sing 'Drink to me only with thine eyes.' 'Fore Heaven, I will remember it till I die."

"Nick Berwick," she said. "Oh! what of him?"

"Ay! he was there; he came in with Master Will Shakespeare, and he sat aside—not speaking to any, watching and listening. He was there when the party had thinned out, still silent. I mind his face, 'twas white as death at a feast. Not half an hour ago—an' there were but ten of us left—a man—one from 'The Rose,' they told me—I knew him not by sight—leaped to a chair and, with a goblet filled and held high, called out to the rest—

"'Come,' he cried above the noise of our voices. 'Come, another toast! Come, merry gentlemen, each a foot on the table! I drink to a new beauty. For as I live 'twas no man, but a maid, who was on the boards at Blackfriars i' the new play, and the name o' her——'"

The girl caught her breath—"Darby!—Darby!"

"Nay, he said no more, sweet; for Nick Berwick caught him and swung him to the floor."

"'Thou dost lie!' he cried. 'Take back thy words before I make thee.' While he spoke he shook the fellow violently, then on a sudden loosened his hold. As he did so, the player drew a poniard from its sheath at his hip, sprang forward, and struck Berwick full i' the throat. That is all," Thornbury said, his voice dropping, "save that he asked incessantly for thee, Deb, ere he fainted."

The coach stopped before a house where the lights burned brightly. Opening the door they entered a low, long room with rafters and wainscoting of dark wood. In the centre of it was a huge table, in disorder of flagons and dishes. The place was blue with smoke, and overheated, for a fire yet burned in the great fireplace. On a settle lay a man, his throat heavily bound with linen, and by him was a physician of much fame in London, and one who had notable skill in surgery.

Debora went swiftly toward them with outstretched hands.

"Oh! Nick! Nick!" she said, with a little half-stifled cry. "Oh! Nick, is't thou?"

"Why, 'twas like thee to come," he answered, eagerly, raising up on his elbow. "'Twill make it easier for me, Deb—an' I go. Come nearer, come close."

The physician lowered him gently back and spoke with soft sternness.

"Have a care, good gentleman," he said. "We have stopped the bleeding, and would not have it break out afresh. Thy life depends upon thy stillness." So saying, he withdrew a little.

"Oh! move not, Nick," said the girl, slipping to the floor beside him and leaning against the oaken seat; "neither move nor speak. I will keep watch beside thee. But why did'st deny it or say aught? 'Twould have been better that the whole o' London knew than this! Nay, answer me not," she continued, fearfully; "thou may not speak or lift a finger."

Berwick smiled faintly, "Ah! sweet," he said, pausing between the words, "I would not have thy name on every tongue—but would silence them all—an' I had lives enough. Yet thou wert in truth upon the stage at Blackfriars—in Will Shakespeare's play—though I denied it!"

"Yes," said Deb, softly, "but 'twas of necessity. We will think no more of it. It breaks my heart to see thee here, Nick," she ended, with quivering lips, her eyes wide and pitiful.

"Now that need not trouble thee," answered the man, a light breaking over his gray, drawn face. "'Fore Heaven, I mind it not."

"Thou wilt be better soon," said the girl. "I will have it so, Nick. I will not have thee die for this."

"Dost remember what I asked thee last Christmas, Deb?"

"Yes," she said, not meeting his eyes.

"Wilt kiss me now, Deb?"

For answer she stooped down and laid her lips to his, then rose and stood beside him.

"Ah! Deb," he said, looking up at her adoringly. "'Twill be something to remember—should I live—an' if not, well—'tis not every man who dies with a kiss on his lips."

"Thou must not talk," she said.

"No," he answered, faintly, "nor keep thee. Yet promise me one thing."

"What would'st have me promise?"

"That thou wilt return on the morrow to Shottery. London is no place for thee now."

"I will go," answered the girl; "though I would fain take care of thee here, Nick."

"That thou must not think of," he replied. "I will fare—as God wills. Go thou home to Shottery."

The physician crossed over to them and laid his white fingers on Berwick's wrist.

"Thou dost seem set upon undoing my work," he said. "Art so over-ready to die, Master Berwick? One more swoon like the last and thou would'st sleep on."

"He will talk no more, good Doctor," said Debora, hastily. "Ah! thou wilt be kind to him, I pray thee? And now I will away, as 'tis best, but my brother will stay, and carry out thy orders. Nay, Nick, thou must not even say good-bye or move thy lips. I will go back to Dame Blossom quite safely in the coach."

"An' to Shottery on the morrow?" he whispered.

"Ay!" she said, looking at him with tear-blinded eyes, "as thou wilt have it so."

X

It was early morning of the next day and Debora Thornbury was in the upper room at Mistress Blossom's house. She folded one garment after another and laid them away in the little trunk that had come with her from home.

Darby entered the room before she had finished, and threw himself wearily into a chair.

"Thou hast brought news," she said, eagerly; "he is better—or——"

"Nay, there is no great change. The Leech is still with him and makes no sign; yet I fancy he hath a shade of hope, for no further hemorrhage hath occurred. Nick sent me back to thee; he would not be denied."

"Ah!" she cried, "I am afraid to take heart. I dare not hope." Then, after a moment's pause, "Tell me, Darby; I must know. Who was it that struck him?"

"'Twas a player I know by reputation," replied Darby, "yet, as I told thee, never met till yesternight. He is one Dorien North, and hath the very name that Sherwood discarded—with ample reason, if what report says of this man be true. It seems they be first cousins, but while Sherwood is a most rarely good fellow, this other, albeit with the same grace o' manner and a handsome enough face, is by odds the most notorious scamp out of Newgate to-day. He hath a polish an' wit that stands him in place o' morals. Of late he hath been with the Lord High Admiral's men at 'The Rose'; but they were ever a scratch company, and a motley lot."

The girl moved unsteadily across to her brother. She grasped the velvet sleeve of his tabard and gazed into his face with eyes great and darkening.

"One thing follows on another o'er fast. I am bewildered. Is't true what thou hast just said, Darby?"

"Egad, yes!" he replied, wonderingly. "I would have told thee of North the day thou swooned, but 't went out o' my mind. Dost not remember asking me why Sherwood had changed his name on the bills o' the play? Yet, what odds can it make?"

"Only this," she cried, "that this Dorien North, who has so painted the name black, and who but last night struck Nicholas Berwick, is in very truth little Dorien's father. So goes the man's name the Puritan maid told me. Moreover, he was a player also. Oh! Darby, dost not see? I thought 'twas the other—Don Sherwood."

"'Twas like a woman to hit so wide o' the mark," answered Darby. "Did'st not think there might chance be two of the name? In any case what is't to thee, Deb?"

"Oh!" she said, laying her face against his arm, "I cannot tell thee; ask no more, but go thou and find him and tell him the story of Nell Quinten, and how I thought that Dorien North she told me of was he; and afterwards if he wilt come with thee, bring him here to me. Perchance he may be at Blackfriars, or—or 'The Tabard Inn,' or even abroad upon the streets. In any case, find him quickly, dear heart, for the time is short and I must away to Shottery, as I promised Nick,—poor Nick,—poor Nick." So she fell to sobbing and crying.

The young fellow gazed at her in that distress which overtakes a man when a woman weeps.

"Marry," he said, "I wish thou would'st give over thy tears. I weary of them and they will mend naught. There, cheer up, sweet. I will surely find Sherwood, and at once, as 'tis thy wish."

It was high noon when Darby Thornbury returned. With him came the player Sherwood and another. The three entered Master Blossom's house, and Darby sought his sister.

"Don Sherwood waits below," he said, simply. "I met him on London Bridge. He hath brought his cousin Dorien North with him."

"I thank thee," the girl answered. "I will go to them."

Presently she entered Dame Blossom's little parlour where the two men awaited her.

She stood a moment, looking from one to the other. Neither spoke nor stirred.

Then Debora turned to Don Sherwood; her lips trembled a little.

"I wronged thee," she said, softly. "I wronged thee greatly. I ask thy pardon."

"Nay," he said, going to her. "Ask it not, 'twas but a mistake. I blame thee not for it. This," motioning to the other, "this is my kinsman, Dorien North. He is my father's brother's son, and we bear the same name, or rather did so in the past."

The girl looked at the man before her coldly, yet half-curiously.

"I would," went on Sherwood, steadily, "that he might hear the tale Darby told me. To-morrow he sails for the Indies, as I have taken passage for him on an outward-bound ship. He came to me for money to escape last night, after having stabbed one Master Berwick in a brawl at 'The Mermaid.' It may be thou hast already heard of this?"

"Ay!" she answered, whitening, "I have heard."

"I gave him the passage money," continued Sherwood, "for I would not either have him swing on Tyburn or rot in Newgate. Yet I will even now tell the Captain under whom he was to sail that he is an escaping felon—a possible murderer—if he lies to thee in aught—and I shall know if he lies."

The man they both watched threw back his handsome, blond head at this and laughed a short, hard laugh. His dazzling white teeth glittered, and in the depths of his blue eyes was a smouldering fire.

"By St. George!" he broke out, "you have me this time, Don. Hang me! If I'm not betwixt the devil and the deep sea." Then, with a low bow to Debora, raising his hand against his heart in courtly fashion, "I am thy servant, fair lady," he said. "Ask me what thou dost desire. I will answer."

"I would have asked thee—Art thou that Dorien North who deceived and betrayed one Nell Quinten, daughter of Makepeace Quinten, the Puritan, who lives near Kenilworth," said Debora, gravely; "but indeed I need not to ask thee. The child who was in her arms when we found her—hath thy face."

"Doth not like it?" he questioned, with bold effrontery, raising his smiling, dare-devil eyes to hers.

"Ay!" she said, gently, "I love little Dorien's face, and 'tis truly thine in miniature—thine when it was small and fair and innocent. Oh! I am sorry for thee, Master Dorien North, more sorry than I was for thy child's mother, for she had done no evil, save it be evil to love."

A change went over the man's face, and for a moment it softened.

"Waste not thy pity," he said; "I am not worth it. I confess to all my sins. I wronged Nell Quinten, and the child is mine. Yet I would be altogether graceless did I not thank thee for giving him shelter, Mistress Thornbury."

Sherwood, who had been listening in silence, suddenly spoke.

"That is all I needed of thee, Dorien," he said. "You may go. I do not think from here to the docks there will be danger of arrest; the heavy cloak and drooping hat so far disguise thee; while once on ship-board thou art safe."

"I am in danger enough," said the other, with a shrug, "but it troubles me little. I bid thee farewell, Mistress Thornbury." And so saying he turned to go.

"Wait," she cried, impulsively, touching his arm. "I would not have thee depart so; thou art going into a far country, Master North, and surely need some fair wishes to take with thee. Oh! I know thou hast been i' the wrong, many, many times over. Perchance, hitherto thou hast feared neither God nor the law. But last night—Nicholas Berwick was sorely wounded by thee, and this because he defended my name."

"Yet 'twas thou who played at Blackfriars?" he questioned, hesitatingly. "I saw thee; it could have been no other."

"'Twas I," she answered. "I played in my brother's place—of necessity—but speak no more of that, 'tis over, and as that is past for me, so would I have thee leave all thy unhappy past. Take not thy sins with thee into the new country. Ah! no. Neither go with bitterness in thy heart towards any, but live through the days that come as any gentleman should who bears thy name. Thy path and mine have crossed," she ended, the pink deepening in her face, "an' so I would bid thee godspeed for the sake of thy little son."

The man stood irresolute a moment, then stooped, lifted Debora's hand to his lips and kissed it.

"Thou hast preached me a homily," he said, in low voice; "yet, 'fore Heaven, from such a priest I mind it not." And, opening the door, he went swiftly away.

Then Don Sherwood drew Debora to him. "Nothing shall ever take thee from me," he said, passionately. "I would not live, sweetheart, to suffer what I suffered yesternight."

"Nor I," she answered.

"When may I to Shottery to wed thee?" he asked.

"Oh! I will not leave my father for many a day," she said, smiling tremulously. "Yet I would have thee come to Shottery by-and-bye—peradventure, when the summer comes, and the great rosebush beneath the south window is ablow."

"Beshrew me! 'tis ages away, the summer," he returned, with impatience.

"The days till then will be as long for me as for thee," she said, tenderly; and with this assurance, and because he would fain be pleasing her in all things, he tried to make himself content.

XI

It is Christmas eve once more, and all the diamond window panes of One Tree Inn—are aglitter with light from the Yule log fire in the front room chimney-place and the many candles Mistress Debora placed in their brass candlesticks.

Little Dorien had followed her joyously from room to room, and many times she had lifted him in her strong, young arms and let him touch the wick with the lighted spill and start the fairy flame. Then his merry laugh rang through the house, and John Sevenoakes and Master Thornbury, sitting by the hearth below, smiled as they listened, for it is so good a thing to hear, the merry, whole-hearted, innocent laughter of a child.

Even the leathery, grim old face of Ned Saddler relaxed into a pleasant expression at the sound of it, though 'twas against his will to allow himself to show anything of happiness he felt; for he was much like a small, tart winter apple, wholesome and sound at heart, yet sour enough to set one's teeth on edge.

And they talked together, these three ancient cronies, while now and then Master Thornbury leaned over and stirred the contents of the big copper pot on the crane, sorely scorching his kindly face in the operation.

Presently Nick Berwick came in, stamping the snow off his long boots, and he crossed to the hearth and turned his broad back to the fire, even as he had done a year before on Christmas eve. His face was graver than it had been, for his soul had had a wide outlook since then, but his mouth smiled in the old-time sweet and friendly fashion, and if he had any ache of the heart he made no sign.

"Hast come over from Stratford, lad?" asked Thornbury.

"Ay!" he answered, "an' I just met little Judith Shakespeare hastening away from grand dame Hathaway's. She tells me her father is coming home for Christmas. Never saw I one in a greater flutter of excitement. 'Oh! Nick,' she cried out, ere I made sure who it was in the dusk, 'Hast heard the news?' 'What news, gossip?' I answered. 'Why, that my father will be home to-night,' she called back. ''Tis more than I dreamed or dared to hope, but 'tis true.' I could see the shining of her eyes as she spoke, and she tripped onward as though the road were covered with rose-leaves instead of snow."

"She is a giddy wench," said Saddler, "and doth lead Deb into half her pranks. If I had a daughter now——"

Thornbury broke into a great laugh and clapped the old fellow soundly on the shoulder.

"Hark to him!" he cried. "If he had a daughter! Marry and amen, I would we could see what kind of maid she would be."

"I gainsay," put in Sevenoakes, thinking to shift the subject, "that Will Shakespeare comes home as much for Deb's wedding as aught else."

A shade went over Berwick's face. "The church hath been pranked out most gaily, Master Thornbury," he said.

"'Twill be gay enough," said Saddler, "but there'll be little comfort in it and small rest for a man's hand or elbow anywhere for the holly they've strung up. I have two lame thumbs with the prickles that have run into them."

Thornbury smiled. "Then 'twas thou who helped the lads and lasses this afternoon, Ned," he said; "and I doubt nothing 'twas no one else who hung the great bunch of mistletoe in the chancel! I marvel at thee."

At this they all laughed so loudly that they did not hear Deb and little Dorien enter the room and come over to the hearth, with Tramp following.

"What art making so merry over, Dad?" she questioned, looking from one to another.

"Nay, ask me not. Ask Saddler."

"He doth not like maids who are curious," she said, shaking her head. "I am content to be in the dark."

Then she cried, listening, "There, dost not hear the coach? I surely caught the rumble of the wheels, and she is on time for once! Come, Dorien. Come, Dad, we will to the door to meet them."

Soon the lumbering coach swung up the road and the tired horses stopped under the oak.

And it was a welcome worth having the two travellers got, for Darby Thornbury and Don Sherwood had journeyed from London together, ay! and Master Shakespeare had borne them company, though he left them half a mile off. As the group drew their chairs about the fireplace, Darby had many a jest and happy story to repeat that the master told them on the homeward way, for he was ever the best company to make a long road seem short.

Deb sat in her old seat in the inglenook and Master Sherwood stood beside her, where he could best see the ruddy light play over her wondrous hair and in the tender depths of her eyes. They seemed to listen, these two, as Darby went lightly from one London topic to another, for now and then Don Sherwood put in a word or so in that mellow voice of his, and Deb smiled often—yet it may be they did not follow him over closely, for they were dreaming a dream of their own and the day after the morrow was their wedding day.

The child Dorien lay upon the sheepskin rug at Deb's feet and watched Darby. His eager, beautiful little face lit up with joy, for were they not all there together, those out of the whole world he loved the best, and it would be Christmas in the morning. What more could any child desire?

"When I look at the little lad, Don," said Debora, softly, "my thoughts go back to his mother. 'Twas on such a night as this, as I have told thee, that Darby found her in the snow."

"Think not of it, sweetheart," he answered; "the child, at least, has missed naught that thou could'st give."

"I know, I know," she said, in a passionate, low tone, "but it troubles me when I think of all that I have of care and life's blessings, and of her woe and desolation, and through no sin, save that of loving too well. I see not why it should be."

"Ah!" he said, bending towards her, "there are some 'Why's' that must wait for their answer—for 'twill not come this side o' heaven." Then, in lighter tone, "When I look at the little lad I see but that scapegrace kinsman of mine; but although he is so marvellous like him, thou wilt be his guide. I fear nothing for his future, for who could be aught but good with thee, my heart's love, beside them."

And presently there was a stir as Nicholas Berwick rose and bid all good-night, and this reminded John Sevenoakes and Ned Saddler that the hour was late. It was then that Berwick went to Deb, at a moment when she stood apart from the others. He held towards her a small leather-covered box.

"'Tis my wedding gift to thee, Deb," he said, his grave eyes upon her changeful face. "'Tis a pearl collar my mother wore on her wedding-day when she was young and fair as thou art. I will not be here to see how sweet thou dost look in it."

"Thou wilt in the church, Nick?"

"Nay, I will not. I have not told thee before, as I would not plant a thorn in any of thy roses, but I ride to London on the morrow. I have much work there, for later on I sail to America to the new Colonies, in charge of certain stores for Sir Walter Raleigh."

She raised her eyes, tear-filled and tender, to his.

"I wish thee peace, Nick," she said, "wherever thou art—and I have no fear but that gladness will follow. I will miss thee, for thou wert ever my friend."

He lifted her hand to his lips and went away, and in the quiet that followed, when Master Thornbury and Darby talked together, Don Sherwood drew Debora into the shadow by the window-seat.

"I' faith," he said, "if I judge not wrongly by Master Nicholas Berwick's face when he spoke with thee but now, he doth love thee also, Deb."

"Ah!" she answered, "he hath indeed said so in the past and moreover proven it."

"In very truth, yes. But thou," with a flash in his eyes, "dost care? Hast aught of love for him? Nay, I need not ask thee."

She smiled a little, half sadly.

"I love but thee," she said.

He gave a short, light laugh, then looked grave.

"'Tis another of life's 'Why's,' sweetheart, that awaiteth an answer. Why!—why, in heaven's name, should I have the good fortune to win thee, when he, who I think is far the better gentleman, hath failed?"

As he spoke, the bells of Stratford rang out their joyous pealing, and the sound came to them on the night wind. Then the child, who had been asleep curled up on the soft rug, opened his wondering eyes.

Deb stooped and lifted him, and he laid his curly head against her shoulder.

"Is it Christmas, Deb?" he asked, sleepily.

"Yes, my lamb," she answered; "for, hark! the bells are ringing it in, and they say, 'Peace, Dorien—Peace and goodwill to men.'"

THE END

Milton Keynes UK
Ingram Content Group UK Ltd.
UKHW020843260624
444769UK00011B/456

Intermediate
GNVQ
Art & Design

Alan W Smith

MACMILLAN

City & Guilds

© Alan W Smith 1997

All rights reserved. No reproduction, copy or transmission of this publication may be made without written permission.

No paragraph of this publication may be reproduced, copied or transmitted save with written permission or in accordance with the provisions of the Copyright, Designs and Patents Act 1988, or under the terms of any licence permitting limited copying issued by the Copyright Licensing Agency, 90 Tottenham Court Road, London W1P 9HE.

Any person who does any unauthorised act in relation to this publication may be liable to criminal prosecution and civil claims for damages.

The author has asserted his right to be identified as the author of this work in accordance with the Copyright, Designs and Patents Act 1988.

First published 1997 by
MACMILLAN PRESS LTD
Houndmills, Basingstoke, Hampshire RG21 6XS
and London
Companies and representatives
throughout the world

ISBN 0-333-66090-0

A catalogue record for this book is available from the British Library.

This book is printed on paper suitable for recycling and made from fully managed and sustained forest sources.

10 9 8 7 6 5 4 3 2 1
06 05 04 03 02 01 00 99 98 97

Printed in Hong Kong

Contents

Acknowledgements vii

Introduction *ix*

1   How this book will help you *1*
    1.1   The language of art and design and of GNVQ *1*
    1.2   Using this book *3*
    1.3   Developing your own approach *4*
    1.4   Study skills *6*
    1.5   Glossary *9*

2   Getting started *10*
    2.1   Personal research and visual resources *11*
    2.2   Introductory design project: a personal log book *13*
    2.3   Introductory art project: still-life line drawing *15*
    2.4   Introductory craft project: mixed media collage *15*
    2.5   Glossary *17*

3   Benefiting from the work of others *19*
    3.1   The importance of theory and practice *19*
    3.2   Inspiration from the work of others *20*
    3.3   Copying methods *20*
    3.4   Case studies *22*
    3.5   Glossary *26*

4   Working with 2D projects *27*
    4.1   Basic design *27*
        – Mark making *27*
        – Lines *29*
        – Shapes *31*
        – Light and form *35*
        – Space *36*
        – Texture *36*
    4.2   Colour *39*
    4.3   Photography as a tool in art and design *45*
    4.4   Exemplar 2D projects *52*
    4.5   Glossary *54*

5   Working with 3D projects *57*
    5.1   3D visual resource development *59*
    5.2   Basic 3D visual studies *62*
    5.3   Exemplar 3D projects *68*
    5.4   Glossary *72*

6 Case study: a college-based project 73
    6.1 Packaging 73
    6.2 Glossary 77

7 Options and extras 78
    7.1 Making the most of your progress 79
    7.2 Project intentions 79
    7.3 The projects 80
        – Painting 80
        – Fashion 82
        – Poster design 84
        – Interior design 85
        – Cultural diversity 86
        – Surface pattern 88
        – Jewellery 89
    7.4 Glossary 90

8 Pulling it all together 91
    8.1 Researching your intended career path 92
    8.2 Your CV and letters of application 93
    8.3 Presentation – your work and yourself 94
    8.4 Interview techniques 95
    8.5 Study through college 97
    8.6 Glossary 98

Appendices 99
    A.1 Equipment list 99
    A.2 Useful addresses 100

Index 101

Acknowledgements

I should like to thank those who have helped at various stages during the preparation of this book, in particular Eric Pascoe, of the Berkshire College of Art & Design, Peter McKenna, of Hirst High School, Ashington, and Pat Shenstone, of the Coventry School of Art & Design. John Lyons, Maggie Montgomery and Lisa Mooney-Smith kindly provided me with the information and illustrations used in the case studies in Chapter 3. Their help and generosity is gratefully acknowledged.

Thanks are also extended to Harvey Dwight, for the majority of the photographs, to David Hawksworth, the Art Librarian, and to other colleagues and friends; to the staff and students of the Bradford & Ilkley Community College GNVQ Intermediate Programme; to Patricia Smith, my secretary, without whose assistance the text would not have emerged; and to my wife and children for their infinite patience and positive encouragement.

The author and publishers wish to thank NCVQ for permission to use material from their publications.

Every effort has been made to trace all copyright holders, but if any have been inadvertently overlooked the publishers will be pleased to make the necessary arrangements at the first opportunity.

Introduction

If you are interested in art, design and crafts and you want to develop your potential, enjoy your studies and if possible obtain a qualification, this is the book for you.

The book will work both for you and with you. You will acquire new skills, and discover your own answers to a range of questions, both practical and personal. Talent and creativity – are they essential? What is a GNVQ? Can *I* acquire one? Am I good enough at art and design? The book is designed to take you through a series of exercises and assignments that will build on existing skills, knowledge and enthusiasm, giving you confidence and bringing insight, whether you intend to work through school or college, at your workplace or from home.

This book will help you to understand school, college and career requirements, and show you how to make the most of your own approach. You can work at your own pace and use your own initiative as you face the exciting challenge of acquiring new skills and understanding.

Try to keep the book beside you throughout your studies. Some of your work will be done *within* this book – don't be too perfectionist with it: just relax and enjoy it. But don't expect the work to be easy: it will take effort to develop your skills. So try hard – and my best wishes for your success!

Intermediate GNVQ

This workbook is based on the requirements of the General National Vocational Qualification at Intermediate level. To achieve this students must successfully complete four *mandatory* units, three *key skills* units, and two *optional* units.

You will concentrate on practical activities, underpinning your knowledge, and on the necessary skills associated with art, design and craft achievements. Key skills are also referred to: don't underestimate their potential in bringing success in your personal development. Key skills are as important as your art and design ability, as demonstrated through your portfolio – you need to work just as hard to develop your literacy, numeracy and communication skills. Key skills combined with common sense give you *transferable skills*: whatever career changes you may make, you will always benefit from these skills. They form the basis for success in work as well as in everyday life.

In your studies as in working life you will need to be part of a team: you will need to relate well to other people. One aspect of this is learning to receive and pass on messages and other information clearly. For your own safety and the safety of others you must also become aware of safe working practices and general health and safety issues.

How this book will help you

As well as developing your skills and knowledge of art, design and crafts, you are also preparing yourself for the successful achievement of an Intermediate GNVQ. In order to make the most of your studies you will need to know the *purpose* of each activity. It is the same as in art, design and craft work: one of the main assets when tackling problems is a clear understanding of what is required of you.

This book will help you with the different requirements of art, design and crafts work. You will read other books, too, for more specific advice. Organisations that can provide this extra advice are listed in Appendix A.2 at the back of this book.

The National Council for Vocational Qualifications (NCVQ) has prepared a series of publications. One of these, *Mandatory Units for Intermediate Art & Design*, should be read alongside this book. It explains what GNVQ Intermediate in Art & Design is, and what you need to do to achieve one. It also gives explanations and guidance.

This book will cover all the necessary ground to prepare you, and you will learn the terminology. For the time being, be relaxed about your approach: just enjoy the exercises and projects. Gradually you will become familiar with the GNVQ side of things.

1.1 The language of art and design and of GNVQ

A number of words used in this book are part of the specialist language of art and design. As each of these new words is introduced it will appear in **bold type**, and you will find it explained in the glossary at the end of the chapter. Some of the terminology may be daunting, but as with any specialist language, or jargon, you will come to understand it as you use it, and you will gradually see that some of it can help you to explain your work. The specialist words will be used as a framework of visual language as you work through the book.

We will start with the words that describe the components of an Art & Design GNVQ Intermediate programme. The diagram shows the requirement for the award of Intermediate GNVQ: the completion of nine **units** – four mandatory **vocational** units, along with three mandatory **key skills** units, and two optional **vocational** units.

Intermediate GNVQ

⬆

TESTING

U + U

OPTIONAL UNITS

U + U + U

KEY SKILLS UNITS

U + U + U + U

VOCATIONAL UNITS - MANDATORY

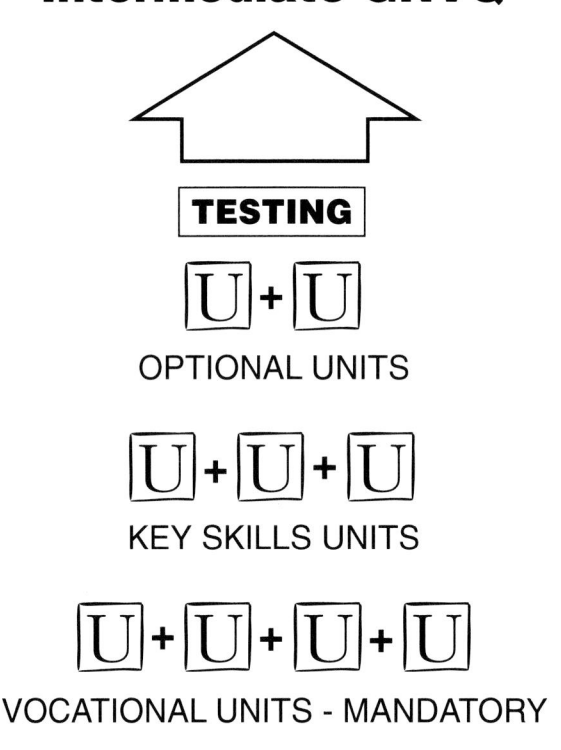

The various units that together comprise the Intermediate GNVQ have some standard features:

- they are all described in the same way;
- consistent language is used throughout (see the glossaries);
- they contain **elements** (the unit contents);
- they require a similar level of work;
- they have **performance criteria** (statements of what you are expected to be able to do after studying the unit);
- they usually show the **range** of activities likely to be covered;
- **evidence indicators** are stated (these aim to show that you can carry out tasks at an appropriate level);
- **amplification** expands and makes clear the requirements, in particular of the range;
- finally **guidance** gives further help.

GNVQs are offered by three awarding bodies: the Business & Technology Education Council (BTEC); City & Guilds; and the Royal Society of Arts (RSA) Examinations Board. All programmes are similar, and all require external as well as internal **assessment**.

Assessment

The purpose of assessment is to evaluate your progress. Your progress is measured by the evidence that you present. You are independent: your assessment is very much your own business. If you are working alone, it is an even bigger responsibility – *you* produce the **outcomes** and then *you* assess the achievement yourself! Sometimes this is a difficult task. Try to get help from others who have appropriate experience; if you can, be consistent in who you use. If you are studying in a school or college, your work will usually be assessed by your tutors. If you are a GNVQ student, assessment procedures are covered by *internal* **verifiers** and overseen by an *external* verifier.

For assessment to be an effective part of your learning process you need a clear idea of the criteria against which assessment is made. If these criteria have been laid down by someone else (as in the GNVQ), don't be afraid to ask questions if anything is unclear. If you are assessing yourself, make sure that you fully understand the brief and its requirements or outcomes before deciding which features you are going to assess.

Most of the projects and some of the exercises in this book have assessment criteria. These should help you to work out suitable assessment criteria for yourself when you are doing self-generated work.

Grading

Grading is another important feature of GNVQs. There are three possible grades: *pass*, *merit* or *distinction*.

Grading is applied both to **process** and to the quality of outcomes. Process covers three main areas of activity: planning, information handling and evaluation. These are all key features of your independent learning skills.

To qualify automatically for a *pass* grade you will need to have:

- completed all tasks required by the nine units that comprise the programme;
- successfully compiled a **portfolio** and a **personal log book**;
- successfully completed all the **external tests** (these tests do not contribute to *merit* or *distinction* grades).

How well you complete all parts of your studies will affect your chance of receiving a *merit* or *distinction* grade.

Testing

As you work through this book you should achieve the basic requirements for Intermediate GNVQ. If you wish to register for, and *receive*, a GNVQ, however, you will need to work through an approved centre. Most such centres for GNVQ are schools or colleges. It is in these centres that testing is carried out.

1.2 Using this book

This book is to work *with* and to work *in*. Some activities will be aimed at outcomes: these will be used to demonstrate your skills and abilities to others. Other activities can be done within the book, in the spaces provided. You will return to the book from time to time, and you may be tempted to improve on the work done in it – but *don't* change it unless it is obviously wrong. Later on you will find it encouraging to see how easily you can cope with exercises which were more difficult first time round.

As you progress through the book you will see **icons** in the margin. Some tell you how long a particular activity is likely to take; some warn you of hazards; others remind you to keep your work as evidence.

You need to build up the sort of evidence that will allow others to assess your ability or to provide **accreditation** of your work, which you will need as you progress to employment or further education. If you are working from home, make sure you follow carefully the advice about collecting evidence. The responsibility for collecting and keeping evidence of your abilities lies with you alone.

In particular, remember to keep your rough work and your ideas during development. Why keep these? Chiefly because your circumstances may change. If you decide later to study full-time or part-time at your local college, the staff there will need to look at your evidence and your **portfolio**, in order to give proper accreditation to your achievements. They will be interested not just in the end results but also in your ideas and developmental work.

You should also keep notes which will help you to explain to others *how* you have developed your ideas. It is important that you record your thoughts about the work you do and the judgements you have made about your practical work. This also helps to show your planning abilities, and can contribute towards GNVQ grading. This will become clearer as you complete the activities in the book.

A key feature of the work you are now doing is **communication**. Although much of this will be *visual*, both your *oral* presentation and your *written* material will benefit from a careful and consistent approach in your working method. You will develop good work habits as you work your way through the book: but you need to be rigorous and methodical in these so as to develop good **professional practice**.

1.3 Developing your own approach

Artists, designers and craftspeople can be seen as *interpreters*. They use their vision of the world to help others appreciate life more fully. Looking, seeing, touching, using ... being aware, in tune, sensitive, *alive*. Most of us have good days and bad days: when did *you* last jump for joy, or feel exceptionally that it was good to be alive? When did you last stop to wonder at some natural thing, or touch a surface, or try to recover a memory prompted by something you had seen, smelled or heard? As an aspiring artist, craftsperson or designer you need continually to cultivate your awareness of the natural and the fabricated world in which you live.

Try to *observe* rather than just look; try to see and to understand. Think of the space you occupy – stretch out your arms and legs, be aware of the physical nature of form and space. Handle things and think about the way they feel: rough, smooth, weighty, light – is it what you expected to feel, could it be improved on? Make notes of what you think, and sketch or draw as often as you can – preferably every day.

To do all this you will need notebooks, sketchbooks and scrapbooks. Notebooks should be small enough to carry at all times. They are best with plain pages, as you will often need to sketch or to try out new media, as well as keeping written notes. Together your notebooks will form a unique personal record from which you will benefit now and later in your life. Be sure to keep them.

The study of art and design is demanding and exciting. If you pursue it seriously, the rewards can be high. Increased awareness of this world you live in and of the environment people create, combined with the pleasure of creating something unique yourself, will be added benefits.

Why study art and design?

List what *you* think are the advantages of studying art and design. Two possible advantages are shown already. (You will return to this list later.)

> WHY STUDY ART AND DESIGN?
> 1 Art helps me to look at the world in a different way.
> 2 Drawing helps me to explain things to others.

Good practice

The basis of good practice is the transmission to others of our own individual observations, interpretations and imagination, making use of various media and processes. Drawing, painting, modelling and making all offer endless opportunities for us to work at translating what we see around us, or feel within us, for the benefit of others as well as for ourselves.

This book will help you to develop a range of skills, while building your knowledge and encouraging your confidence in your own creative potential. It is intended as a working guide. I hope that it will be the key to a successful career or a rewarding pastime which will stay with you throughout your life.

Getting started

Before you can begin to enjoy the process of developing successfully as an artist you need to assemble your skills, ideas and techniques, together with the tools that will help you to exploit them.

You will need not only a basic *kit* (see Appendix A.1) but an enquiring and investigative *attitude*. You will also need to develop visual *awareness*. This will enrich the way you look at the world, informing the choices that you make and increasing your powers of communication.

There are several key elements which affect all art and design. They include light, colour, shape, form, pattern and style. There are many ways to teach these elements; this book aims to help you study independently, as well as encouraging you to seek advice and tips from those who are more advanced than you.

You will need a special place to work. This can be a part of your bedroom or perhaps a shed or an attic – somewhere you can leave things at the end of one session and pick them up again at the start of the next. You will need to be warm enough in winter and cool in summer. Lighting is important, as are storage and display potential. Wherever you choose, it should be dedicated to your studies.

It may not be possible to get a place that is entirely free from interruptions, but ask the people you live with to help as best they can by encouraging you and allowing you to work in peace.

The professional way

A good start

1.4 Study skills

To achieve good results you need to develop good practice. Clean working, with the appropriate tools and materials, is essential. You also need to develop a methodical approach.

- Are your working space and your working surface clear and clean?
- Do you have everything you need to hand?
- Have you thought about the sequence of the activity and how long it will take?
- Are your ideas, notes, diagrams and other reference material readily available?

Add to this list according to your own way of working and what suits you – for example, do you like music playing or do you prefer silence?

Try to develop a regular routine of study, setting aside periods throughout the week. Mix short sessions and long ones, according to what you want to achieve.

Manage your time carefully

Once you have somewhere to work and have set out your work space and collected your equipment, you need to consider time. How much is available? How best might you use it? This is called **time management**: it is one key to successful progress.

For effective time management you need to know three things:

- what you have to do;
- how much time you have in which to do it;
- when you will do it best.

Plan your work schedule

Some people work better in the morning, others in the evening. Are you an early bird or a night owl?

Divide large tasks into short stages. Allocate a set amount of time to each stage. Try to be realistic about how long it will take to do each part, and allow a margin for error. Plan in some proper breaks as well, and make sure you take them – you will be fresher when you start again.

If you stick to your work plan there is no reason why you should not finish the task. There will be need to get into a panic, or wake up worrying in the early hours, or become irritable with other people.

Get a planner

You can buy a planner, use a diary, make a spreadsheet using a personal computer, or design and make your own. You need a weekly and a monthly planner, as well as one for the whole year.

Your planner is there to help you: display it where you can easily see it. Refer to it regularly, updating it as necessary so that it remains effective.

Examples of time planners

Study skills 7

Planning projects

Good time management can be applied over any timescale and over any size of task. It is as important to practise it with a simple task taking an hour as with a complex project taking several weeks.

When you feel overwhelmed by having too much to do, recognise that there is only so much you can do in any one day. Do not panic, but set yourself realistic goals – goals that you know that you can actually achieve. This will help you achieve your work target within the time you have allowed yourself, and avoid any feeling of failure.

- Stage your work to suit your circumstances.
- Allocate your time realistically so that you successfully complete the activity according to your plan.
- Finish what you set out to do.
- Expect sometimes to keep going when the going is good, and to be disciplined when it isn't going well.

Exercises and projects in this book indicate the length of time that is appropriate for each activity. Sometimes a long period is shown, such as '1 week'. This means that you will need to spend a good deal of each day working on the project. Note that these timings are guidelines, not exact requirements.

Skills

To be successful in any career you need a high level of personal skills in addition to the specific professional skills. These are usually referred to as **common skills** or **interpersonal skills**. They are largely to do with how we get on with each other.

Common sense plays its part, too, especially in the areas of health and safety; so do disposition (are you cheerful or gloomy?), attitude (are you keen and reliable or laid back and lazy?) and presentation (are you and your work both clean and attractively presented?).

You will find a list of common skills on page 26: as you work through the book, make sure that you attend fully to common skills requirements and suggestions. Start to compile your **personal log book**. This will prove invaluable if you apply for jobs or college courses. The design of your log book is covered in the first project.

Using this book

This book is divided into ten sections: eight chapters and two appendices. It is important that you start with the study skills and visual research exercises before you move on to the main projects. If you work for about two hours each day, you should cover every exercise and project in this book in less than a year.

When you have worked your way through the exercises and projects, providing that you have practised sufficiently you will have satisfied the practical requirements of the GNVQ Intermediate in Art & Design. Good luck, and enjoy your studies!

1.5 Glossary

accreditation Official recognition; formal acknowledgement of achievement.

amplification Further information offered in explanation of a particular requirement.

assessment Evaluation and marking.

common skills Those skills which are needed in all areas of life and work.

communication The process of imparting and receiving information.

element A component part of a **unit**.

evidence indicator The work produced, or the outcome of an activity, upon which evaluation and assessment can be based.

external testing Formal tests (examinations) undertaken through approved centres.

guidance Information about the GNVQ approach. See the mandatory units for Intermediate Art & Design from NCVQ.

icon An image or visual device, used to represent something.

interpersonal skills Skills relating to relationships between people.

key skills The most important skills: communication, numeracy, and information technology (IT).

outcome The result of your work: a product or a solution, the end result of art, craft or design activity. (Compare **process**.)

performance criteria The requirements defined within a given activity to demonstrate your competence.

personal log book A personal record/diary of your work, including the assessment of your work or skills. The log book charts your progress.

portfolio The collected evidence of your work; or the case in which you keep and protect this work.

process The carrying out of an activity. (Compare **outcome**.)

professional practice The working approach used by professional artists, craftspeople and designers (as indeed by doctors, lawyers, dentists and the like).

range The scope or extent of activities that you are expected to cover.

time management The planned and considered use of the available time.

unit One complete component of the GNVQ programme. A unit comprises several **elements**.

verifiers (**external** and **internal**) People whose job is to evaluate and assess your results if you are working in school or college.

vocational Aimed at a particular career or occupation, as distinct from more traditional academic study.

2 Getting started

Being successful in art, design and crafts is not just a question of 'talent'. Practical ability is important, but so are ideas. Observing, pondering, planning and then making things are all interconnected.

The initial thinking may be triggered by something you see, hear, smell or do; it may be set off by seeing other people's work; or it can come from inside you, as **inspiration**. Your ideas may be unique, or they may be adaptations of someone else's. Both are useful approaches.

2.1 Personal research and visual resources

When you start work you will use your **personal reference material**. Depending on how complex a task you are doing, you may use both **personal research** (PR) and **visual resource** (VR) material. This might make use of drawing, painting, photography, written notes, scrapbooks or **ephemera**.

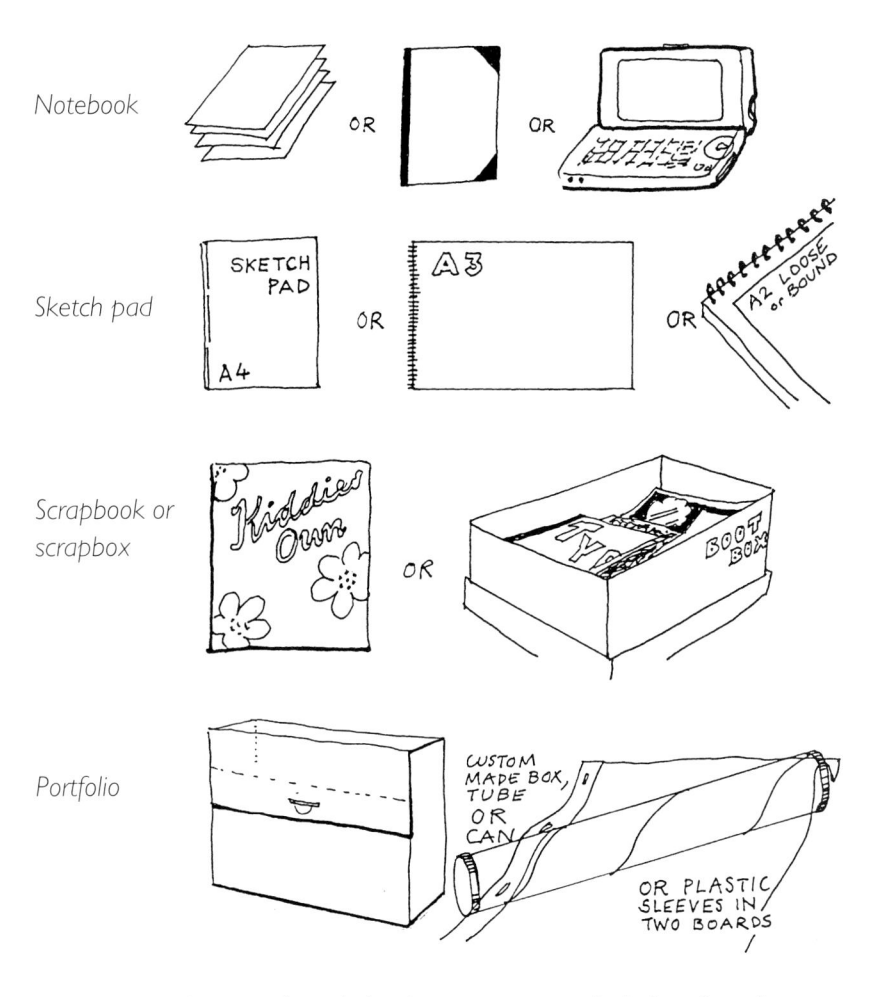

Notebook

Sketch pad

Scrapbook or scrapbox

Portfolio

Your personal research and visual resource as a whole is referred to as your PRVR.

Beginning

Of course as you are in the early stages of your work you may have a very small PRVR. Don't worry: it will grow fast!

The following practical tasks are all introductory activities aimed at gathering and using visual material and recording outcomes. Let's start with recording outcomes.

At this stage, do not expect too much of yourself. You are at the beginning of a demanding programme and you need to concentrate on the basics. Acquire confidence in your skills, your abilities in making things, your approach to identifying, analysing and solving problems. In some cultures artists in training are allowed for two or three years only to draw lines. For such trainee artists, the promotion to drawing circles must be a tremendous step forward! Although this book does not adopt quite this approach, it does assume that you will practise basic skills continually and not be content merely with accomplishing the exercises.

How good are you – a genius or an absolute beginner? The happy medium is ideal. In improving your work you will need to be effectively self-critical. This does not mean that when things are not going well you resign yourself to thinking that your work is hopeless – far from it. It *does* mean analysing what you've done, whether successful or unsuccessful, and learning from it.

Work with simple ideas and appropriate challenges. If you start off by wanting to draw something complicated – a friend, a pet, or a fork in a glass of water – you cannot expect brilliant results. So choose something simpler: try to draw a stock cube, a tulip or a matchbox. You will then have more chance of success. Remember too that every good drawing has its own magic – even when you are skilled you may not always be fully satisfied with your efforts. When you do get a good result, though, you'll know that it has been worth the time practising.

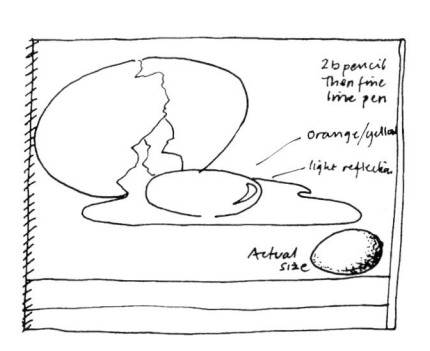

Expect a long-term, gradual improvement. Always strive for the best outcome you can achieve, and be prepared to say why it is suited to the job in hand.

Preparation

One of the hardest things in art and design is to be patient in doing the research and planning for projects. It is always tempting to get on with the practical things as soon as you can.

Take your time. Analyse what it is that you need to come up with. Why? How will you do it? It can be easy to select a wrong outcome – in advertising, for example, one might choose a video to sell double-glazing when information sent by post (a direct mailshot) would be more effective and much less costly.

Start with the **brief**. Is it clearly written? Do you understand it? Then make notes. These will include **ideas development**, perhaps using **brainstorming** and **word association**. Other starting points include writing down the strengths of particular proposals and their apparent weaknesses. Talk to your friends for fresh ideas and consult other people who might be able to help you.

Make some rough drawings, or **thumbnail sketches**. As you work, think

```
Clarify brief and                    Originate ideas
carry out research

    ┌─────────────────┐                  ┌─────────────────────┐
    │ Brief – is it clear? │                  │ How can the objectives of the │
    │ Enough facts?   │                  │ brief/project best be attained? │
    └────────┬────────┘                  └──────────┬──────────┘
             ▼                                      ▼
    ┌──────────────────────┐              ┌──────────────┐  ┌──────────────────┐
    │ What is/are the requirements? │              │ Think-tank or │  │ Word association or │
    │ Narrowly defined or open-ended, │              │ brainstorming │  │ image association │
    │ it will still have some straightforward │              └──────┬───────┘  └────────┬─────────┘
    │ requirements         │                     ▼                   ▼
    └──┬────────────┬──────┘              ┌──────────────────┐
       ▼            ▼                     │ Record of roughs │
  ┌──────────┐  ┌──────────┐               │ and notes        │
  │ Special  │  │ What do  │               └────────┬─────────┘
  │ require- │  │ you need │                        ▼
  │ ments?   │  │ to       │               ┌──────────────────┐
  └──────────┘  │ research?│               │ Selection        │
                └────┬─────┘               └────────┬─────────┘
                     ▼                              ▼
         ┌────────────────────────┐         ┌──────────────────┐
         │ What are the constraints? │         │ Proceed to production │
         │ Processing costs, colour, time, etc. │         │ of finished work │
         └────────────────────────┘         └──────────────────┘
```

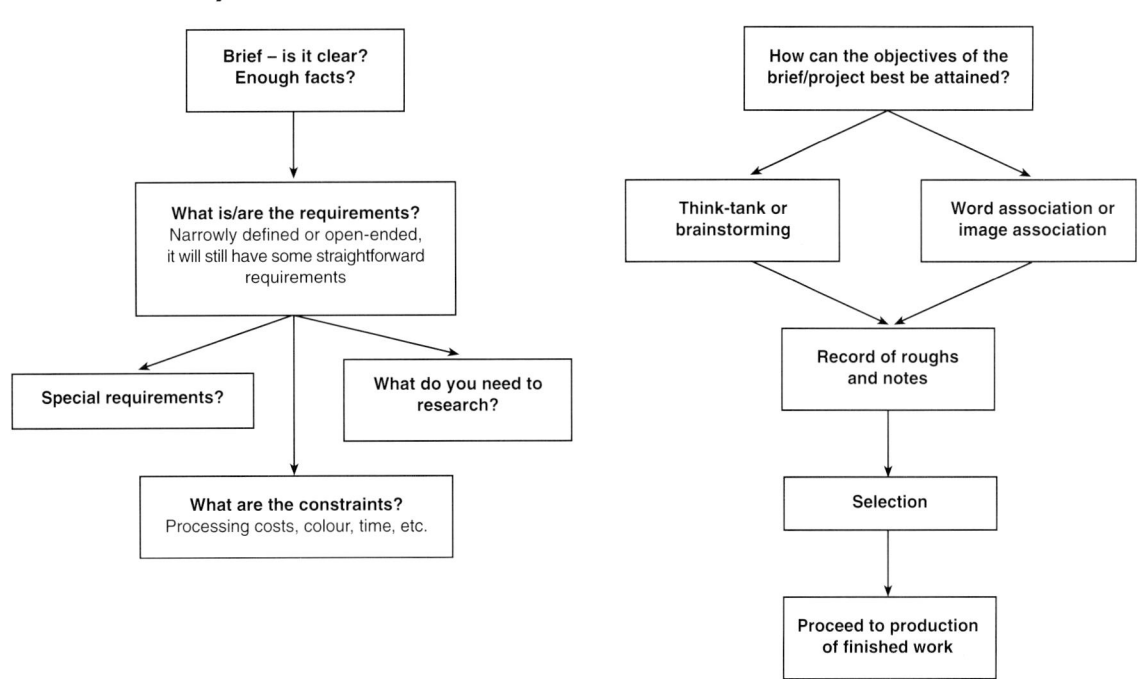

about the impact your proposal will have on the user. The **flowcharts** above may help. Feel free to adapt and improve it. Let your inventiveness and imagination flow.

You will find that your personal approach will benefit from methodical application, and that these good habits will underpin your future work. With experience you may find some shortcuts – but don't look for them now.

2.2 Introductory design project: a personal log book

A key requirement for all artists, craftspeople and designers is the ability to benefit from constructive criticism. As explained already, you also need to be self-critical. You need to analyse and evaluate your progress from activity to activity.

To help with this you should record your efforts in a personal log book. This will provide a record both of progress and of assessment details. The log book will contain A4 sheets.

Brief

Design an A4 self-assessment form to be stored in a ring binder. For each exercise or project that you do, you will fill in your own comments on one of these forms. Gathered together, the forms will make up your log book. As you go along you will use it to assess your progress; when finished it will provide a record of your achievements and of your progress as an artist and a designer.

Some points to consider when designing your form:

▸ What is this introductory project about? What are its aims?
▸ What information will have to go on the form?

- What do other people need to get from it?
- How much space does each bit need?
- Do you have room for notes?
- Have you left room for a statement about other skills you have used (apart from art and design)?
- How well have you used these common skills?
- Is there space for other relevant comments?

Self-assessment review

When you have finished, apply the assessment form to the job you have just done. You will probably want to improve the design after you have used it once or twice. Keep the original, as well as your later attempts: they will help you to see that you are improving.

Some questions to help you assess your work:

- Does the form look OK?
- Was it easy or difficult to design?
- How did you do? How can you best show this?
- When you have to evaluate your work, will you use a 'tick box' approach? Or circle numbers on a scale of 1–5 (poor–excellent)?
- How long did you take? How long do you think you should have taken?

Add your own questions, answers and comments on this first design project.

Evaluation

Now look at this example. How does yours compare with it?

When you have studied both for a while, decide whether or not to re-design yours. Write down your reasons if you change things.

Once you feel satisfied with your self-assessment form, make about six copies. Later on, if you are still happy with the form, you will make further copies, but be prepared to amend your design if this proves necessary.

SELF-ASSESSMENT SHEET

Name   Date

Exercise/Project title

GNVQ Unit No.   Associated units   Time allocated   Time taken

Requirements of Exercise/Project

Points to follow up

Work recorded and in portfolio? Yes ☐ No ☐   If not, why not? → Action Plan

Indicate which Key or Common Skills were used

Assessment	weak									excellent
Planning	1	2	3	4	5	6	7	8	9	10
Evaluation	1	2	3	4	5	6	7	8	9	10
Outcome	1	2	3	4	5	6	7	8	9	10

Self-Grading   Pass   Merit   Distinction

Notes

Will you need a second attempt? If so, remember to complete another sheet.

2.3 Introductory art project: still-life line drawing

Brief

Select an apple, an orange and a banana, or three other simple items from the kitchen or your tool box. Place them on a piece of white A4 paper.

Draw them in 2B pencil, as near to life-size as you can within an A3 sheet. Don't shade them in! The result is called a **line drawing**.

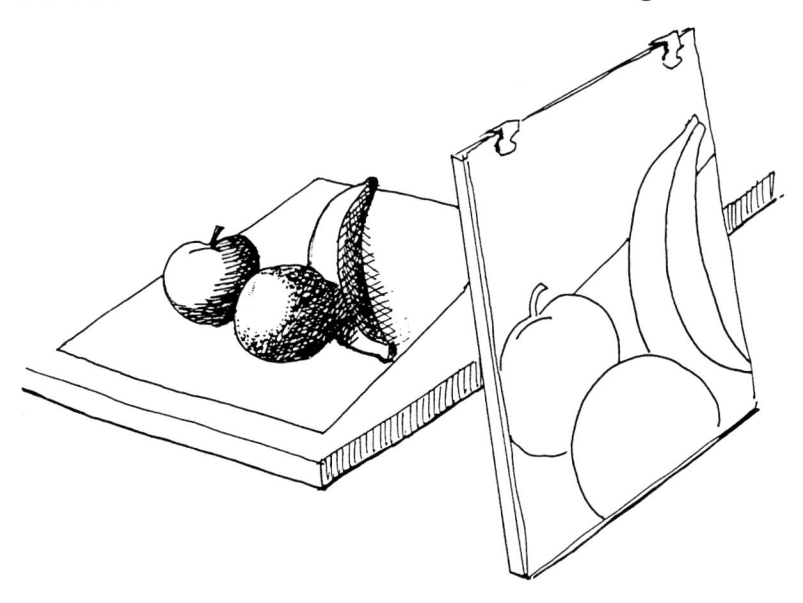

Some features your line drawing should show:

- clean, confident lines;
- a good overall composition;
- essential qualities of the objects drawn, such as form, texture and scale, so that these are obvious to the viewer.

How did you do?

Fill in one of your assessment forms. Be fair but firm with yourself. If you have not made a good job of the drawing, mark your sheet low. State why you have done so.

Keep your work, whether it is good or bad. You will need it later.

Often your feelings about your early drawings will change as you develop in confidence and experience. This is a sign of progress: your evaluation is becoming more effective.

2.4 Introductory craft project: mixed media collage

Brief

This project requires you to make a **collage** – a design, an image or a picture made from assembled material glued onto a piece of card or paper or some other suitable base.

You will have seen such work, or made it yourself at school. At its simplest, a collage may be composed of torn scraps of paper. Some collage, though, is more elaborate, composed of cereals and grains or of fabricated objects such as watch or clock pieces. A similar approach to image making is found in mosaic work, in which small pieces of coloured material are set in a base material to form patterns or images.

You are going to work at a more imaginative level: your collage is going to be a **mood-board** too. Mood-boards are used in fashion work to set the scene for garments as they are being designed. They have a theme, supported by the choice of colour and by the inclusion of images and ephemera to complete the overall effect.

Your collage is going to use the mood-board approach because you are going to create an image that evokes an occasion or activity that you took part in. This could be a journey or a holiday, a visit to the cinema or a shopping expedition. It could be falling in love, a celebration of your favourite pop group, or a political protest. Choose your title, write it down and get to work!

Preparation

Start by collecting plenty of material connected with your chosen event. Bearing in mind your title, work towards evoking the mood. Try to communicate your feelings about the event, using the medium of collage.

Examples of collage

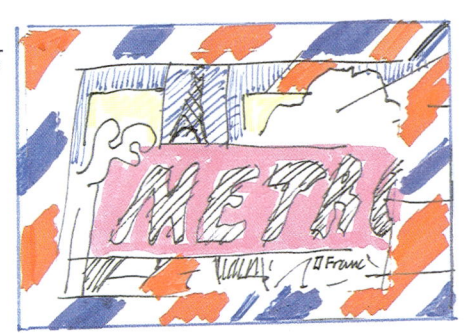

Making the collage

Work to A3 size, on cartridge paper or card. Make sure you use the right adhesive for the materials.

As well as making an appropriate image, pattern or design, remember to try to evoke a mood. If you need to *add* colour you may, but a more effective result will be achieved if you select the right colours from your collected material.

Do not try too hard to make a realistic picture – the idea is to evoke feelings in the people who look at the finished work. Torn strips of old firework wrappers put together to form a bonfire or firework picture, for example, may better create the image of bonfire night than a painted scene.

Enjoy your work. Keep the surface clear of excess glue or paste, and do not try to stick heavy objects on frail supports.

Self-assessment review

You should now complete an assessment sheet for your collage exercise. Put it alongside those you have already done for your drawing and your personal log book design.

Make sure you are as honest and clear as you can be when filling in your record. You will find that you are able to criticise your work effectively if you record your thoughts soon after completing each task. This sort of self-assessment will also help you to see where you need to put in some extra study.

It is unlikely that your work at this stage will fully satisfy you. Nevertheless, do resist the temptation to *overwork* your attempts. Once you have finished, particularly if you are within the allocated time for that exercise, move on. Remember to write down or sketch any ideas that grew out of doing the work; you may be able to make use of them later.

Go back over your first three completed assessment forms and ask yourself the following questions:

- Does the form work OK?
- Is there enough information?
- How well can I assess my own work?

How well are the self-assessments going? If you are not clear, talk to someone about your problems and write down your concerns. This is an essential part of your development as an artist, a designer or a craftsperson. Does your form cover all the points that you feel are important? If it does, stick with it. If it needs amending, change it.

You should now move on to the next chapter. Make a note in your planner to turn back to your log book in a month's time and review your efforts.

2.5 Glossary

brainstorming A process of sharing spontaneous ideas about a problem.

brief Instructions for a task, an assignment or a project.

collage A picture made by gluing materials onto a background.

ephemera Things of only short-lived relevance.

flowchart A diagram representing the steps of a process.

ideas development Progressing your creative thinking, a process that usually incorporates making rough sketches and recording word associations.

inspiration A creative force or influence; a brainwave or an instinctive feeling.

line drawing An illustration in pencil or ink which has no greys (half-tones).

mood-board A collection of colours and images, collage or multimedia, evoking a feeling. Used mainly in fashion design, to communicate style and colour range.

personal reference material Your own collection of material, gathered over time, which may be used to check specific topics or more generally to stimulate your imagination.

personal research Finding out more about a specific topic.

thumbnail sketch A simple small sketch, to convey the general idea without going into detail.

visual resource A collection of images, items and artefacts used to provide inspiration.

word association A process of stringing together lists of words that remind you one of another.

Benefiting from the work of others

Good art, design and craftwork is the product of a combination of both skills and knowledge. It grows out of practice and theory.

Much of the theory comes from studying and analysing the work of others. This theory, whether mainstream or supporting study, is often referred to as **contextual study**.

3.1 The importance of theory and practice

When you are working on contextual study it is vital that you strengthen your design thinking and creative processes at the same time. Theory and practice are both essential: to inform creative workers they must be combined.

Knowledge and skills must be built as you go along, improving your confidence and your ability. Be methodical. Plan how you are going to approach your study. Always present your work as clearly and attractively as you can.

To prepare for career development you will also need to understand professional practice. How do contemporary artists, craftspeople and designers work? What sort of practice do you know about? Where did your understanding come from? How can you benefit from visiting professionals?

In the process of finding out about professional practice, be sure to keep good records. As well as being useful in their own right, these will provide some evidence for the second element of the key skills units, 'Communication', about which you will learn more later.

Work with your notebook and your image collection; keep up to date with your log book and your personal resource collection. Take opportunities to visit museums, galleries, libraries and studios, as well as studying at home.

Be aware of what you come across, in books, magazines and papers, on television, the radio and film. Be alive to the world about you, and the myriad information sources. If you have access to a personal computer, especially one with CD-Rom, this will prove very useful in the analysis, collection and retrieval of data.

Is your communication effective? Whether written or visual, does it work? How can you judge this? Analyse your results and be as honest as you can in your self-criticism: enjoy those aspects that proved successful, learn from those that did not.

3.2 Inspiration from the work of others

By studying work produced by past or present artists, designers and craftspeople, you can explore their ideas and learn from their techniques. The GNVQ requires that you carry out six **case studies**. The six must include at least one artist, one designer and one craftsperson.

Remember to keep records of this activity, using your notebook and your visual diary. Add relevant images to your resource collection. Watch out for postcards and posters which could supplement the photographs or scrapbook items you collect.

3.3 Copying methods

Treat all research material with respect. It is selfish (and illegal) to deface library books and journals. Librarians can help to arrange photocopying; in addition, you can copy the work of famous artists by hand. This will help you to appreciate their work even more fully.

Squaring up

One effective way to copy work accurately is to 'square up'. Take a piece of **translucent** or transparent material large enough to cover the image to be transferred. You will also need a fine-tipped pen or pencil.

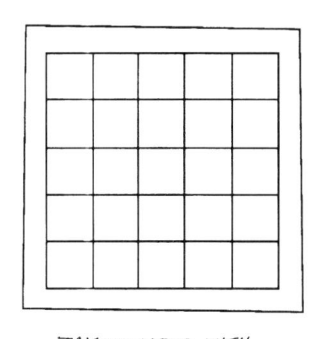

TRACING PAPER WITH
1 CM GRID DRAWN ON

TRACING PAPER GRID IN
PLACE OVER IMAGE.

1. Select the original to be copied.
2. Select a grid size suitable for the job you are doing. (In this example, a 1 cm grid is used.)
3. Lay the grid over the image you are copying, and trace off the key features in each square. 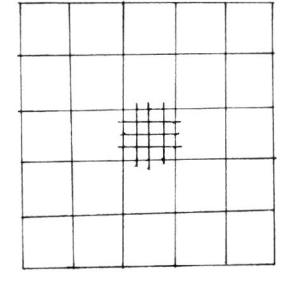
4. If you need even tighter detail, you can square up your tracing further. Use as much or as little detail as you need.

Benefiting from the work of others

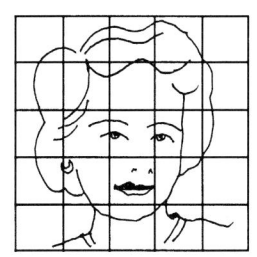

5 You can use the tracing as it is for a same-size copy, or you can now enlarge or reduce the image simply by changing the scale. To enlarge, draw a grid in soft pencil (2B or softer) to the scale required and copy from each square on your tracing on to the corresponding larger square.

6 This simple grid system can also be used to *distort* images, by altering the scale ratios – for instance, 1 cm on one axis to 2.5 cm on the other.

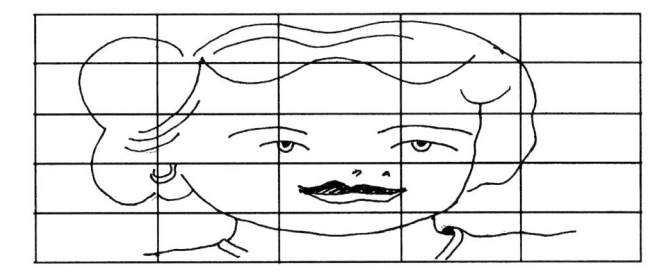

7 Once you have successfully transferred the image, draw over it with ink or felt tip and then clean away your pencil grid.

You will experiment with colour and tone later on – you can then have fun changing shapes and effects if you wish. Find out about tracing visualisers and pantographs, which were designed to help with such work.

Using a computer

You may like to make more experiments with distortion or repeated images. On a computer it will be quick and easy once the image is in the machine, but unless you have a scanner you will still need to make the initial copy by hand. The alternative is to confine yourself to standard images already in the computer plus your own drawings made on it, but it is valuable and instructive to work with the pictures of great artists.

Registration marks

When tracing, put **registration marks** on the photocopied image you are tracing from (remember: never deface the *original* materials). These will help you to replace your tracing medium exactly, and so get an accurate result.

Types of registration marks: left, at the corners; right, at the top and bottom and at the sides

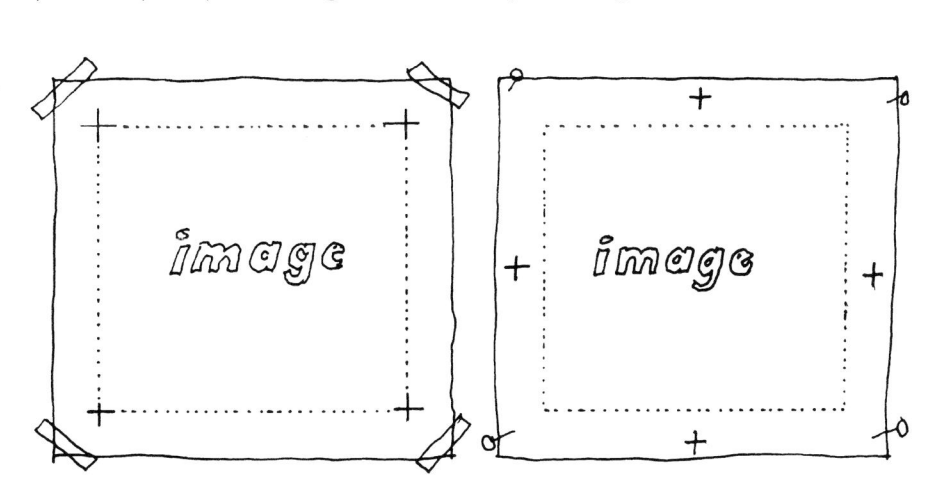

Copying methods 21

When you have laid your tracing medium over the image and taped or pinned it down the first thing to do is to copy the registration marks. If necessary you can now take the tracing up and lay it back down again as many times as you wish, without being confused by the complexity of the image.

As you look at the work of famous artists, designers or craftspeople, remember to note down which you especially like, and why. Why write these things down? In the first place, because making written notes will help you pay closer attention to the work and think more carefully about it. And in the second, because making notes involves practising some of the key skills.

3.4 Case studies

The following pages show examples of case studies of contemporary practitioners: an artist, a craftsperson and a designer. This is not the only way of organising and presenting the material, of course, and you may wish to develop your own model. Be sure that it includes sufficient detail to enable you to make your own comments about the working approaches of the people you have chosen.

The layout used here is a fairly typical one. It lends itself to **catalogue** production, it is easy to file, and it is only A4 in size. Samples of work, photographs and other additional material can be filed with the case study in an A4 clear sleeve.

As you begin your own case studies, write down your reasons for choosing *these* subjects.

- Is it that you know them?
- Do you like their work? If so, why?
- How do you know the work?
- Have you other reasons for admiring them?

Don't be nervous about writing down things that might appear superficial or unimportant, such as 'saw him/her on TV' – but do record the details (the programme, the channel, the date and time).

Be as clear and concise as you can with these notes. In making them you are strengthening your communication skills and developing your planning ability – both major ingredients in the GNVQ recipe for success.

ARTIST/WRITER

case study number 1

name	John LYONS
address	10 Something Road, Anytown
telephone number	012 345 6789
extension	—
internet address	—

school/college attended	Goldsmiths & University of Newcastle
date of birth	1933 (Port of Spain, Trinidad)
main area of work	Painting
brief description of current/past activities	John is a prolific writer and painter. He enjoys reading his work in galleries where his work is being exhibited. He is a lyrical colourist and revels in mythology of his Trinidadian home island. Broadcaster and authority on cross cultural activity. Lively lecturer. Great entertainer. Paintings rich in story content and paint.
evidence (catalogues, prints, articles, postcards, etc.)	Good catalogues and several articles in pack.
quick quotes/notes	Likes working with young people.

Case studies

CRAFTSPERSON

case study number 2

name	Maggie MONTGOMERY
address	16 Something Close, Inatown
telephone number	098 765 4321
extension	—
internet address	http:inter.net.address

school/college attended	Bradford & Ilkley Community College
date of birth	9/4/47
main area of work	Sculpture
brief description of current/past activities	Works with small groups of artists in an old mill building near Bradford. Studio address is An Arts Studio, An Old Mill, Near Bradford. Has won travel awards and worked in Paris at the Pompidou Centre. Worked in USA with artist/blacksmith (and in Scotland). Lots of exhibitions and work in collections. Was on Tony Hart show on TV.
evidence (catalogues, prints, articles, postcards, etc.)	See in pack. Lively work, fun and thought-provoking. ('Cows' on 'Sustrans' cycle route near Bath.)
quick quotes/notes	Visitors welcome. She also does residencies and teaching in school or college. Very nice and helpful. 'Exciting time for artists, designers and makers. This Internet means we can meet and discuss our ideas and work.'

24 Benefiting from the work of others

DESIGNER

case study number 3

name	Lisa MOONEY
address	A Cottage, Smallvillage, Fictionaltown
telephone number	024 680 13579
extension	—
internet address	—
school/college attended	Arnold & Carlton College of FE, Notts Mansfield College of Art Gwent College of HE
date of birth	9/2/66
main area of work	Quality outdoor gear for under-fives
brief description of current/past activities	Lisa was a video installation artist who moved into children's clothing design and production when she wanted specific items such as warm, comfortable and accessible clothes for her own kids. Lisa has worked as a lecturer in many situations from special needs to degree. She has travelled extensively and done some tough jobs (British Steel in South Wales!). 'Great personality and an enquiring mind, a good teacher and a warm-hearted colleague' – Head of Bradford Art College.
evidence (catalogues, prints, articles, postcards, etc.)	Catalogue in folder & CV and photographs
quick quotes/notes	'Talking to my accountant sharpens my mind: good design sells but there is a lot of graft too!'

Case studies

This sort of exercise develops other skills, as well. Notice the terms 'common skills' and 'key skills'. Why do you think these terms are used?

An important feature of the common skills developed by GNVQ study is that they are **transferable skills**: they have wider application in life, in both work and leisure.

Write out a list of your own transferable skills.

<u>TRANSFERABLE SKILLS</u>

Did your list include some of these?

- Accurate data collection
- Note taking
- Report writing
- Using the telephone
- Using information technology (IT) tools
- Sketching
- Explaining things to others
- Drawing maps and charts
- Listening
- Being a team worker
- Decision making
- Working safely
- Planning
- Speaking clearly
- Problem solving
- Presentation

3.5 Glossary

case studies Records of people's activities and achievements.

catalogue A complete or extensive list of the items in a collection.

contextual study The study of the cultural, historical, social or economic factors that affect the main area of interest. (In the case of art, design and textiles, these factors often merge.)

registration marks Marks made alongside an image to allow the exact placement or alignment of copies of the image.

transferable skills Skills learned in one area of activity that can be used also in other areas.

translucent Allowing some light to pass through: semi-transparent, like tracing paper.

4 Working with 2D projects

This chapter contains some more advanced practical projects. You will have better results all round if you work carefully through the exercises in basic design and colour first. 'Practice makes perfect' may not always be true, but regular practice can certainly help to improve outcomes in art, design and craft.

4.1 Basic design

Give time to the exercises in this section, which are fundamental to all further work. Some of it may seem familiar, but the creative process is one of continuous change through improvement and refinement.

Mark making, the experimental use of colour and basic drawing should all show evidence of your personal motivation. Concentrate on developing your individual way of looking, working, and presenting your results. Do not copy the basic design work of others even if you wish to do the same kind of work: find your own way.

Visual language

You need to develop a vocabulary for your visual language to enable you to express your ideas through drawing.

This visual language is composed of *marks*, *lines*, *shapes*, *textures* and *colour*, amongst others. In GNVQ these are known collectively as **formal elements**. For basic design activities you will concentrate on working with just some of the formal elements.

Mark making

Pencil

Pencils are probably your most easily available means of making marks. There is a wide range of pencil grades. Start by finding out which pencil will give you a certain type of mark. For example, a 2H pencil, which is relatively hard, will give a quite different mark from that made by a B pencil, which is softer, when applied to the same paper with the same pressure.

Working in the grid on the left, and using a different pencil in each left-hand square, make some small marks in order to try out the various pencils.

Other drawing media

Now try other, similar drawing media, such as conté crayons, charcoal and pastels. Keep within a **monochrome** range. Record which medium you have used in each square.

Other mark-making objects

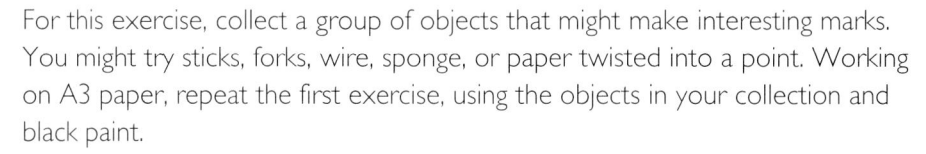

For this exercise, collect a group of objects that might make interesting marks. You might try sticks, forks, wire, sponge, or paper twisted into a point. Working on A3 paper, repeat the first exercise, using the objects in your collection and black paint.

Self-assessment review

Look back at your work. What have you learned? Fill in a self-assessment form.

Surfaces

The surface you are working on will affect the mark considerably.

Collect several different types of paper, such as newsprint, cartridge paper, sugar paper, tissue and coated paper (like that used for glossy magazines). Use the same media.

Mount the results in grid form, noting your findings underneath each sample.

Working with 2D projects

Lines

Lines can give a feeling of rhythm. The spaces between lines, and the position in which lines are placed, can change this rhythm. Thickness of line may be constant or may vary. Varying the length, the type and the direction of line can give a feeling of movement:

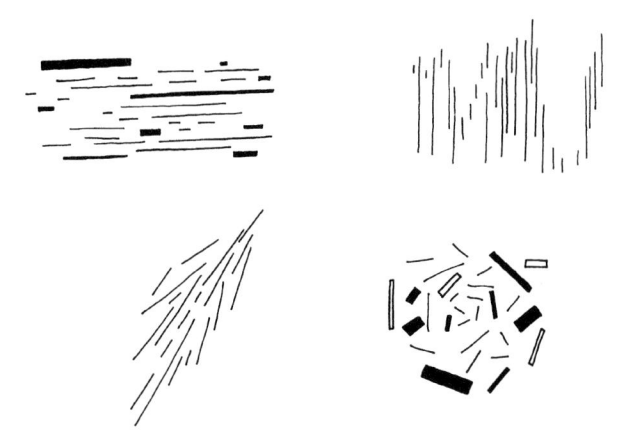

Movement may also be suggested by changing the flow of a line:

Experiment with the rhythm of single repetitive units:

Similarly, experiment with the rhythm of interchanging units and spaces:

Brief

It is important to get a feeling for the visual effect of differing lines, and to practise producing the effect you want.

From the following list, choose six words.

construction growth happy sad excited running large swirling weak ribbon aggressive meandering

Now try to illustrate your six words using lines. (You may also use colour in this exercise if you think it would help.)

VISUAL EFFECTS OF LINE

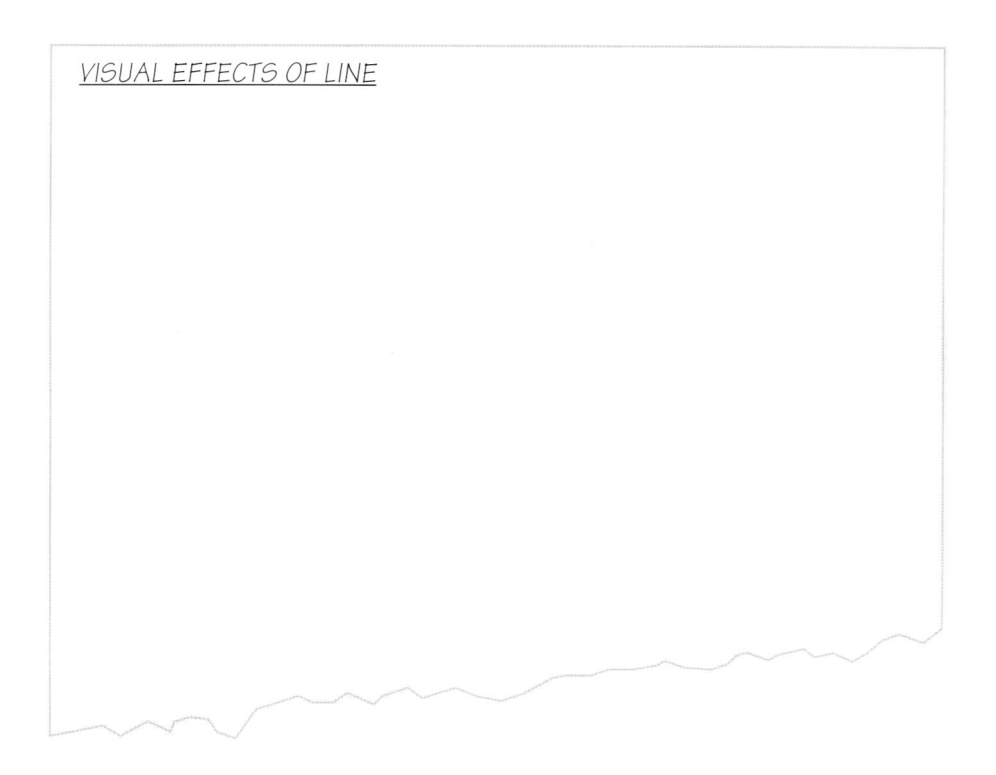

Examples of line

———————— *straight* calm, orderly

⌒ *curved* smooth

∿∿∿ *zigzag* angular, excited, moving

ℓℓℓℓ *looped* continuous, flowing

∿∿ *wavy* continuous, flowing

⌢⌢⌢ *scalloped* continuous, flowing

━━━━ *thick* weighty, strong

──────── *thin* delicate, passive

━━━━ *uneven* unsteady, uneven

──────── *even* steady, unbroken

∿∿∿ *continuous* smooth, unbroken

─ ─ ─ ─ *broken* irregular, broken

⋯⋯⋯ *dotted* moving

⌐⌐⌐⌐ *patterned* varied, interesting, detailed

──────────── *long* continuous, directional

- - - - - *short* busy

▬▬▬▬ *fuzzy* indefinite, soft

════ *open* strong, but could also be negative

──────── *horizontal* passive; could indicate width

│ *vertical* dynamic, strong, directional

Working with 2D projects

Line drawings by Eric Critchley (1941–82)

Shapes

Kinds of shape

An area enclosed by a line becomes a shape. The three basic shapes are a *square*, a *circle* and a *triangle*:

These are all simple shapes. When combined to form new shapes they become complex or compound shapes:

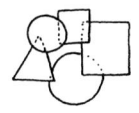

In these shapes the line is predominant, whereas the plane in which they are drawn has less impact:

In these shapes, however, it is the plane that is more predominant and that has more impact:

Basic design

Context

The size of a shape is relative to the size of the background on which it is placed. A small spot may look lost on a large ground, whereas placed on a background only slightly larger than itself it appears quite large:

The position in which a shape is placed on a background is also important. When one or more shapes are placed within another shape, tension is created.

- When a shape is placed towards the bottom of the background shape, it can appear to be falling out of the picture.
- Placed at the top, it may appear to float.
- Placed in the centre, it is static.
- The eye is drawn to the part of the picture containing the most interest. Bear this in mind when deciding where you wish to create a focal point.

Shape and form

Shape can have both 2D and 3D meanings, but usually the word **shape** is used to mean a flat, defined area in two dimensions. When a shape has depth, length and width, it is called a **form**.

There are two basic categories of shapes: geometric and organic. The *geometric shape* is precise, ordered and sharply defined. It can be simple, like a circle, a square or a triangle, or complex, such as a hexagon, a pentagon or some other many-sided construction. All geometric shapes can be drawn exactly, using rulers, compasses and other drawing aids.

Much of what humanity produces is based on geometric shapes – think of architecture and much product design, for instance. Nature too has geometric forms, in plant cells and in regular structures such as the honeycomb. Most natural forms, however, grow organically, producing a variety of precise yet irregular shapes. (Even those that appear to be irregular, however, often relate to a precise mathematical formula.) Organic forms are frequently deformed or altered by various processes: wear and tear is continual in the natural world.

Interrelationships

When working on surface design or in pattern making, always consider the relationship of one shape to another. Spaces *between* shapes are just as important as the shapes themselves and need equal consideration. Within a pattern, for example, a secondary or background shape can create an unwanted focal point. This may emerge to the eye of the observer, unsettling the rest of the design. Take care that this does not occur in your own work.

Space gives emphasis to a pattern. A small, patterned area well placed in a design can look better alone than when surrounded by other patterns, but

Working with 2D projects

small shapes sparsely scattered may look meagre if the background dominates them.

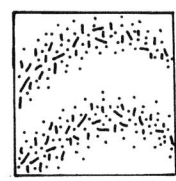

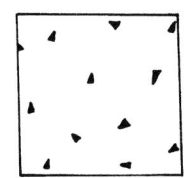

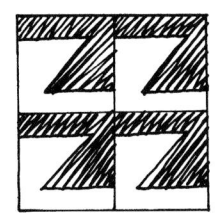

When considering shapes within a drawing or painting, the spaces between them – the negative shapes – often help in leading to accurate observation. Look at the key shapes of the objects you are studying. Then look with equal care at the spaces *between* the objects.

Kinds of shape and form

The various shapes and forms can be put into categories with particular properties.

Curved and angular shapes

The leaning position of an *angular* shape suggests movement, and increases the power of the shape. *Curves* are seen rapidly as the eye sweeps uninterruptedly along a form.

Open and closed forms

Open forms can be looked into or through; *closed* forms are self-contained and solid in appearance.

Positive and negative shapes

These are the visual elements that make it possible to recognise and understand the shapes and forms we see.

Your hand, for example, is a *positive* shape: it is solid and tangible. Spread your fingers and the spaces between the fingers – the *negative* shapes – provide a good illustration of positive and negative shapes working together. A plant against a window pane provides another example: choose a plant with a strong shape, like a bromeliad, a Swiss cheese plant or a dandelion. Likewise, you might also look at a stool, a table or a ladder: each has clear, regular lines and spaces.

Smooth and textured shapes

The surface of a shape determines the speed at which we look at it. Smooth forms tend to accelerate our eye speed, whereas textured surfaces slow us down.

Interesting patterns can be formed by repeating simple shapes. The repetition also creates rhythm.

Basic design 33

Counterchange is a term used when a design and the **ground** are interchangeable.

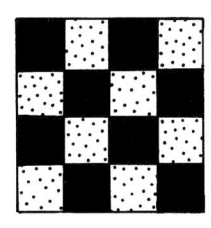

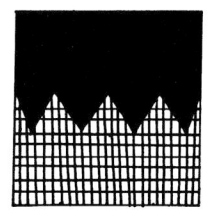

Repeat pattern

Repeat interchange can form interesting repeat patterns.

Brief

Using the information on shapes, choose at least two interlocking shapes and produce designs for a repeat pattern.

Cut the chosen shapes, in relief, from halved potatoes. Paint the raised areas with gouache, and print down on A3 paper.

Lino printing

Information and technique

Lino can be used to create repeating patterns or single images which can be printed many times. When printed the design will be laterally **inverted** – a mirror image. Any lettering to be printed must therefore be *cut* as a mirror image. This is easily done by tracing.

Roll ink in all directions

Ink bed

To give an even thin film.

The rubber roller is moved up, down and across the surface to create a smooth 'bed' of ink

1. Areas of lino that are cut away will *not* print, remaining areas *will* print. Before you start to cut, think carefully about which areas to leave and which to cut away.
2. Draw a design onto lino. You may use tracing paper or some other transfer method, such as chalk or carbon paper, or you may draw freehand.
3. The surface of the lino is quite soft. Cut into it with lino-cutting tools.
   Take care! Always keep your hands behind the cutting tool!
4. When the lino is ready, prepare the ink for printing. Squeeze ink out onto a flat, clean surface, such as a glass, metal or perspex sheet. Using a roller, roll out the ink until it is smooth and flat.
5. Place the roller, loaded with ink, onto the uncut surface of the lino. Roll it backwards and forwards until all of the raised surface is covered with a flat layer of ink.
6. Turn the lino over and press it down firmly onto the paper or fabric.
7. Repeat the process to print further copies.

Experimental techniques using the lino block

Lino can be used for **frottage** – the process of transferring a texture by rubbing.

1. Try the following exercise. Place the lino cut side up, and lay a sheet of paper over it. Rub the paper firmly with a wax crayon, a wax candle, an oil

Working with 2D projects

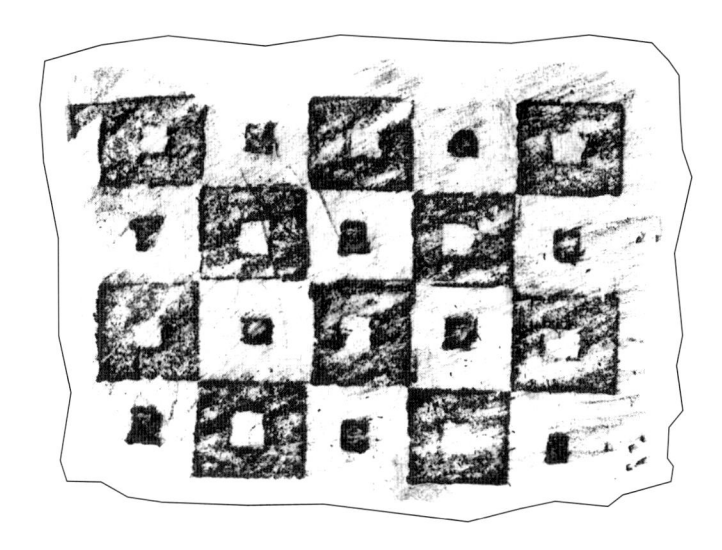

pastel or a pencil crayon so as to transfer the design. Now paint over your rubbings with liquid colour, such as an ink or a dye. The wax will act as a **resist**, creating interesting surface textures.
2. Paint the lino with PVA glue. Print this down; then sprinkle the print with a loose material such as sand, glitter or grains.
3. Paint the lino with bleach. Print this down onto dark paper, material or tissue: the bleach will remove the colour. The bleached area could then be painted with another colour. **Remember that bleach is a hazardous substance.** Before you start, find out how to use it safely.
4. Experiment further using these examples as a starting point. Keep good samples for your visual resource. Write up your notes to remind yourself how you arrived at these effects.

Transparent, translucent and opaque shapes

With **transparent** objects our view is unimpeded: we can see both the inner and the outer aspects of the form. In some cases this can make it hard to distinguish the form from its surrounding environment. With translucent shapes, which are only partially clear, some blurring of the shapes occurs. With **opaque** forms the eye rests on the outer surface.

Soft and hard forms

Softness and hardness are easily recognised – by touch, certainly, but almost as easily by looking. Softness suggests flexibility, while hardness implies durability.

Soft forms include animal fur, material, and clouds. Hard forms include buildings, tools and machines.

Light and form

Without light nothing is discernible to the naked eye. Low light affects our perception of shapes and forms: we tend to lose most of the detail and see only the overall shape, as with a silhouette. Strong directional lighting, on the other hand, clearly illuminates objects and reveals both the form itself and the shape it casts: the shadow.

Space

We live in a 3D world. Objects are solid and occupy space. Many people think of space as a void, as nothingness, but in design space is an important consideration.

- *Actual space* exists in a 2D composition, for instance within the borders of a painting, and in a 3D form as spaces around or inside a sculpture.
- *Pictorial spaces* are illusory spaces seen in a 2D work such as a painting or a drawing.

A feeling of spaciousness can be created by the choice of materials used. Transparent materials can give a particular feeling of endless space.

One of the most effective ways to decide upon **spatial relationships** is to cut shapes from paper and then move them round until you find a pleasing result.

Texture

Texture is inseparable from other elements of design. It can be thought of in two ways:

- as a 3D **tactile** quality – an actual quality, which you can feel;
- as a 2D surface quality – a visual quality, which you can see.

Texture enriches surface design and adds variety. Below are some examples of physical texture – what else can you think of? Write them down.

>   <u>PHYSICAL TEXTURES</u>
>
>   sandpaper
>   corrugated cardboard
>   polystyrene
>   embossed paper
>   wood
>   wire netting
>   concrete
>   fabric
>   fur

Brief 1

1. Collect several samples of textures from your list.
2. Draw an A3 rectangle. Construct a border around it using one of your textures. This is your picture frame.
3. Inside this border, compose a pattern of geometric shapes. Fill these with different textures.

Brief 2

1. Set up a still life, using a mixture of natural and artificial objects.
2. Using line only, draw the shapes of the objects in your composition.
3. Fill in the shapes with textures, either hand-drawn or using frottage.

Equal-sided flat shapes

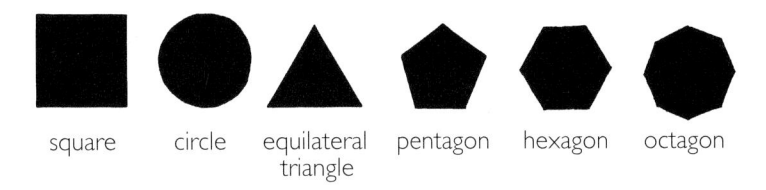

square   circle   equilateral triangle   pentagon   hexagon   octagon

Unequal-sided flat shapes

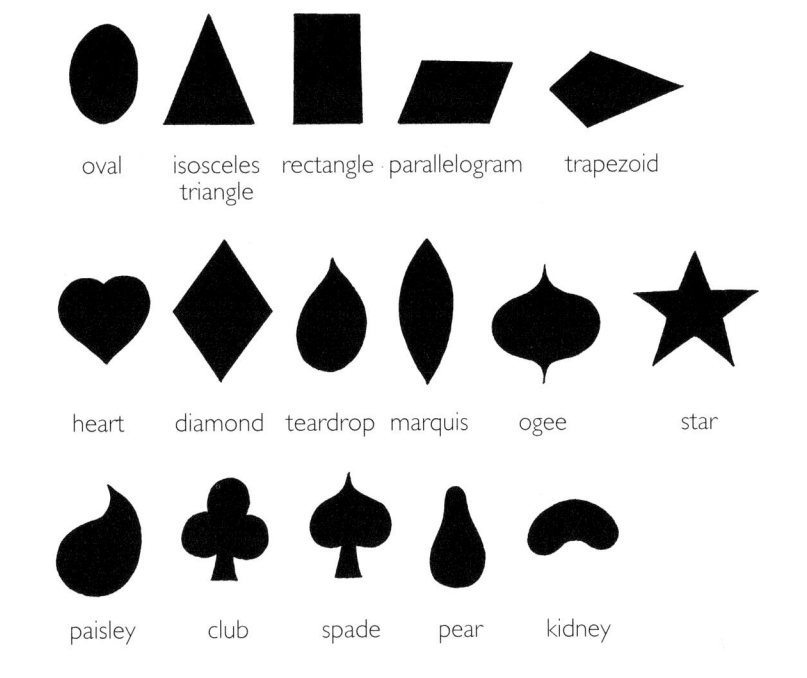

oval   isosceles triangle   rectangle   parallelogram   trapezoid

heart   diamond   teardrop   marquis   ogee   star

paisley   club   spade   pear   kidney

Equal-sided volume forms

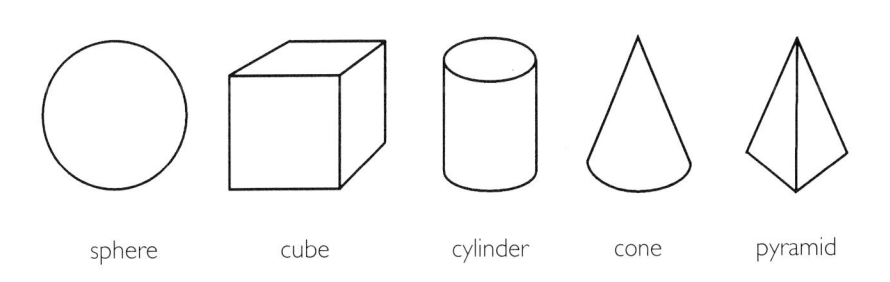

sphere   cube   cylinder   cone   pyramid

Basic design

Some shapes that fit together

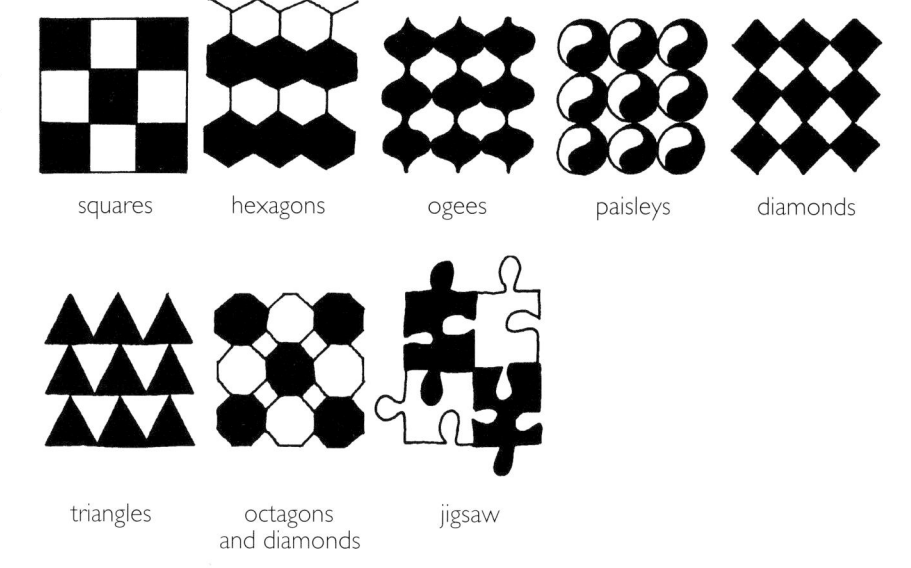

squares   hexagons   ogees   paisleys   diamonds

triangles   octagons and diamonds   jigsaw

Project

Texture enlivens and gives identity to an area, a shape or an object.

Preparation
Collect a variety of objects that have texture. Possibilities include sandpaper, corrugated card, bubble wrap, polystyrene, foam, wallpaper, netting (wire or fabric), wood, foil, fabrics and knitting. You could also *make* surface textures, by gluing sawdust, woodshavings, sugar and so on onto thin card.

Exercise 1
Cut your examples of texture into equal-sized rectangles. Stick them onto this grid.

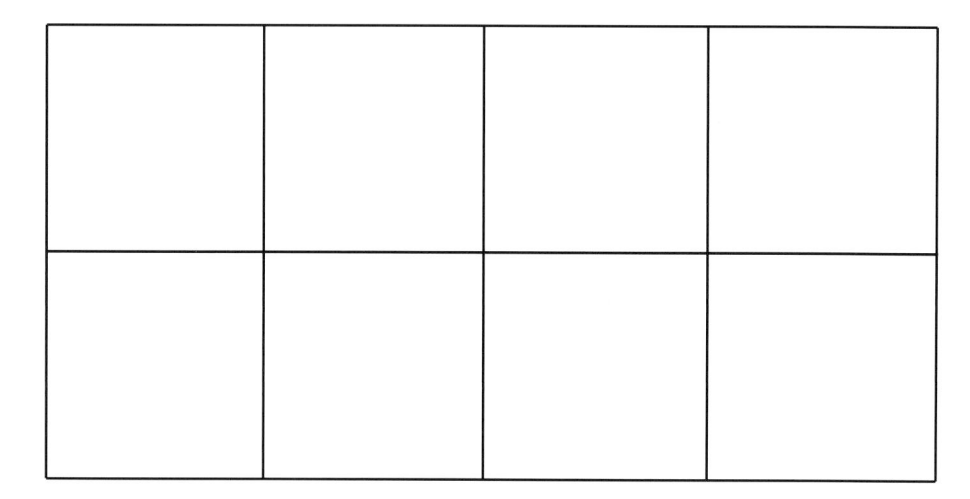

Exercise 2
Using suitable and varied media, try to re-create several of the textures from your sample sheet. Using A3 paper, draw the textures at least twice the original size. Allow one to run into another so as to create an all-over effect on the sheet. Dry the sheet fully and apply fixative. Put the sample sheet in your portfolio.

Exercise 3
Collect together several objects from the following group:

shells   marbles   bark   fruit   pebbles   fish   leaves

Working with 2D projects

Using the knowledge you have gained from the first two exercises, draw these objects using suitable media. Concentrate on the surface textures of the objects. Use A3 or A2 paper. Keep the result in your portfolio.

Outcome: relationship to GNVQ

This project will have covered the following units, elements and performance criteria:

- Unit 1: element 1.1 (performance criteria 1–3, 5);
  element 1.2 (performance criteria 1–5).
- Unit 4: element 4.3 (performance criteria 1–6);
  element 4.4 (performance criteria 1, 2, 5, 6).

The evidence required is:

- Studies showing the use of 2D visual language – mark making and 2D formal elements.
- An explanation of 2D formal elements.
- Discussion of the use of visual language in your own and others' work.
- Indication that you are aware of and have followed 2D health and safety procedures.

Self-assessment review

Discuss and review the effectiveness of your use of media, technology processes and techniques. Fill in your self-assessment form, and put it in your log book.

4.2 Colour

Colour is a quality of visible **phenomena** distinct from form, light and shade. It is an essential part of the visual language for artists and designers. This section considers **pigment** colour. This is light reflected from coloured objects, rather than direct light scattered by a prism.

Colour is one of the most important aspects of art and design. You need to develop confidence in using colour and in making it work for you. Most people are continually influenced by colour in their daily lives: as designers we need to know how to exploit this.

The following exercises afford a simple introduction to colour theory. You will start by filling in a *colour circle*, or *colour wheel*. This is a basic layout showing how colours relate to one another. The colour circle used above was developed by Johannes Itten, working with Bauhaus artists. Our version has been simplified to give six, rather than twelve, tertiary colours. You will achieve better colour values with paint than the printer has here.

The colour circle

This exercise requires you to paint the appropriate colours to match the diagram. On A3 paper, draw a neat copy of the colour circle. (Leave enough space for complementary scale and grey scale exercises on page 41.)

The colour circle comprises a sequence of colours in an orderly progression.

- In the middle are the three **primary colours**, *red*, *yellow* and *blue*. Primary colours are so called because they cannot be mixed from other colours, but if combined can produce nearly every other known colour. (This is the theory: in practice it is surprisingly difficult to mix some colours, which is why so many different colours are offered by artists' suppliers.)
- Next come the **secondary colours**, *orange*, *green* and *violet*. Each is obtained by mixing two primaries in equal amounts.
- On the outside of the diagram are **tertiary colours**, each a combination of a primary and a secondary colour. These are named according to their components: *yellow-green*, *blue-violet*, and so on.

Painting the colour circle

Think carefully before starting the exercise and ensure at each stage that your colours and brushes are clean.

Mix up the colours, starting with the primaries and progressing through the secondaries to the tertiaries. Mix your colours carefully, to a creamy consistency. Ensure that the paper is completely covered so that no white can be seen.

Different colours have different staining powers. To achieve a balanced green you will probably need more yellow than blue. It is best to start with yellow and gradually to add the blue. It is always easier to start with the lighter colour and to add the darker one.

1. Start with the three primary colours: *blue*, *yellow*, *red*.
2. Paint in the secondary colours. These are made by mixing together two primary colours:
    - ▶ *blue + yellow → green*
    - ▶ *yellow + red → orange*
    - ▶ *red + blue → violet*
3. Finally, add the tertiary colours. Each is a mixture of one primary and one secondary:
    - ▶ *yellow-green*
    - ▶ *red-orange*
    - ▶ *blue-violet*
    - ▶ *yellow-orange*
    - ▶ *red-violet*
    - ▶ *blue-green*

These colours form the basic colour circle, and mixing and painting them will have helped you to see how one colour relates to another.

Complementary colours

Each colour has a **complementary colour**. This is the colour opposite to it on the colour circle:

- *red — green*
- *blue — orange*
- *yellow — violet*

Working with 2D projects

Each pair of complementary colours together co[ntains all the primary]
colours, and thus all the colours of the spectrum. [Mixing a pair of]
complementaries will make a neutral grey.

If a colour you have mixed looks too strong, add a [little of its complementary]
colour. This will reduce its strength.

To make a colour appear stronger within a design, pla[ce its]
complementary nearby. If you stare at a colour for a wh[ile and then close your]
eyes you will see an *after-image*. This will have the comp[lementary colour.]
(Surgeons wear green overalls and during an operation th[e patient is covered]
with green cloths. This counteracts the effect of looking at [the red] of the blood,
helping to reduce the after-image.)

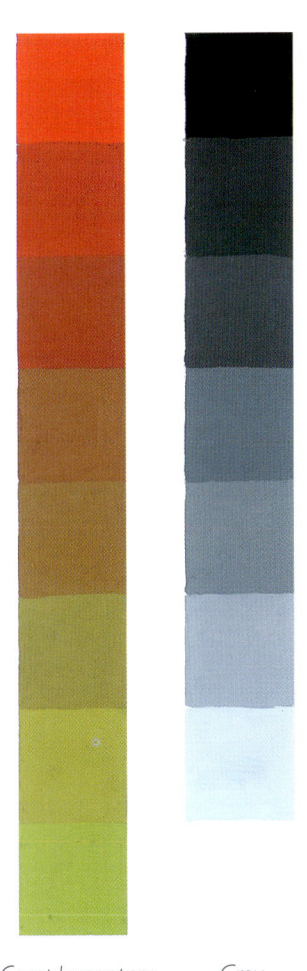

Complementary scale
1 Choose a pair of complementaries (e.g. red and green).
2 Prepare the two paints.
3 Starting with red, paint a small area of colour (approximately 2 cm square).
4 Add a small amount of green, and paint another small area.
5 Continue, adding green and painting small areas, until you reach green. (It may help to paint a splodge of green at the beginning, so that you know when you reach true green.)
6 When dry, cut out the patches and arrange them into a strip to show a gradual change from red to green.

Grey scale
A *grey scale* shows the shades and tones, or the value, of a colour. The grey scale comes from the system devised by A. H. Munsell early this century: in this, colours are arranged three-dimensionally according to *hue*, *value* and *chroma*. The greys show the *value* of the colour, from light to dark.

1 Paint out a grey scale, as you did for the colour scale, from black to white.

Colour perception

A given colour is hardly ever seen as it really is – our perception is always influenced by the other colours that surround it. This next exercise shows how this happens.

1 Cut out, or paint, four squares (approximately 10 cm square) of different colours.
2 Cut out four small squares (approximately 1 cm square), all of the same colour.
3 Stick one of the small squares in the centre of each of the larger ones.
4 Look at the two colours against a white background.

You can see in each of the examples to the right that, because of the backgrounds they are seen against, the small patches appear to be different colours.

Complementary scale

Grey scale

Colour

Colour mixing and matching

You need to be able to mix paint to obtain an exact colour. This is sometimes extremely difficult, so you must practise until you are confident.

1 Choose a colour postcard, a piece of fabric, or a magazine cutting. Stick it onto paper, with white all round.
2 Now try to mix and match the colours as closely as you can, painting out onto the white alongside the image.

Terms commonly used in talking about colour

Like all specialist studies, art and design has its own language. At first this can appear to be a difficult 'code', but like any specialist language it has grown in response to the needs of practitioners: it allows them to talk to each other with precision and without misunderstanding. As you study, and talk with other designers, craftspeople and artists, you will quickly find yourself both understanding and using the jargon.

The following list of terms and definitions accords with most dictionaries and textbooks. To make it work for you, take time to rewrite any definitions that you find difficult, using your own words.

Some terms are used loosely; others, such as *intensity* and *saturation*, are almost interchangeable. Use the word that serves your purpose. For example, in a garden lit by the noonday sun the colours of the flowers may be 'intense'. The same flower bed in the late afternoon may have 'saturated' colour.

In some cases you may need to wrestle with the meaning of a term, trying to clarify the meaning and express it in simple words. Keep at it – the process of refining the definition is a very effective way of learning.

achromatic Without chroma – *black*, *white*, *greys*.

analogous colours Related colours; colours with a common hue. Such colours are adjacent on the colour wheel, for example *blue*, *blue-green* and *green*.

chroma (Greek for *colour*) Usually used in a scientific context: a quality that embraces **hue** and **saturation**.

Working with 2D projects

chromatic Having colour – reds, greens, browns, pinks.

colour or **hue** A visible quality of something, distinct from form, light and shade.

colour circle or **colour wheel** A systematic mixing guide showing a sequence of colours in an orderly progression.
- **primary colours** *Red, yellow* and *blue*. Called primaries because they cannot be obtained by mixing other pigments; combined they can produce nearly every other known colour. When all three are mixed they make black.
- **secondary colours** *Orange, green* and *violet*. Obtained by mixing two primaries in equal amounts.
- **tertiary colours** *Yellow-green, blue-violet*, etc. Combinations of one primary and one secondary colour.

colour perspective Colours appear less bright in the distance, and bluer.

colour scheme Any plan to use colour within some chosen limits.

colour solid A 3D colour system showing not just the aspects depicted by the colour wheel but also progress in value from black to white.

complementary colours Optically opposed colours. Such colours are opposite each other on the **colour circle**, for instance *blue* and *orange*, *red* and *green*.
- Any two complements can either cancel or intensify each other. To *reduce* the intensity of colour, add a touch of its complementary. To make a colour look *more* intense without adding another hue, place its complementary nearby.
- Any two complementary colours of paint, mixed in the proper amounts, will produce a neutral grey.

(Again, the adding of colours of *light* differs from the adding of colours of *pigments*. Any two colours of light are called complementary if together they produce white light.)

harmonious colour scheme A scheme that avoids strong values and intensities.

harmony and disharmony The juxtaposition of colours that go well together results in harmony; the juxtaposition of colours that clash with each other yields disharmony. Colours that clash may appear to be jumping out of the picture. Any colour combination can be made more harmonious by subduing a tone or two, or by making one tone warmer or cooler.

hue The colour of something. The term is often used when describing similar colours, which are said to be close in hue.

intensity The purity, strength or saturation of a colour.

monochrome A colour scheme using tints and shades of only one hue.

normal value The most characteristic value of each colour. The value used in colour mixing systems, such as colour circles. Usually the value of paint.

physical primaries (also **physiological**, **fundamental** or **principal primaries**) *Red, green* and *blue*. The primary colours for light are not the same as the primaries for pigments: red, green and blue light together produce white light. Colour television makes use of this by illuminating red, green and blue dots. (Edwin Land, the inventor of Polaroid film, has further reduced the physical primaries to *two* colours, which together produce a natural-looking colour range.)

pigment A coloured substance used in paint.

saturation The degree of vividness of a colour.

shade A value darker than the normal value. Usually, therefore, a colour to which black has been added. For example, *maroon* is a shade of *red*.

spectrum The full range of colour, from violet to red. It can be seen by shining white light through a prism. (A rainbow is a spectrum made when raindrops act as prisms for sunlight.)

tinge An infusion or stain of a colour.

tint A value lighter than the normal value. Usually, therefore, a colour to which white has been added. For example, *pink* is a tint of *red*.

tone The lightness or darkness of a colour, such as *lemon yellow* and *yellow ochre*, sometimes referred to as the **value**. Tone is often used to suggest a mood.

value The lightness or darkness of a colour, which measures variation among the greys. Any area or line of colour can vary in value, for example *red* can vary between *light pink* and *dark maroon*.

warm and cool colours If you look at your colour wheel you will see that it falls into two halves. Reddish and yellowish colours are considered warm – they remind us of fire. Bluish and greenish colours are seen as cool – they remind us of ice.
- All hues can be made warmer by adding red, orange or yellow, and can be made cooler by adding blue, green or white.
- In paintings, warm colours come forward, whereas cool colours recede. In interiors, cool colours make rooms look larger and more peaceful, whereas warm colours make them look smaller and cosier.

Light and colour

Without light there is no colour. Light is a form of energy. It behaves like a wave, and the colour depends on the wavelength. White light appears white because it is a combination of all of the colours of the visible spectrum. It is a mixture of all the different wavelengths.

When white light strikes a surface, one of two things may happen.

1. The white light may be reflected unchanged. In this case we see the surface as white. This happens when the surface *is* white, but also in parts of the highlights seen on wet fruit, polished metals, mirrors, lustrous satin, shimmering water and the like.
2. Pigment in the surface may absorb some of the wavelengths in the white light. The wavelengths *not* absorbed are reflected, and it is these that we see. The colour we attribute to a surface depends on the reflected light.

Various consequences follow from this, which the artist or designer must understand.

- If white light strikes a surface that has no dye or pigmentation, all wavelengths are *reflected* and the surface appears white.
- If white light strikes a surface that contains pigments sufficient to *absorb* all

wavelengths, then because none are reflected the surface appears black.
- If light contains more blue and green and less red and yellow (as do street lights and fluorescent lights), then people will look less than healthy, and lipstick, skin and hair will look dull and greyish. Blues and greens, however, will look brighter.
- If light contains more red, orange and yellow and less blue and green (as with sunlight, candlelight and incandescent light bulbs), then blues and green will be duller but yellows, oranges, and reds will be more intense. People tend to look better in warm lights, which give a warm glow to the skin.
- Surfaces can reflect only the colours that strike them. Thus a white surface illuminated by green light will appear to be green. Similarly, green light striking a grey surface will be partly reflected as a darker, duller green. Green light striking a black surface will be absorbed and the surface will appear very black. This phenomenon can be exploited: for instance a blue light striking a blue-and-white patterned fabric will make the fabric appear all blue, so on stage simply changing the light can completely change a costume.
- Very bright, intense lights can make colours seem duller, whereas softer lights can make the colour appear brighter again.
- As a light dims, reds and oranges darken more quickly. Blues and violets (colours with shorter wavelengths) are still reflected at lower light intensity.
- The level of illumination and the colour sensitivity of the individual's eyes also affect perception of a colour. In bright white lights, colours lean towards yellow and seem warmer; yellow can look almost white. In low lights, colours lean towards blue and seem cooler.

4.3 Photography as a tool in art and design

As an artist or a designer you need to accumulate a great deal of visual imagery for your resource collection – some of it rare or beautiful, much of it ordinary and expected. You will sift through this material from time to time as you seek to trigger ideas for creative solutions to art and design problems.

Photography can be a valuable asset both in personal research and in building your resource collection. The camera is an essential tool for all artists and designers.

The quality of the camera isn't crucial – what matters is how you use it!

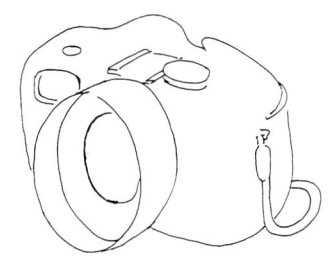

The photography exercises in this section have two main aims:

- to establish the camera as a recording instrument which you can use to build your visual resource collection;
- to introduce you to the portrait, and to a task which you will then need to assess.

Professional practice

You are already beginning to form some essential good habits, or 'professional practice'. These habits need to be carefully developed. Here are some of them:

- Plan your proposed activity – before you start work make a note of your intentions.
- Look at the work of other photographers – what do you like or dislike? Write down their names and your thoughts on their work.
- Negotiate with people who may be affected by your plans – your model, users of the space you want to work in, and people responsible for the locations you will be 'shooting' in.
- Record your activities as you go along – this is one of the hardest things to do, especially if you are enjoying yourself!
- Tidy up, and thank those involved in making your activity work for you.
- Analyse your outcome – is it as you expected, did it fulfil the criteria given at the outset?
- How will you improve next time? Again, write it down.
- Carefully store, mount or frame your photographs.

Can you see the importance of a **holistic** approach?

To achieve a good GNVQ result you will need to understand how the various parts of the GNVQ interact with each other. This will mean continually asking questions, cross-referring, and re-examining what you do. Do keep all your work, your notes, your ideas – *including* your less successful results. Together these will quickly guide you to better products.

Creative photography

Photography can be used to record things, but it can also be used as a creative medium. The camera helps you to record images which can stimulate your thinking, allowing you to store them and to bring them to mind again later.

Before this century visual images were stored by sketching, drawing and painting. Nowadays you can take photographs, but like the illustrators of the past you will often need to add a note or two to supplement your images. Carry a pocket notebook when taking pictures, and be sure to record specific data such as the film type and speed, along with details of the camera settings.

Be methodical about your photographic recording. Think about colours, too, as these may be distorted in the processing: some delicately coloured lichens photographed on a field trip may look like sulphurous yellow and lime green chemical spillage on the prints!

Your notebook might say, 'Found this wonderful lichen, never seen it before. Reminded me of an end paper – try marbling soon. Useful for fabric printing?' Such notes develop your creative thinking and establish a design-conscious approach to your work.

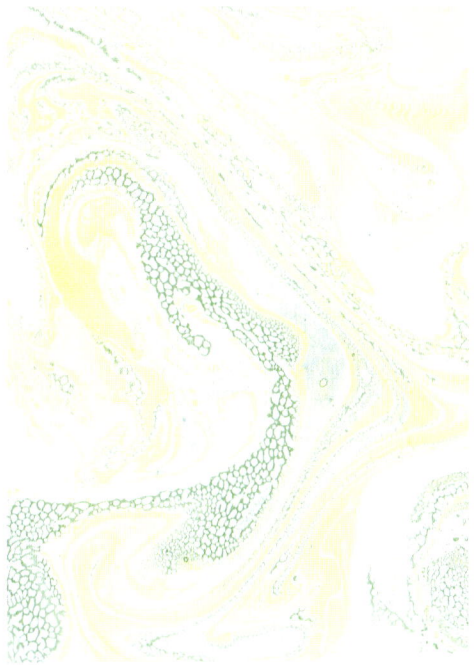

Add the date, the time, the reason for your visit, the weather conditions and your comments on the location generally. As well as being useful in their own right, such records are evidence of your ability to store, retrieve and use information.

You will gradually develop a catalogue of visual stimuli. Look for themes or other logical categories of image associations, as you did earlier with your drawing and visual research.

The theme of 'change'
The effects of weather, time and usage on things, places or people can be fun to study, as well as providing you with rich visual imagery.

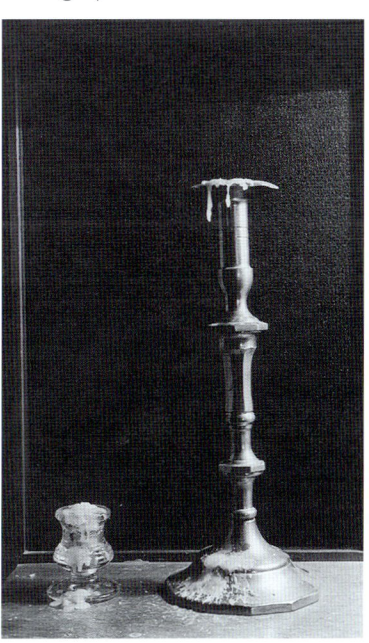

Working with 2D projects

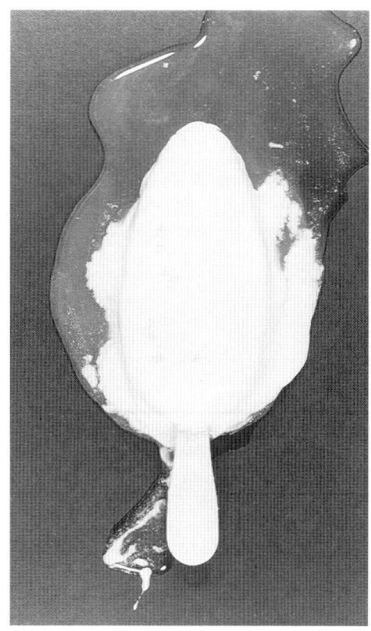

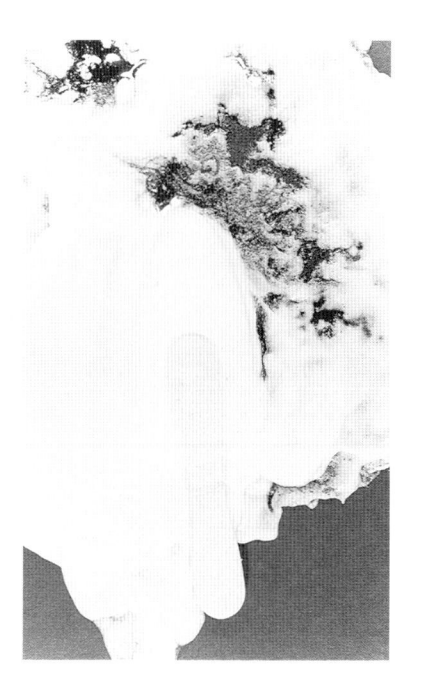

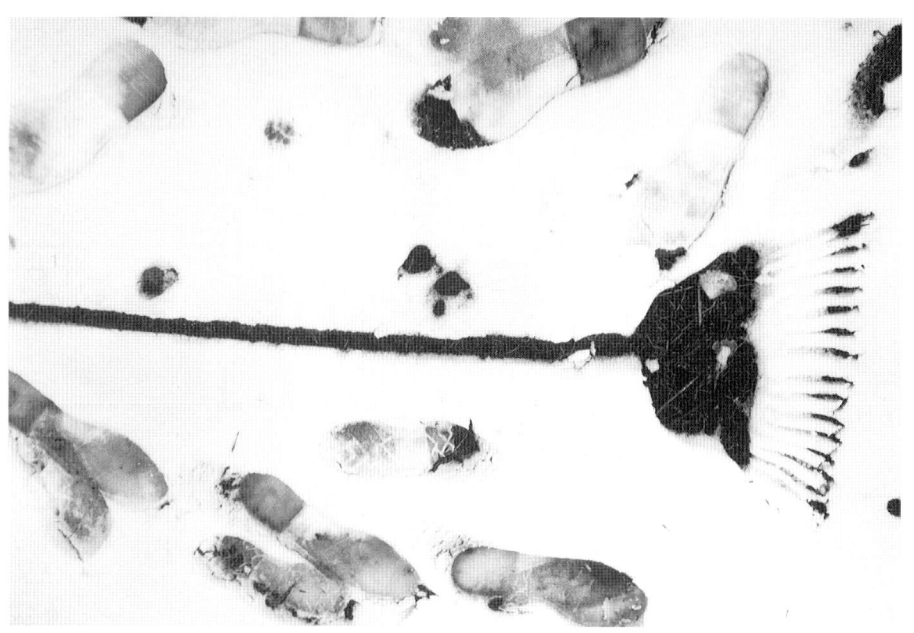

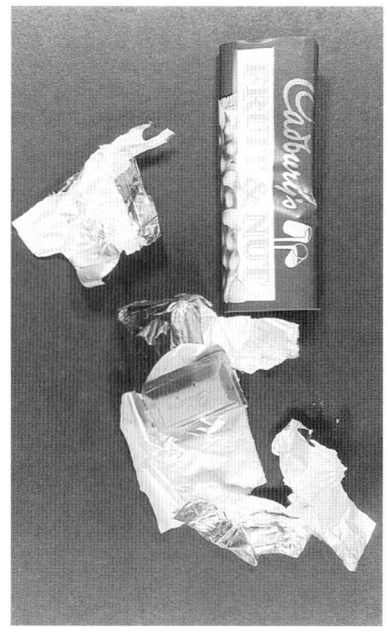

Developing your ideas

Use your camera to your advantage. Although any camera can be useful, you need to know the limitations of the one you are using.

The throwaway camera, for example, will work wonderfully in well-lit open locations, when used to photograph views, people and large objects. It won't work well, however, in extreme close-up, for long-distance detail, or in less bright light conditions.

With your photographs, keep a note of your results. Say what you think about them, and perhaps add other media to reinforce your point.

This photo of a tree fungus was taken in winter. The photo shows the fungus clearly. Can I make a good pattern from it?

When copied in black and white, the fungus photo reveals an interesting set of shapes. Develop as a painting or a surface pattern?

Photography as a tool in art and design

A repeat pattern can be developed from an **abstract** image.

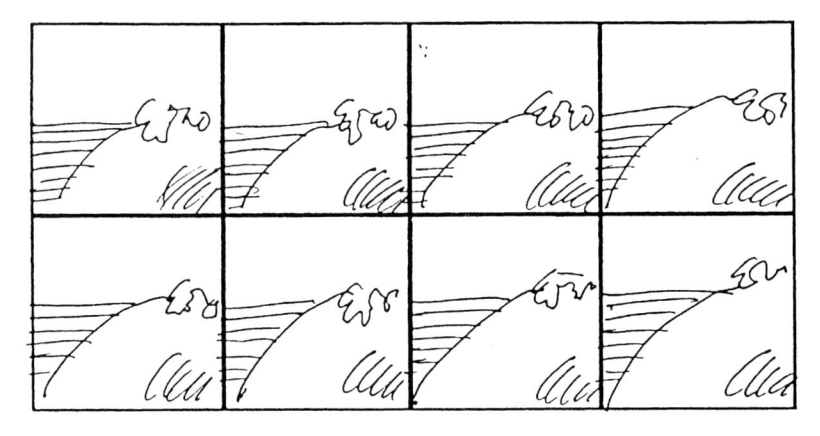

Note: I have used the photocopier to build up my repeat designs. I could instead have traced some elements, or used a black and white copier at an earlier stage, and still have arrived at a suitable final image.

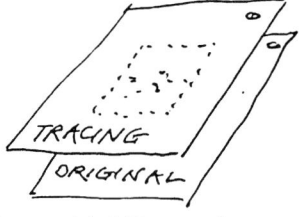

1. Trace with HB or softer pencil 
2. Turn the tracing paper over. 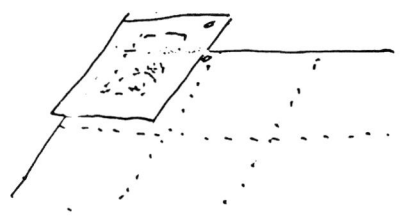
3. Position accurately over the grid and draw over your lines. 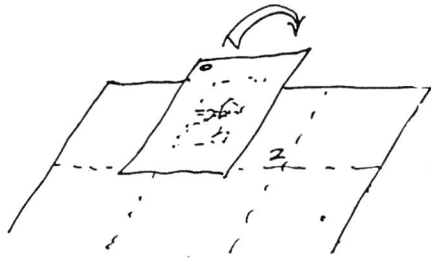
4. Turn tracing paper and repeat in space 2. 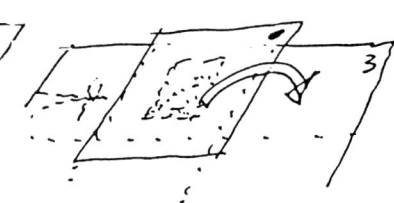
5. When done turn again to repeat on space 3. Continue until you have full sheet of repeat pattern

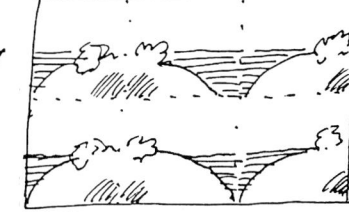

Chiarascuro

Use light to improve your results. In your early tonal drawings you concentrated on achieving strong contrast by working only in black and white. Try to achieve the same tonal contrast with your camera in the next exercise.

Brief

This is a simple photographic exercise based on a portrait study of a friend or a member of your own family. The idea is to show **chiaroscuro**, the art of working with light and shade.

1. First take a shot of your subject in normal light. In this picture show your subject with a normal, cheerful expression.
2. Build up to a high-contrast side-lit one. Take it a little further, if you like, by going for a dramatic result. In this second picture, show your subject with a sombre, grave or mysterious expression.

Working with 2D projects

Visual literacy

By carrying out these exercises you will have achieved some competence in the use of photography as a tool. You will also have exercised key skills and increased your **visual literacy** – your awareness and understanding of visual images.

Checks

- Look back through this section. Do you clearly understand what you have learned?
- Have you entered your achievements in your personal log book?
- Have you transferred relevant notes from your notebook to your visual diary?

Keeping your records up to date

During this section you will have acquired evidence to show your ability in the following:

- Operating a camera with confidence, without shake and in a controlled way.
- Responding to instructions and achieving the expected results.
- Keeping records of your activities.
- Keeping notes of visual research.

If you are satisfied with your results, transfer them now to your portfolio.

Can you see that this way of working can be applied to other topics, and with other media and materials? (This is one example of a transferable skill.)

Personal log book

Self-assessment review

Complete your self-assessment form. Did you meet the criteria? Do you need to redo any work?

If you have learnt from your mistakes you will be able to decide confidently whether to redo part or all of your work. You don't need to go for excellence in everything, but you must recognise when you need extra practice. It is useful to be able to say to yourself not just 'This isn't good' but 'because . . . (too dark, too small, etc.).'

Time management

Did you hit your time targets? If not, try to work out why not. Was it to do with things outside your control, or had you prepared inadequately? Did you think things would take less time than they did?

Photography as a tool in art and design

This workbook is based on real-time projects. Each of us has different skills and abilities: the important thing here is to develop self-awareness so that you can make realistic estimates of the time you will need for different sorts of activity.

4.4 Exemplar 2D projects

As you work through this book, build on your experience. The projects suggested can all be done at home. Some of them are simple to do, but this does not mean that it will automatically be easy to achieve good results. Try always to incorporate what you have learned already. Use the skills and knowledge that you have to plan, carry out and successfully complete your tasks.

Good results will be most likely to follow good preparation: apply the professional approach to your projects. Decide from the outset what materials you will require, where your practical work can be carried out safely and cleanly, and how much time you will need.

When you have obtained the result you want, take time to tidy up, to clean your equipment, to store away materials and to file your evidence. Complete your self-assessment form, record information in your notebook, collect and store your rough work, and mount and present your best pieces in your portfolio. By now your sketchbooks, your personal research material and your visual resource in general will be growing, and your log book, your visual diary and your portfolio will be starting to show your individual style and ability.

Keep forming good habits as you work. Even when you feel tired and hungry, try to complete your notes and tasks at the end of each practical session. You will be glad that you did so later on. When you are *not* tired and hungry – perhaps the next day, and again a month or two later – reflect on what you have done. Note down what you feel about the work you have done, the way you worked, and what you learned from the process.

Monoprint and relief print: 'Year of colour'

Brief
You are invited to produce a series of coloured images for a chemical company. The company wishes to produce a calendar to help in promoting and **marketing** their products. As a supplier of pigment to paint manufacturers the company also intends to offer the calendar to major paint retailers.

Specification
A minimum of four A4 prints is required. All four must have **portrait orientation**. Full-colour printing is to be used but the company hopes to see effective use of colour ranges, from subtle to strident. Some images could be largely of one colour, others could cover a wider spectrum.

The finished calendar will be A3 overall and wire 'O' bound: allow a minimum of 5 cm at the top and sides. In addition, allow a generous border around your print in order to accommodate the printed additions below your image: the **logo**, the company's name and the calendar dates.

Materials
- Ink (or paint), oil-based or water-based, and solvent.
- An A3 sheet with a hard surface, such as glass, plastic or metal, to act as the ink bed.

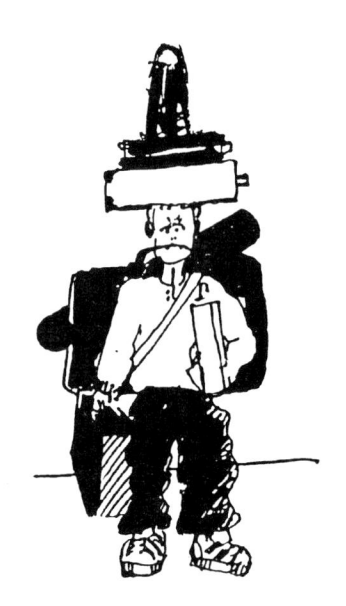

- A roller, to apply the ink.
- Sticks, pencils, brushes and rags.
- Tough paper to accept the print – it will need to be absorbent.

Research

Research the work of artists who celebrate colour, such as Josef Albers, Philip Sutton and Henri Matisse, together with famous **monoprint** users, including William Blake, Edgar Degas, Paul Klee, Pablo Picasso and Max Ernst. Add other artists' names as you discover them.

Process

1. Choose the ink colour (lightest first) to apply to the ink bed. Roll it out to give a thin surface film.
2. Draw into the ink with a stick, a pencil, or solvent and a brush: this will give a white impression.
3. Place your paper on top. Press with your hand or a soft cloth.
4. Draw with a stick or pencil through the paper: this will pick up more ink and give a dark impression.
5. Carefully peel back the paper and leave to dry.

Experiment

Carry on making prints, adding or subtracting colour and using **masking materials**, solvents or water, until you have sufficient images.

Further development

Use the monoprint technique to add a 'painterly' feel to illustrations, posters and surface pattern designs. Mix your techniques. You could make collages out of your scrap monoprints.

Remember to save the results for your visual resource, keeping notes of how you achieved certain textures and effects.

Another type of printing, **relief printing**, is done in its simplest form using the same basic materials.

1. Roll out a thin film of ink on the ink bed.
2. Add torn paper or other materials to block out the ink (feathers, leaves, **perforated metal**, etc.).
3. Place your paper over and rub it to transfer ink to the paper.
4. Peel off the print and let it dry.

Alternatively:

1. Roll a thin film of ink directly onto shaped card or balsa wood which you have stuck down onto board or card.
2. Lay your print paper over the inked-up shapes.
3. Use a dry roller or hand pressure to pick up the image.
4. Remove your print and leave it to dry.

Presentation

Select your four images for presentation. Ask yourself the following questions:

- Do your images look attractive? If not, why not? Write down the reasons.
- Are they clean and properly positioned? If not, correct them.
- As part of the calendar, will they enhance the company's image?
- Will customers like them? Write down your thoughts.
- Do the images suggest anything? Again, write down your answer.

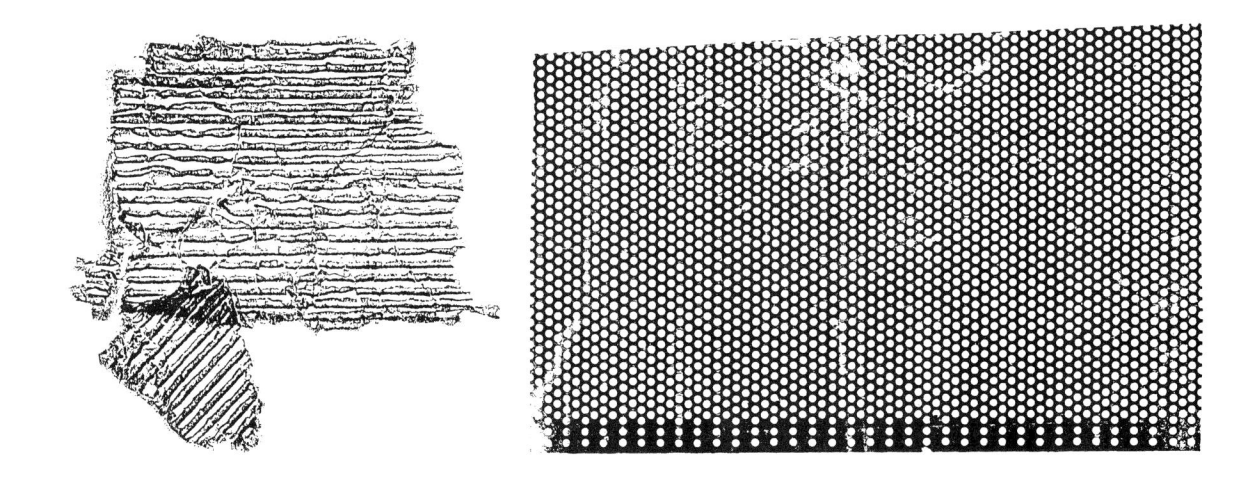

Direct relief prints, using corrugated paper, perforated zinc, and rope

- Did you cover a range of colour?
- Are your prints bright and cheerful or moody and mysterious? Try to record your thoughts about them.

Self-assessment review

Fill out your form and put it in your log book. Did you write down your criteria? If so, did you think about the points listed above? Clearly the main requirements concerning the celebration of colour, the size, and the use of mono or relief print must be correct. The images should be capable of maintaining interest and freshness throughout a month-long exposure.

Outcome

- If your images look clean, if they are rich in colour, and if they are properly presented within the border with a fair level of supporting work: *pass*.
- If the images are clean, well-positioned, celebrate a range of colour in them, and are accompanied by a high level of supporting material, development work, historical notes and detailed descriptions of the process: *merit*.
- If they are as described above, and accompanied by outstanding reference materials; if the images are innovative, fresh and jewel-like, if they are attractive to most observers, if there is good supporting material relating to colour and imagery and a high level of analytical notes; and if you and others want to keep re-examining the images: *distinction*.

This project will have covered the following units, elements and performance criteria:

- Unit 1: element 1.1 (performance criteria 1–6, in part)
    element 1.2 (performance criteria 1–5, in part)

▶ Unit 4: element 4.1 (performance criteria 1–5, in part)
   element 4.2 (performance criteria 1–5, in part)
   element 4.2 (performance criteria 1–6, in part)
   element 4.2 (performance criteria 1–6, in part)

As with all your projects, you should check your achievements by referring to the NCVQ guide, *GNVQ Mandatory Units for Intermediate Art & Design*.

4.5 Glossary

See also pages 42–4.

abstract Representing ideas rather than things. The term is often teamed with 'expressionism'.

chiarascuro Treatment of light or shade in painting.

complementary colours Optically opposed colours, such as *blue* and *orange*. (More information is given on page 43.)

counterchange Interchangeability of the design shape and its background.

form A shape in three dimensions, with depth, length and width. (Compare **shape**.)

formal elements An umbrella term covering visual elements such as line, tone, colour and form, and visual dynamics like balance, proportion and scale.

frottage Rubbing over a textured surface in order to transfer the texture (as in brass rubbing).

ground The surface worked on in painting or a design.

holistic Concerning the whole rather than just one part.

invert Turn upside down.

landscape orientation With the longer side horizontal. (Compare **portrait orientation**.)

logo An organisation's emblem or badge, used in graphics and advertising.

marketing The art of understanding potential purchasers' needs, thereby promoting sales and services more effectively.

masking materials Wax or patented solutions used to block out areas in designs.

monochrome A colour scheme using tints and shades of only one hue.

monoprint A 'one-off' printmaking technique in which ink is transferred to paper by pressure.

opaque Not transmitting light.

perforated metal Usually zinc, with regularly placed holes in it.

phenomena Observed or apparent objects or occurrences.

pigment A coloured substance used in paint.

portrait orientation With the longer side vertical. (Compare **landscape orientation**.)

primary colours The three basic colours of pigment (*red*, *yellow* and *blue*), which cannot be obtained by combining other colours.

relief printing The process of covering a raised surface in ink and pressing it against a material such as paper.

resist A barrier against acid or ink penetration. The resist is dissolved once the process has been finished, leaving the original surface exposed.

secondary colours The three pigment colours made by combining pairs of primary colours (*orange, green* and *violet*).

shape A defined area in two dimensions. (Compare **form**.)

spatial relationships The companionship or otherwise of solid objects one with another in a given space.

tactile Relating to the sense of touch.

tertiary colours The pigment colours formed by combining a primary colour with a secondary colour (e.g. *yellow-green*).

transparent Able to be seen through.

visual literacy Awareness, understanding and appreciation of visual images.

5 Working with 3D projects

The products of 3D activity in art, design and crafts are all around us: everything we use has undergone the design process. Even illustrations which we usually think of as 2D can draw on the 3D skills and creativity of sculptors and model-makers, puppetry artists or special-effect designers.

The range of formal elements for 3D includes most of those used in 2D visual language, with some additional ones. The main difference between 2D and 3D is the very straightforward and obvious one: 3D works occupy space and can be seen from all angles, whereas 2D work often has to simulate 3D qualities as each piece can only be viewed from the position chosen by the artist or designer.

Remember from your 2D studies that 2D works have shape and 3D works have form. By definition 3D works are objects: their forms occupy space. Drawings, photographs, paintings and prints, in 2D, are in one **plane**.

Certain formal elements, like colour and texture, are common to 2D and 3D work, although they may work in different ways. Texture, for instance, can be physical as well as visual: in 3D we can use the sense of touch as well as that of sight. In 3D, therefore, a material has a tactile quality.

You will have worked in 3D applications already. What experience have you had? Make a list. Model-making, carving and shaping, knitting and dressmaking are all examples.

<u>3D APPLICATIONS</u>

Now think about your list. Can you analyse any main feature shared by these 3D experiences? Are they all assemblages (the 3D equivalent of 2D collages)? Are they all sculpture, made by putting bits together as well as by taking bits away (carving)? Do you use **objets trouvés** (French for 'found objects')? Or have you had experience with building or construction toys like Lego, Meccano or Quadro?

The exercises and projects that follow will give you a range of different outcomes. Some you will find easier or more interesting than others. Remember to write down *why* you like some more than others, *why* you have reacted as you have. Also record in your notebook what you think are the reasons for and against the quality of your results.

5.1 3D visual resource development

Storage and retrieval: a design problem

There are many similarities between the requirements of your 3D studies and those of your 2D work. As well as gaining new skills and understanding and learning more visual language you will draw on existing skills and knowledge.

Materials will be more important than media in this section of the book. This means that your visual resource will become bigger and harder to store and to access.

This in itself creates a design problem: it is a fundamental issue for interior designers, architects, and display and exhibition designers. Instead of reducing the real world and its objects into a manageable 2D frame, they have to take the real world objects – perhaps reduced in size – and arrange them in an effective and interesting way. This can be a lot harder than at first appears.

Design factors

For your first exercise in 3D, therefore, you need to decide how you are going to continue to add to your visual resource, while effectively storing it and accessing it as necessary. How you will catalogue what you have?

One of the key problems in 3D exercises and projects is that of **scale**. Scale is more significant in handling 3D work than in handling 2D because solid objects are more intrusive. A drawing or painting is limited by the size of wall you are working on – it may be big, but it's only in the one plane.

Where do you sleep now?

Another problem is cost. Depending on the materials used, costs for 3D works can be very high. Architects, artists and designers get round this by making models or **maquettes** of their proposals, which accompany their drawings. The models help others to understand the sometimes complex **spatial** concepts under consideration.

Much of your 2D work can be stored in folders, envelopes or portfolios, in drawers or plan chests or simply under the bed. But what about 3D work? Yet you do need to handle and work with different materials if you are to understand their properties and their potential.

A compromise is therefore needed. When you do 3D work you will be able to keep the 2D materials: the rough ideas sheets and the working drawings. But you may not have space to keep your finished 3D work. You must therefore *record* it – the process, and the outcomes.

So draw it or photograph it. Concentrate on establishing a record of its main qualities. The record can be enhanced by your use of light or tone: think back to your portrait exercise. This is where a Polaroid camera can be very useful – it provides a quick reference. If the essential characteristics of your work don't come through, reposition the work and alter the lighting until you get the effect you want.

Refining the brief

It is important that you collect objects, as well as images, to provide inspiration. You also need materials for reference, and you need materials from which to make things.

Good organisation is essential, and it's likely that you will need to review your collection ruthlessly from time to time. For the review you will need a bin bag!

It may be better to specialise in some areas rather than to try to cover a great range of materials or objects, but don't throw things away without thinking carefully first.

List the sort of things you think will be essential. Are they natural, organic or synthetic? Will you be content with pebbles, shells and feathers, or do you want things which have been used, deformed, worn or decayed? Will you put together things of one colour? Will you separate the natural from the fabricated? How will you store the fragile or degradable items?

Write about your ideas. As always, explore the ways of doing things that are personal to you. It may not be easy to communicate what you think in writing alone, so use sketches and samples too.

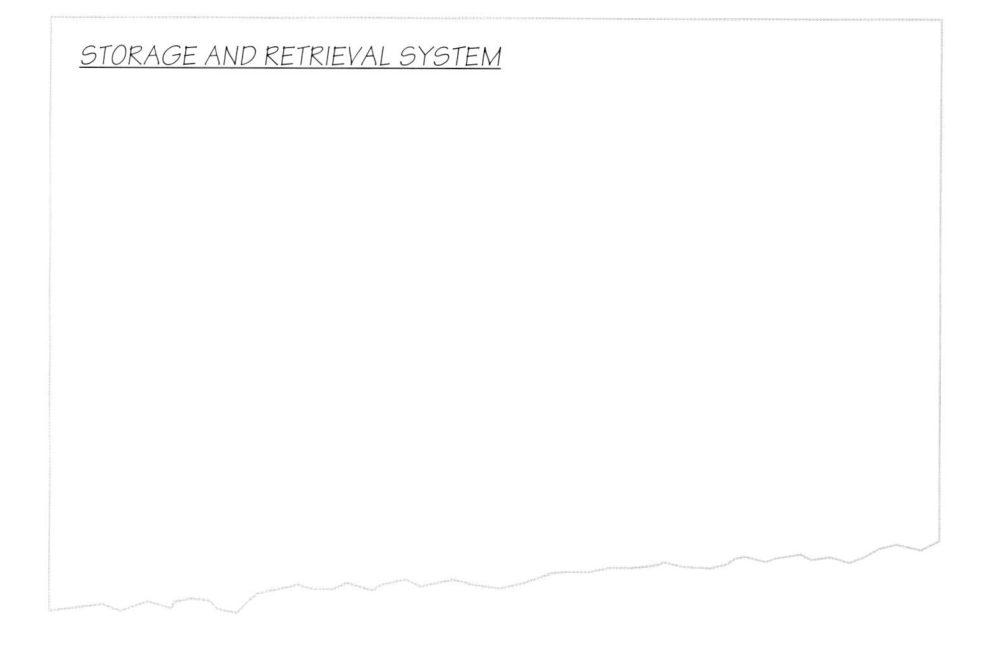

STORAGE AND RETRIEVAL SYSTEM

Be inventive and imaginative with your storage ideas. What can you use that is cheap and safe and that can be recycled? Your local supermarket is a source of free boxes; you can easily adapt empty coffee jars or plastic containers.

Look around in your work space, your bedroom or your shed. Is there empty space that you could **utilise**? Many people have **mobiles** hanging from the ceiling: other things can be hung up too – models, materials and light sculpture.

You will certainly need interpersonal skills if you are to convince members of your family that you need part of the garage! You will need to remind yourself (and them) that what is inspirational material to you might appear to them to be junk.

Designing

You are being creative as well as inventive. To complete the storage and retrieval system you will need to use making and fixing skills as well as key skills. Remember how you should tackle a brief.

Storage and retrieval system: brief

First of all, clarify the brief and carry out research. Are you clear about what you need? Write down facts and your requirements in your own way. What are the main constraints? Write them down. Do any necessary research. Note any new requirements that become apparent.

Ideas

How can you best solve the storage problems? And what about the retrieval one? Do your own thinking, and ask other people for *their* ideas. Write down possible answers; make any plans or sketches.

If you have your own computer, that might help with cataloguing and retrieval. If you don't, choose another type of inventory or indexing system, such as a card index system or photographs with notes on the back.

Don't regard these tasks as a diversion: they are an essential part of the design process, helping you to organise and plan effectively.

Classification

Classifying everything in your 3D resource is a big job – even bigger if you add in your 2D collection! But don't let that put you off.

Decide how many levels of classification you need – a general category such as 'old metal junk' or detailed sub-categories right down to each tiny sub-group of junk? General terms, such as 'Flotsam and jetsam', or descriptions for each part of your collection, such as 'Shell types', 'Rope', 'Plastics', 'Driftwood' and so on?

Making the storage and retrieval system

Having done the research and developed the design, put your ideas into practice!

Evaluation

Having made your storage and retrieval system and perhaps used it for a while, analyse its effectiveness. Write down what would improve it. If money were no object, how would you adapt it?

Self-assessment review

Fill in a self-assessment form for your personal log book. Don't be too hard on yourself – you aren't a museum or a library, after all: if the system works for you then you have satisfied the requirements of the brief.

5.2 Basic 3D visual studies

Do the following simple exercises in your sketchbook, on your layout pad or on a sheet of cartridge paper (minimum size A4) before transferring them to the spaces provided in this book. Concentrate on the form or solidity of the objects. Use a drawing medium of your own choice, but bear in mind that you will need to do a lot of shading – don't choose too fine a point. Felt tips, charcoal or broad soft pencil would be easiest.

Drawing

In the space provided, draw the following forms.

FORM

cube sphere pyramid

Add shading to emphasise the *form*.

Remember to imagine a simple light source outside your picture: keep it in the same place for all three forms. Work out in each case where the deepest shadow would be. For the purpose of this part of the exercise, however, do not put in the cast shadows.

light source

shadow

cast shadow

cone

Working with 3D projects

Make one or two rough attempts in your sketchbook before drawing in this book. Try to work freehand at this stage. Once you feel comfortable with your drawing, move on to the next exercise.

Composition

In your mind, arrange your three objects in different ways. Then make some rough sketches which change the scale, the proportions and the spatial relationships (their position relative to each other).

Choose two to draw up in the space provided. The two examples you choose should try to evoke different moods or feelings through the composition.

COMPOSITIONS

Put in writing what you think they communicate to you, or what you hope they would communicate to someone else looking at them. Use the sort of language that describes emotions and feelings. Are they calm, overpowering, surreal? Is the scale awesome? Do you feel bigger or smaller than the things that you have drawn?

Have you achieved an effective representation of the solidarity and scale of the cube, the sphere and the pyramid? Which did you do best? On your self-assessment sheet, write down your answers and give reasons if you can.

Through your study of other artists' drawings, you should be now be able to differentiate between the many types of drawing and to talk about the drawing of artists: **fine art drawing**. 'Fine art' doesn't mean 'really excellent art' (although it often is): it means different from other types of drawing. It is different in that it expresses something unique: the artist's vision. It therefore communicates in a way that a plan or sketch doesn't. Fine art is more than just objective drawing; it has more to do with drawing the essential quality of things. Each drawing is **imbued** with a special quality, which affects the feelings of the observer beyond the mere looking and seeing. Fine art can *move* the viewer emotionally, as can music or literature.

Techniques in making

There are five performance criteria for Unit 2 of the Intermediate GNVQ: the first of these concerns **making techniques**. What does the term cover?

Below is a list with three making techniques – can you enlarge on it? Remember to associate words with one another. (A few examples are given: you will think of more.)

MAKING TECHNIQUES

CUTTING   Suited to the work you are doing – scissors for paper and fabric, files and hacksaws for metal, saws and chisels for wood, knives for modelling, shaping and carving soft materials.

FORMING   Plastics, clay and dough.

JOINING   Fixing and fastening for all materials.

Think of the sorts of activities that use these techniques. Add to the list as you come across new examples.

3D study: techniques in manufacture

1 hour

Find an empty cereal or juice pack or carton. Carefully take it apart, analysing what techniques were used to make it. (Use your list as a memory jogger.)

3D study: stages in manufacture

3 hours

Study a chair or sofa for a while. Then make a series of four or five drawings in comic strip style to show how it has come from basic materials to the finished job. (Again, refer to your list of making techniques.)

Basic 3D visual studies

STAGES IN MANUFACTURE

3D study: construction

Choose a kitchen appliance and make a cut-away drawing to show its construction. As far as you can, name the materials and techniques used by the designer and manufacturer. (This is intended as a short exercise of about one hour at maximum, so choose a simple item like a kettle rather than something complex like a fan-assisted oven!)

CONSTRUCTION

Wherever you are, think about these making techniques. Sitting on the bus, for instance, you will be able to touch different materials and recognise different techniques all about you. Stitching, riveting, bolting and sealing allow us to utilise many varied materials with their individual qualities of softness or hardness, opacity or transparency, and so on. How have making techniques ensured safety, comfort and convenience? Keep your notebook with you, and record what you see.

5.3 Exemplar 3D projects

Project: junk sculpture

Read through the brief and analyse it. Do you clearly understand its aims? When you do, and your ideas begin to flow, start to collect your materials, and begin to make roughs. This is a big project, which will take at least 36 hours of your time.

Junk City: brief

Design a landscape set for a television advertisement launching a new 'Space Age' drink aimed at 9–14-year-olds. The landscape should include figures or machines, also designed and made by you.

Apply your normal working approach to the brief, and try to cover the following aspects.

Materials

Junk, plus fixing and fastening materials. Card, plastic, sand and other suitable landscape components.

Techniques

Include an element of market research – devise a questionnaire which will enable you to target your project successfully at the correct section of the market: young people of 9–14.

Ideas

Seek inspiration from your visual resource. Make notes and collect visual material, referring to contemporary and historical advertising. Look at 'Space Age' ideas in films, science fiction magazines and so on. Research contemporary robots and robotic machines.

Development

Make rough drawings and imaginative layouts. Collect and experiment with suitable materials for the construction of figures and machines. (These could include electrical components, old radio parts, wires, wood, plastics and other 'junk'.)

Consider making techniques, including cutting, forming, and joining with glue guns and soldering irons if these are available.

Take initial drawings and research work through to detailed working drawings for figures, machines and landscape. Use suitable media.

Then move on to construction of the finished 3D models.

Art direction

You now need to photograph your work for your presentation.

Set up your landscape, and position your models in it. Then photograph your set. (Bear in mind that the advertisement will need text and titles.) Take the photographs in such a way that they include the background, which should enhance the models. The photographs should suggest both realistic and imaginative scenes – the stuff of fantasy.

When your photographs have been processed, choose the best one and enlarge it on a colour photocopier to A4 size (laser print).

Decide on a name for your 'Space Age' drink. Superimpose it over your print.

Then file the finished design into your portfolio. Store your 3D props too, if you intend to keep them.

Self-assessment review

Fill in your self-assessment form and add it to your log book. Remember to think carefully about the key activities you have covered, especially in terms of application of number and communication skills.

Finally, look at the work produced by two youngsters from the target age group. The designers were 13-year-olds with no special tools or advantages; the robots were made in a bedroom on a bedside table. How do you think they did? Evaluate their attempts on the next page. (They later made the metre-high robot shown on page 57.)

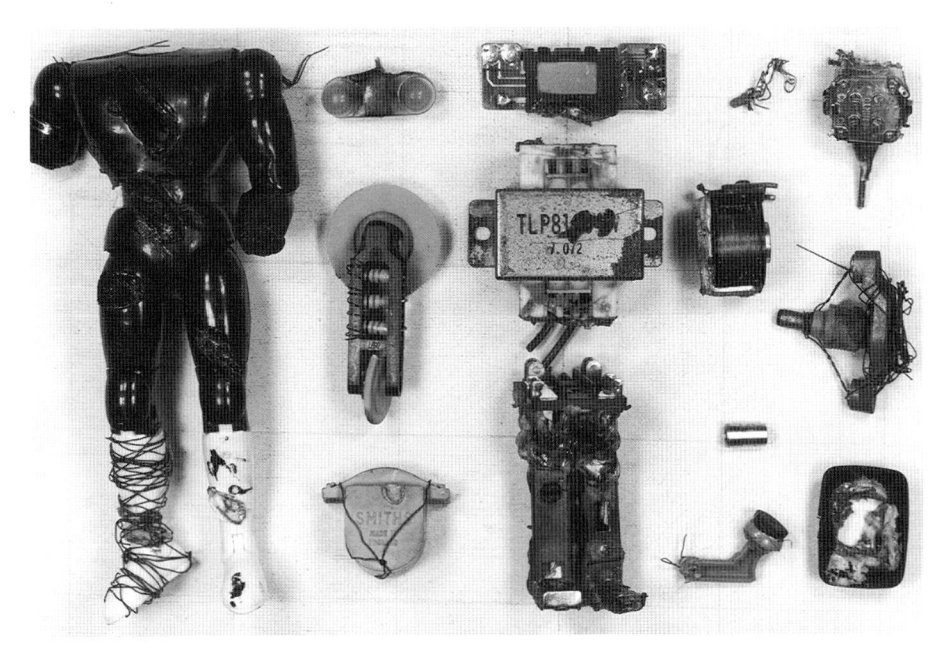

Exemplar 3D projects

EVALUATION

Outcome

This project will cover the following units, elements and performance criteria.

- Unit 1: element 1.1 (performance criteria 1–6);
  element 1.2 (performance criteria 1–5).
- Unit 2: element 2.1 (performance criteria 1–6);
  element 2.2 (performance criteria 1–5).
- Unit 3: element 3.1 (performance criteria 1–4).
- Unit 4: element 4.1 (performance criteria 1–5);
  element 4.2 (performance criteria 1–5);
  element 4.3 (performance criteria 1–6);
  element 4.4 (performance criteria 1–6).

Project: Russian Futurism

'New Russia 2000': brief

Design and make a maquette for a telecommunications tower to be used at 'New Russia 2000', an international event in Moscow. The tower will be a main feature of the exposition. It will be a real, working tower and will continue to be used after the exposition has finished.

Materials

Card, balsa, wood, glue, wire, plastic, and foil.

Ideas

You must thoroughly research imagery associated with Russian Futurism and the City of Moscow. You will also need to familiarise yourself with existing telecommunications architecture and towers, such as the Skylon and the London British Telecom tower. You may find local telecommunications towers on high ground near where you live or work.

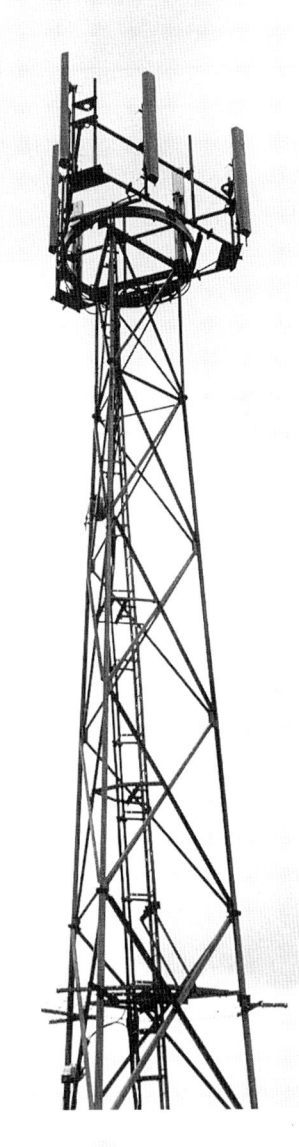

Development

Begin your work with research and drawing, using notebooks, sketchbooks and A2 paper. Finished work should also include photographs, photocopies or sketches of actual architecture, and examples of the Futurist movement – these will show the range of research undertaken, as well as the results of your design work.

Outcome

This project will cover the following units, elements and performance criteria:

- Unit 1: element 1.1 (performance criteria 1–6);
  element 1.2 (performance criteria 1–5).
- Unit 2: element 2.1 (performance criteria 1–6);
  element 2.2 (performance criteria 1–5).
- Unit 3: element 3.1 (performance criteria 1–4).
- Unit 4: element 4.1 (performance criteria 1–5);
  element 4.2 (performance criteria 1–5);
  element 4.3 (performance criteria 1–6);
  element 4.4 (performance criteria 1–3, 5, 6).

Evidence required

- Action plan.
- Research, including written notes.
- Developmental ideas, showing the use of media and techniques.
- Finished designs.
- The finished 3D maquette.

5.4 Glossary

fine art drawing The work of an artist (as distinct from a sketch or a technical drawing).

imbued Invested, soaked, saturated.

making techniques How materials are altered by a process in order to achieve a particular outcome. Techniques include carving, casting, soldering and sewing.

maquettes Preliminary models or sketches.

mobile A hanging decoration which moves.

objets trouvés French for 'found objects'; usually pebbles, driftwood, feathers and the like.

plane A flat surface (in any direction).

scale The overall size and the relative dimensions.

spatial Relating to space.

utilise Make use of.

6 Case study: a college-based project

The project discussed in this chapter was carried out at a large school of art, design and textiles, by students studying for Intermediate GNVQ. Although their course is similar to this workbook in its content and aims, such students do have some advantages over individuals studying alone. One principle advantage is the opportunity for group discussions and **critiques**; another, of course, is the resources available within a large specialist college.

Despite these differences, however, you will readily identify with the processes used and follow the students' thinking as they work towards their individual outcomes and assessments.

6.1 Packaging

This project set out to link directly the application of art in design, and to make students more aware of the infinite source material available around them.

The project ran concurrently with a series of lectures which stressed the importance of mixing theory with practice, of attaining a visual awareness

Word translation

alongside knowledge of art and design, and of gaining experience of historical contexts so as to enrich one's resource and creative response to design problems.

At this particular college, the department has a strong cultural mix, so it was decided that in addition to the design process described an 'East–West' culture workshop would be established. This incorporated an exploration of *word translation* for its meaning, its shape and its sound, **calligraphic** style, colour and application.

The Packaging Project

The students were asked to design items of packaging – bags, boxes or other containers to be used by retail outlets. The containers were to be well constructed, to use letterforms in an imaginative way, and to be colourful and exciting.

The project took three weeks. During this time, in addition to completing the project, students attended contextual studies, computer studies and tutorials. These sessions were integrated into the project. The tutorials allowed work done to be checked by both tutor and tutor groups.

Week 1

The work began by unscrambling the project – what was required? What was the brief?

Monday am For background and inspiration, lectures were given on contemporary packaging, the use of colour, and historical letterforms.

Monday pm Students produced three sheets of words associated with three themes: *food*, *fashion* and *cosmetics*. From this brainstorming 'key words' were identified in preparation for Week 2 of the workshops.

Tuesday am Students researched design in the 'marketplace', gaining first-hand knowledge. They collected both information and samples, from shops, stores and other retail outlets. This was an opportunity to see how packaging appears to the consumer: how effective were the designs? The students made visual notes of colour, use of symbols, signs, words, shapes, forms and materials used.

Tuesday pm The students discussed their findings and organised them into the three areas: *food*, *fashion* and *cosmetics*.

Tutors then led a discussion on packages as 'objects of quality', showing examples of good design application both in 2D and in 3D.

Wednesday Tutorials offered a chance to discuss the project so far and check that it was progressing satisfactorily.

Thursday Students constructed a 'dummy pack' for three different designs using **nets**, diagrams to show how packages are cut, creased and fitted together. They considered the **mechanics** involved in converting a 2D flat pack into a 3D package, and the package's suitability for carrying effective imagery.

Friday The students now used all of this first week's research and findings to produce three postcard-sized mood-boards to distinguish the kinds of images, colours, shapes and so on that they were looking for. They used these key words:

- *Food:* fresh, bright, clean.
- *Fashion:* style, mood, atmosphere.
- *Cosmetics:* elegance, taste, adornment.

Week 2

The second week was an intensive 'workshop' experience. The emphasis in workshop activities is on learning new skills, techniques and crafts, while engaging in experimentation, exploration and creativity. Many skills were utilised and developed in the following activities:

- printmaking and stencilling;
- collage;
- calligraphy;
- frottage;
- computer graphics.

The source images for these workshops were specific words and letterforms taken from the earlier brainstorming exercises.

Workshop products helped to form a source idea from which students were able to develop further their finished designs.

Week 3

As the students approached the **realisation** of their designs, they identified a clear principle: *one theme, one package*.

They now used a selection of images to produce rough design sheets. Visual analysis of the workshop results had made them aware of 'fitness for purpose'. All elements were now brought together in forming the final designs.

Each word chosen — such as *tasty* for food — was now explored, a visual image being drawn to show its application to the 3D package.

These rough visuals, or thumbnails, would lead to the larger-scale, finished visuals, and would finally be developed as a 3D 'mock-up' presentation.

The following approach was used:

Points to follow
1 Establish a 'dummy pack' to test and confirm the shape of the pack.
2 How does the graphic image fit the shape? Pay attention to scale, position, and the dynamics of the design.
3 Choose the colour, the texture, the kind of paper, board, lamination, etc.

3D visual
1 View the package in many positions.
2 Apply the design in the flat (2D).
3 Make up the flat design into the final package (3D).

Evaluation On A4, give a short description of any modifications and improvements that could be made. Consider the following criteria:

1 Planning.
2 Information seeking and information handling.
3 Evaluation.
4 Quality of outcomes.

6.2 Glossary

calligraphy The art of beautiful lettering.

critique A critical analysis, usually made by more than one person, of alternative creative solutions.

mechanics How things work: the routine technical aspects of things.

net A diagram that shows how to cut and assemble a package.

realisation A clear understanding converted into actuality.

7 Options and extras

The material in this chapter will assist you in developing your own optional units. The chapter includes a range of additional sample projects, with subject matter broad enough to cover the optional units you may choose to design and carry out yourself.

The projects all contain elements of the mandatory units too. By now you will appreciate that all art, design and craft activity interrelates; where you find cross-references between units, draw attention to these in your self-assessment notes. This will help you evaluate your progress.

These activities ask more of you than much of the earlier work: although there are some similarities in the projects the level of skill required is higher and the outcomes are more demanding. In addition, you will by now be more self-critical.

7.1 Making the most of your progress

Use this chapter to extend your specialist knowledge, polish up your skills and refine your key skills. You will be introduced to extra projects and you are encouraged to devise further projects of your own.

When you have finished the work in this chapter, your practical activities for now are complete. Of course, as art, craft and design activities always benefit from development and practice you can *never* sit back and say that you are on top of it all! Do continue to explore your own work and that of others. Seek out harder design problems to solve, and practise your drawing, painting and craft skills.

The final chapter will help you to make the most of your work and yourself in order to progress. Whichever career direction you take, it is vital that you develop a substantial body of work.

7.2 Project intentions

The projects in the next section relate to the requirements of Unit 1, '2D visual language', and Unit 2, '3D visual language', together with some of the optional units. They also include essential elements of the mandatory Unit 4, 'Applying the creative process'.

As should be clear by now, the secret of success in art, design and craft project work is a good brief. Often, though, a client will ask the designer to do something that is unclear to both parties. This must be sorted out at the beginning of the discussion. If you are not sure, ask questions. (This is part of Element 4.1, 'Clarify brief'.) You must be clear before you can tackle the problem.

Seemingly simple problems may be critical, so never be afraid of asking what may seem to be too basic a question. There is no magic process which transmits the client's needs into your brain. Communication is a two-way process; time taken in ensuring that you understand the client's needs is time well spent.

Once you do understand what is required, write it down. You can then start your research in earnest. Use your favourite approach, such as 'unscrambling', 'word association' or 'brainstorming', or look through your personal visual resource for information and inspiration. As ideas occur to you, remember to get them down in note form.

As you move forward into producing your solution, try to keep a visual and written record of your progress. Remember to cost your activities: if you have to buy materials or services, keep the receipts. Test out your ideas among your friends or colleagues. Try to analyse their comments and let these inform your self-criticism.

When you have carried out the practical parts of your work, bearing in mind health and safety issues, decide how best to present the work. Again, you may want to go back to your personal resource, or you may have a terrific original idea. Or, of course, you might feel that the work speaks for itself, and settle for a crisp, clean presentation. Don't be afraid to seek the opinions of others, but be prepared finally to stand by your own judgement – it's *your* project.

Finally, evaluate your work using your self-assessment form. Record your progress and the outcome with suitable images – especially if the work cannot itself go into your portfolio.

The projects that follow should be seen as exemplars: you are not just free but *encouraged* to develop others, to be imaginative and inventive. Don't be too ambitious, however, in scale or scope: it is better to have some complete well-executed simple projects than a number of complex half-finished grand ideas.

7.3 **The projects**

Painting

This project aims to encourage your research activities and to develop your painting skills.

You will need:

- cartridge paper (A3), loose or in a sketchpad;
- paint – gouache or acrylic;
- brushes, a rag, water, a **palette** or a plate;
- a drawing board;
- **gummed strip**, a sponge or cloth, scissors.

Preparation

The day before you need it, stretch an A3 sheet of cartridge paper onto your drawing board.

1. Cut lengths of gummed strip, a little longer than the edges of your paper: two for the sides, and two for the top and bottom edges.
2. Lay the paper on the (clean) board.
3. Gently wipe a wet sponge or cloth across the surface. Mop up any excess water.
4. Turn over the paper and repeat.

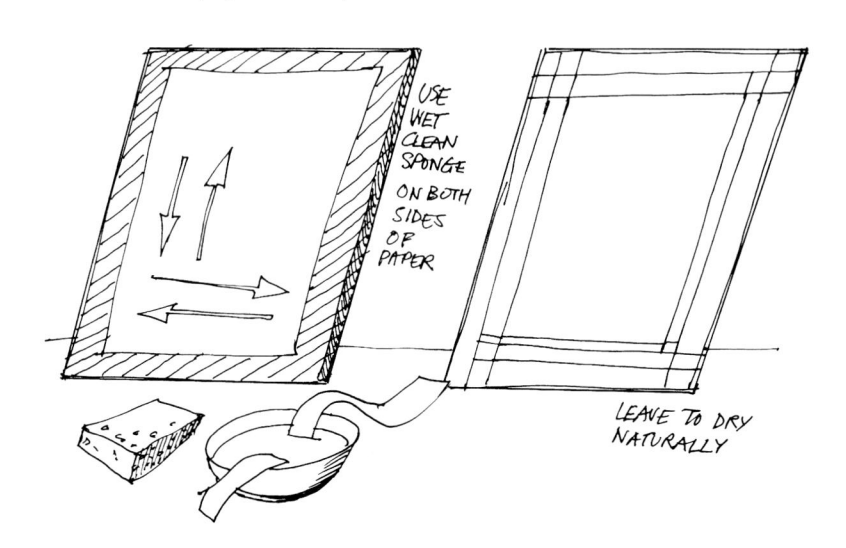

Options and extras

5. Lay the paper centrally in the board. Again, mop up.
6. Wet the gummed strip, one piece at a time. Overlapping the paper edge by about 2 cm, stick the strip to the board. Continue for the other edges.
7. Mop up any surface water.
8. Put the board and the paper to dry naturally. Note: never dry stretched paper by direct heat – this would cause the paper to distort.

Stretching paper prevents it from cockling when you work on it with water-based materials. It should be done in advance so there is time for it to dry properly.

Requirement

You are to paint two small pictures in the styles of two different artists.

1. Draw two 12 cm squares on your sheet, allowing borders on all sides.
2. Think back to your 'getting started' line drawings. Now set up a similar, simple image. This could be a view from your window or a still life set up on your table.
3. Choosing only the key shapes and lines, draw a basic composition in each of the squares.

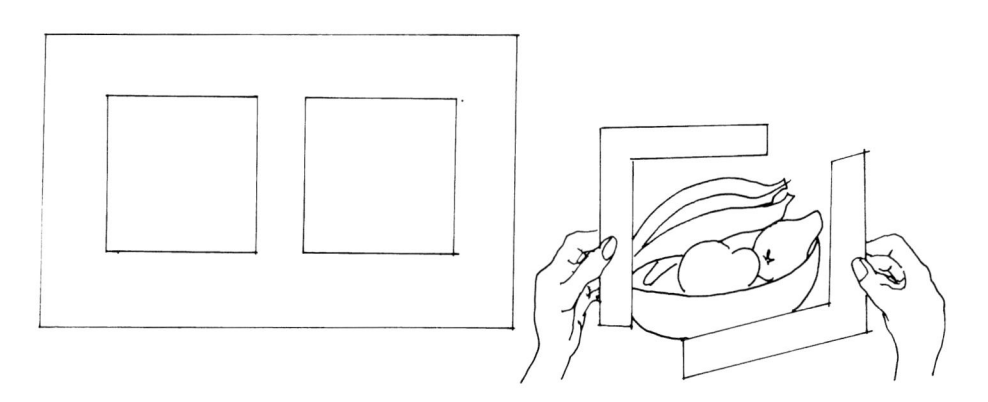

4. Using gouache or acrylic paints, paint one picture in the style of an artist of one of the following movements:
   - Impressionist;
   - Cubist;
   - Surrealist;
   - Expressionist;
   - Fauvist.
5. When you have finished, paint the other picture, choosing another artist with a different style.

Research

Look at examples of the work of painters in these movements. Compare the work of artists within each movement, making notes of your findings. Who do you like best, and why? Why do you prefer one movement to another? Read about the artists and try to write down key facts about them.

Outcome

If you are successful first time in capturing the spirit of the artists and their styles, well done! If not, try again. When you do have a good result prepare the paintings for your portfolio. In doing this work you will have covered elements of units 1, 3 and 4.

The projects

Assess your work. Try to analyse what you are assessing: what do you think are the key criteria for assessment? You should be thinking of a number of points, including these:

- effective planning and preparation;
- good practical work: clean, accurate, and achieved within the time allowed;
- the range of material studied and the quality of the notes taken;
- communication (do others recognise the style and artists you chose?);
- the layout and appearance of the final product.

Grading

Pass Completion of the tasks within the time. Demonstration, through the portfolio and the notebook, of understanding the requirement, carrying out the process and achieving the expected outcome.

Merit All of the above, but with a good number of supporting notes and visual references such as postcards and photocopied samples to illustrate points in research. An attractive, well-presented outcome.

Distinction The above points, plus evidence of a high level of research achieved, independent conclusions reached, and persuasive communication both visual and written. Excellent presentation, and a high level of painting skill exhibited.

Further developments

When you have completed your self-assessment, logged it and carefully stored your work (written and practical), you may wish to carry out further painting, in your own style, of the same subject matter. Keep all notes and sketches of this extra work: you will have a chance to reflect on your learning and your skills progress in a month or two's time. Reflecting on your own achievements is a necessary and enriching activity from time to time.

Fashion

This project picks up threads from other activities and calls on all the GNVQ units. It will build upon your research and recording skills, extend your visual language, develop your skills in textiles, 2D studies and communication, and introduce you to the exciting and demanding world of fashion. It is in two parts.

Part 1

Context
Betty Jackson is one of Britain's most well-established and well-known fashion designers. She works mainly in the field of women's wear. She was made a Royal Designer for Industry in 1988. In her own words she believes 'in simple, beautiful clothes that make women feel good'.

Requirements
Design a two-page illustrated layout about Betty Jackson for a local evening paper. It should highlight the lifestyle of today's woman: you need to put her fashion message across. Headlines, punchy statements and illustrations (from magazines and your own drawings) should all combine to give a 'Betty Jackson' feeling to the double-page spread.

You will need about 250 words and four or five illustrations. The double-page spread should be in proportion to a tabloid newspaper, but a quarter-sized reduction. The finished rough may be colour laser-copied to achieve a realistic published appearance.

Part 2

Choose any designer whose work you admire and carry out research similar to that which you carried out for Part 1.

Requirements

1 Write out the key features that identify your chosen designer's work. Collect visual references and make drawings if you cannot find enough magazine examples. Develop a strong fashion statement about your designer, using quotes if you wish, and write it up in not more than 100 words.

2 Draw up a mood-board (A3) featuring your designer's visual strengths and themes.

3 Design three garments in the style of your chosen designer. Present them together as sketches on an A3 sheet, complete with colour, fabric samples, wool, buttons or other supporting items. Remember it is often the *detail* of garments that gives them their 'designer signature'.

Outcome

Assess your work and complete your notes. The quantity and depth of research that you have had to carry out will have made this a major project.

You are required as part of Intermediate GNVQ programmes to be competent in developing your own projects and briefs. This book illustrates different project layouts and different approaches to the gathering of assessment evidence, but you should be aware of essential common features of good projects. What does the brief demand? How do you plan to achieve a good outcome? How will you organise the process, record your activities and assess the results? Refer constantly to the GNVQ publication *Mandatory Units for Intermediate Art & Design*, which will help you to develop a methodical approach to planning, creating, evaluating and recording.

Poster design

All students of art, design and crafts enjoy being commissioned to do real jobs. Such work is good preparation for a future career and is the best test of professional ability. For many beginners the first commission is in the form of a poster design.

This project will work best if you have a real event to advertise. Think of groups with whom you come into contact, who might be pleased to have a design specialist at hand: local sports centres, shops, churches, charity events and car boot sales. They all need your services!

If you cannot do a real poster project, design a poster for a simulated job. Choose from the following list:

- An anti-crime poster.
- A rock or pop concert promotion.
- A sports event in your town.
- A hobby club meeting.

Guidelines for poster design

Rule 1
Posters need to convey these main items of information: Who? What? Why? Where? When? How much?

It is up to you to put these items in order of importance. It is also important that you listen carefully to your **client**. The client may wish to stress a particular aspect, such as an entrance fee or a change of date; often, though, clients just ask for a poster, as cheap as possible, and provide the details on the back of an envelope.

It is up to you to organise liaison with the client, to develop the brief, to design the poster, to oversee its production and to calculate your fee. You have to do all of this in a professional manner, and to give each job equal attention.

When you discuss your clients' needs, be prepared to advise and help them. If the poster doesn't do its job you might as well not have bothered to design it. On the other hand, if the poster is a success everyone will be happy – and you may attract further commissions!

Rule 2
Make your design simple, clear and attractive.

Rule 3
Your design must be legible.

If the client wants a hand-painted two-metre-long poster, however, you might think very carefully about whether or not you want to be involved! So . . .

Rule 4
Don't bite off more than you can chew.

Printing can be costly, and clients always seem to want everything for as little as possible. In this introductory poster project we will look at a cheap but effective approach: the photocopied A4 sheet in black and white, with a little added **spot colour**. This is suitable for 100 posters or fewer.

Requirement

Produce a poster suitable for photocopying, with one area of spot colour.

First design the poster, including all of the information. Then decide which bit you wish to be eye-catching and plan a simple use of colour. Make sure that a broad felt-tip pen, used by an amateur, is sufficient to add this eye-catching detail.

If unskilled people are to add the spot colour, it must be *easy* and *quick* to do. Think of a child's colouring book: provide enclosed spaces, whether for lettering or an image, for them to fill in. Do a sample one yourself for each colourer.

Further development

We are surrounded by advertising and publicity material. Collect your favourite slogans and images, and write up why you like them. Put them with your visual resource.

Develop some more graphic design projects. Write out the briefs, do the work, and record and assess your endeavours.

Interior design

The study of interior design is demanding and rewarding. It involves work with teams of people: artists, developers, architects, craftspeople and clients. Building inspectors, surveyors and engineers will also contribute, advising you of relevant regulations – as well as structural safety features such as fire escapes and adequate roof supports, there will be factors affecting interior design, such as whether materials are flammable. Legal and insurance issues affect design, as well as artistic and creative ones.

For this project you will need to collect samples from soft furnishing and decorator's shops. Although this project is less demanding than a whole building, you may be lucky and get to carry out your scheme for real.

Requirements

1. Choose a room that you know well. Draw it up, from measurements, in plan form. Show the floor plan and a general **perspective** of the room from one corner. Mark on the floor plan the positions of the main items of furniture, as well as permanent fixtures. If possible take photographs too, from the same corner as your perspective view.
2. Re-design the room layout and show it redecorated. Colour co-ordinate the walls, carpets and soft furnishings. On an A3 sheet mount your 'before' and 'after' floor plans, and set out the two perspective sketches similarly.
   - Use any suitable media to colour your sketches, but include paint charts and swatches of wallpaper, and soft furnishings.
   - Cost your proposal.
   - In your notebook record the reasons for your choices.
   - If it is possible actually to put your ideas into practice, re-photograph the newly designed room. It will be interesting to compare the 'before' and 'after' shots!

Assessment

When you fill in your self-assessment form, ask yourself these questions:

- Was the floor plan accurate?
- Was the perspective sketch good, adequate or bad?
- Did you do sufficient research into style?
- Did you use an ideas development sheet?
- Was lighting a factor? Was it good or bad previously? Has the design improved it?
- Do your notes show advantages of the layout changes you have made?
- Did you increase storage or make other improvements?
- Did you try an innovative scheme, or did you merely freshen up the old one?
- Is your visual resource bigger now?
- Which journals or magazines did you study?
- How many common or communication skills did you use?
- Did you cross-check in which elements of other units you gained experience?
- Did you note these extra elements on your assessment form?
- How well does your presentation look? Does it demonstrate your talents? Would it convince anyone to employ you? If not, how could it be improved?

Cultural diversity

This project offers you the opportunity to be inventive and to draw from cultural influences other than European ones.

Context

Imagine that to mark the 'International Year of Friendship' the Arts Council of England, together with a major construction company, have decided to celebrate the many ethnic groups who together form the people of the United Kingdom. You have been chosen to design structures to occupy five important sites throughout the country.

Brief

For the project, concentrate on just *two* locations.

Make presentation visuals for two contrasting sites: one within a large city, on the banks of a river; the other in a rural situation. Each will celebrate one continent's culture. Design suitable structures and show how they will look when built.

Unusually, money is not a problem: National Lottery funding has ensured that the budget is set at several million pounds. Naturally the construction company wants to show off its capabilities: it wants you to make use of contemporary materials and construction techniques. (For example, the company will be happy to use helicopters, cranes and explosives if needed.)

Each structure should utilise 'grace, space, light and site', as the directors put it. The structure can be temporary or, like Stonehenge, built to last.

Requirements

Any media can be used for the presentation visual, including photography, collage, painting or drawing. The cultural identity of each structure should be recognisable. To quote the Minister who opened the competition, structures should 'have dignity and aim for a spiritual impact: at least an uplifting and joyous translation of its origins, at best a brilliant reminder of our mixed cultural heritage'.

There is to be an official celebration two years from now. As well as the structures which will be visited, you are also asked to design the souvenir badges and gifts, and invitations to one of the openings.

Design development. Ideas for the freebies

MUGS

Ceramic BADGES too!

TIES

Head Squares & Hankies

Little notebooks

The projects 87

Notes, images and ideas sheets will be required, as well as your presentation visuals and the 'freebies' you have designed for the opening ceremonies.

Outcome

In your self-assessment give yourself a good grade if you manage to achieve a successful outcome. This is a difficult project and the assessment criteria will have to take account of:

- innovative thinking;
- aesthetic qualities;
- cultural identity achieved;
- great artistic vision – these structures, after all, are to mark the best in cultural representation of the major groups of the world's peoples and to point to a different future: to hope, to a change for the better, to a new design for all of us!

Surface pattern

Requirements

Design a series of wallpapers, with co-ordinating borders, for use in kitchens.

Techniques to be employed: research, drawing, lino printing, **resist processes**.

Process

Research
Before beginning this project do some research to familiarise yourself with wallpaper and border designs, both contemporary and historical. Make use of shops, catalogues, magazines, television, library, slides, and so on.

Development

1. Set up a still-life arrangement, using tomatoes, apples, oranges, spring onions, celery, watercress. Cut one of the fruits in half.
2. Use pastel and soft pencil crayon on an A2 white or coloured ground. Draw a frame to your work: a freehand rectangle, about 2 cm in from the outer edge of the sheet.
3. Using your chosen media, complete a drawing which fills the framed area. Plan your drawing carefully, using a neutral colour, to ensure that the proportions and positions of the objects are correct. Decide the overall composition and lightly mark it in before beginning any detailed drawing.
4. When your drawing is complete, move on to design development. From your drawing, extract and simplify important elements so as to create suitable patterns. Use layout paper: this will enable you to redraw quickly as you try out ideas. (A light box, a window pane, a Grant projector or a Copy-scanner could also be helpful, if available.)
5. Draw out each design idea at least twice. Try out colour combinations and variations.
6. When you feel happy that you have a suitable design idea, cut a lino block for it. Use this for experimental work. Try out ideas both for the wallpaper and the border.
7. This project is intended to be experimental: try to come up with several ideas. The brief asks for kitchen wallpaper and a border design, but you may

find that some of your designs could be applied to packaging, cooking implements, teatowels and the like. Push your ideas as far as you can.

Outcome

This brief will cover the following units, elements and performance criteria:

- Unit 1: element 1.1 (performance criteria 1–6);
  element 1.2 (performance criteria 1–5).
- Unit 3: element 3.1 (performance criteria 1–4).
- Unit 4: element 4.1 (performance criteria 1–5);
  element 4.2 (performance criteria 1–5);
  element 4.3 (performance criteria 1–6);
  element 4.4 (performance criteria 1–6).

Jewellery

This is a design and research project which includes a case study of a contemporary designer's professional practice.

Requirements

Design and make a collection of fun jewellery under the title 'South Sea Island'. Use **Fimo**, a pliable substance in a wide range of colours which can be baked to a hard finish.

The project is divided into two sections.

Part 1

Gather information about a freelance jewellery designer of your choice. As far as possible, include details of the types of work, the kinds of clients, and aspects of the business – running costs, premises, production, selling, legal requirements, financial requirements and so on.

Present your findings neatly in a special file. Include illustrations, photographs, written notes and information from relevant agencies.

Part 2

Alongside your research into the business of being a professional designer, gather information for your own design project, 'South Sea Island'. This could include photographs, photocopies, drawings, colour studies and a mood-board.

Working from the information you have gathered, design and make your own range of jewellery. Your finished work should include research sheets, design development work, finished design sheets, and jewellery.

Outcome

The project will cover the following units, elements and performance criteria:

- Unit 1: element 1.1 (performance criteria 1–6);
  element 1.2 (performance criteria 1–5).
- Unit 2: element 2.1 (performance criteria 1–6);
  element 2.2 (performance criteria 1, 2, 4, 5).
- Unit 3: element 3.1 (performance criteria 1–4);
  element 3.2 (performance criteria 1–5).
- Unit 4: element 4.1 (performance criteria 1–5);

The projects

element 4.2 (performance criteria 1–5);
element 4.3 (performance criteria 1–6);
element 4.4 (performance criteria 1–3, 5, 6).

7.4 Glossary

client Someone who uses someone else's services.

Fimo A pliable substance sold commercially for modelling. It is often used in jewellery.

gummed strip Paper strip, gummed on one side with water-soluble gum.

palette A portable smooth surface on which colours can be mixed. (A plate is adequate.)

perspective The art of drawing so as to suggest a sense of depth and distance.

resist processes Processes that involve applying colour to paper or fabric after first applying a substance (such as wax) which will protect areas from the colour. This *resist* is later removed. Batik, etching and screen printing are all resist processes.

spot colour The use of flat colour, as distinct from full-colour or four-colour process printing.

8 Pulling it all together

How can you make the most of your potential for progression as an artist, designer or craftsperson? It may be that you intend to apply for the first time to a college, or that you are moving on within a college to Advanced GNVQ or some other further education (FE) course. You may be ready for an Art & Design Foundation Course in preparation for higher education (HE).

Whether or not you are looking towards FE or HE or wishing to seek work or further your employment, the advice and information in this chapter will be relevant. It considers work presentation, portfolio enhancement, and personal presentation (drawing on your work on common skills). To ensure that you are well prepared for interviews and that you can make a good impression, some activities will concentrate on these points.

Being realistic, it has to be recognised that although many students will become successful practitioners of art and design, not everyone has the combination of imagination, inventiveness, flair, skills and business ability to make a livelihood from what they enjoy doing. The work you have done so far will help you to decide now whether you will benefit from further study. A career in art and design is not a soft option: you will need great commitment. On the other hand, if you are successful in what you do the rewards can be high.

8.1 Researching your intended career path

Do you have a clear ambition? If so, you should now concentrate on achieving your goal. Will you look for work? Or do you intend to study further? Whichever route you choose, seek advice in order to make the most of your next step.

If you are broadly interested in an art, design and craft career but have not yet decided on a particular job, it would be wise to remain on a diagnostic type of course, such as Advanced GNVQ.

Before going to your local careers officer or to the nearest further education college for advice, prepare yourself. Write down your career ambition. Write out your intentions for improving your chances. Then list your strengths and weaknesses (as on page 92). This preparation will help you to become clearer and will also assist the people trying to advise you.

CAREER AMBITION

I want to be a graphic designer working in a small company.

STRENGTHS	WEAKNESSES
Good drawing	I don't know how companies use their designers or how
I mix well with people	they take on junior staff
I like designing Fanzines	I don't know much about printing or computer
Passed my driving test	typesetting

Pulling it all together

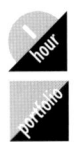

When you go for advice, take your portfolio and this written evidence with you. If you then decide to apply for a job or for a specific educational programme, write a letter of application and send it off together with your **curriculum vitae** (**CV**) to the company or college of your choice.

8.2 Your CV and letters of application

Curriculum vitae

Whenever you need to let someone else know of your experience and ability, you will need a CV. This is a personal history listing details such as your date of birth and your address, together with facts about your experience.

Fill in the following CV now, and add to it over time as you gain qualifications and experience.

	CURRICULUM VITAE
Give your full name	NAME DATE OF BIRTH ADDRESS
Married or single; mention any dependants	STATUS
Include the STD code, and fax number or e-mail address if you have these	TELEPHONE NUMBER
Names and addresses of schools or colleges (with dates)	EDUCATION
List any qualifications (with dates), such as Foundation GNVQ, NVQ, GCE or GCSE	QUALIFICATIONS
Can you use a computer? Do you have one? Do you have word-processing or desk-top publishing skills?	IT SKILLS
Record work placements and any holiday or part-time jobs. Any craftwork or design work commissioned? Do you have a current driving licence?	WORK EXPERIENCE
Include sport and other leisure activities, and interests such as reading, music, films and television	INTERESTS/HOBBIES

Letters of application

Whether you are applying for a job or for a place in a college, you need to communicate certain key messages to the reader.

At all times you need to present yourself in the best possible way: the reader of your letter needs to be interested enough to pay attention to what you are saying. To command and keep the reader's attention you need to be positive, concise, neat and accurate.

To ensure that the employer or admissions tutor wants to meet you, you also need to engage the reader's interest in you as an individual. Your CV must contain the necessary information, and your letter must draw attention to relevant details so that you will be seen as an applicant with appropriate experience. Try to convey not just your experience but your *enthusiasm*. It will also help if you can show that you are aware of any special features of the business or special strengths of the course.

Try to keep your letter to one side of A4 only. Lay it out in a conventional way, showing your address (including the postcode), your telephone or fax number if possible, the date, and any heading or reference used by the company or college. If you are writing to a named person, address this person by name and sign 'Yours sincerely'. If you are writing to 'Sir or Madam', as with an unknown post-holder (such as a personnel officer or a course tutor), sign 'Yours faithfully'.

If you are writing to a college or a company on your own initiative, rather than in response to an advertisement, it is a good idea to include a stamped, addressed envelope. This shows your professionalism and you are more likely to get a reply.

IT tip

Unless the person or organisation to whom you are writing has specifically asked for a handwritten letter, it is best to word-process your communication. Most personal computers offer standard layouts (templates): if yours doesn't, it's a good idea to develop your own. If you do not have your own PC you can often get access to one through a local library or job centre.

Store your letter and CV on disk so that you can easily amend and reprint them as necessary.

8.3 Presentation – your work and yourself

Throughout this book you have been concentrating on good practice. Each of your practical exercises and projects has been prepared in a clear and professional manner. If you are invited for an interview, select from your work, review its condition, and remedy any poor presentation.

Try to make this selection of work when you are not under pressure. You will need time to think about the appropriateness of your portfolio contents and to clean up or re-mount work that is showing its age with tatty corners or creasing. Window mount your best work, as shown opposite.

Your decisions on the content of your portfolio will be informed by your research into the interviewing organisation. Include at least some work that shows clearly how you would benefit from getting the job or the college place. But remember that ideas development work is also interesting to interviewers, so include some evidence of this. Show your working process: brief, ideas, roughs and finished work.

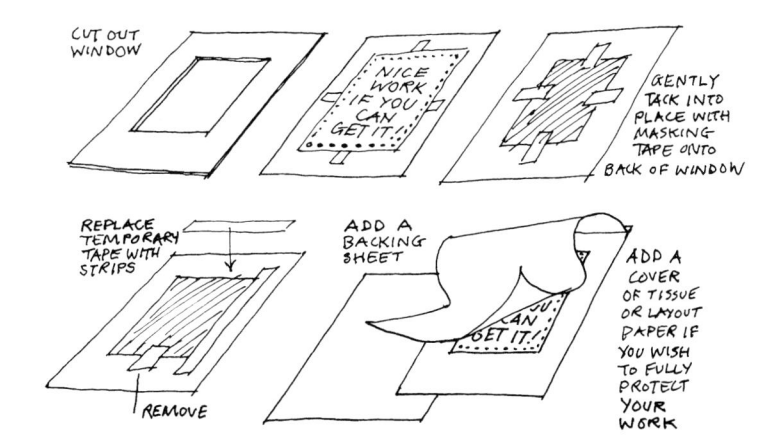

Don't swamp your interviewer with work, however: select good-quality examples and concentrate on putting in work about which you feel confident. At the interview you will need to talk about your examples, and this will be an opportunity for you to expand on your abilities. If you are at all doubtful about whether to include particular pieces of work, leave them out.

Label your portfolio pages, and individual items, clearly. Present your work **chronologically** and adopt a simple classification such as '2D', '3D', 'live projects', and so on.

Take along those records which are most appropriate, but always include a *recent* sketchbook, photographs of work that is too large to carry, and your personal log book.

You should feel comfortable with your portfolio. It will help if you rehearse what you want to say about your work. Choose someone with whom you feel reasonably at ease and ask her or him to **role-play** an interviewer while you talk through your work. Practise using this talking time to introduce information about yourself as well as about your work.

Time your efforts. Try for five to ten minutes at the outside: in a real situation questions will be asked which will quickly fill the allocated time.

If your role-playing interviewer has done a good job, ask for further help later. Get feedback now and try to rehearse until any shortcomings identified have been sorted out.

8.4 Interview techniques

Whether you are interviewed along with other candidates or in a one-to-one situation, there is one key point to get across: that *you* are the best person they could have! If you are methodical about your presentation and answer the main points of the questions asked of you, you are halfway there. For the other half, you need to demonstrate good interpersonal skills and to appeal to the interviewers as the sort of person that they feel would benefit their organisation as well as benefiting from it – would you be a talented employee, or a talented student?

As well as your skills and experience, you will be assessed on your manner and appearance. Try to wear clothes which fit with the impression you are trying to

STRENGTHS AND WEAKNESSES

create. List the strengths or **attributes** you think you have. Then put down your weaker characteristics (such as, 'I sometimes get tongue-tied').

Did you list your interpersonal skills too? If you missed any, go back to your list and amend it.

Show the completed list to some of the people you know and ask for their comments. You need to have a good idea of your personal abilities as they appear to others, not just to yourself. Try to be honest – if the truth hurts a little, be encouraged: it probably indicates that you are sensitive and responsive too!

Now review your list. What do you need to do to balance your strengths and weaknesses? Write up an action plan if you need to.

Finally, recognise that you will not automatically get the job or the place: you may have to keep trying. Maintain your enthusiasm and commitment. Each interview can be a valuable learning process, building your experience.

If you don't have a successful outcome, do write to or telephone the interviewer and ask what let you down. Was it your personal qualities? Or a lack of experience? The answers should help you prepare to be a better applicant next time. If you really want valuable feedback, never moan about the experience: be polite, courteous and appreciative. That's being professional.

8.5 Study through college

Induction

Wherever you study you are likely on arrival to receive an information pack. This should include a student's handbook – a guide to your rights and responsibilities – as well as the sort of information that will enable you to make the most of your situation. If you have not been given a copy automatically, ask about the student charter.

Tuition

You will probably have a course tutor, a general tutor and a personal tutor. However, you will not be taught much using the traditional 'chalk and talk' approach; sometimes you may even feel undertaught. In competence-based courses such as art and design, your independence is a key feature. Within UK institutions there is a student-centred ethos in these subjects. Learning by doing, 'hands-on', is coupled with theoretical studies.

The Intermediate GNVQ builds on foundations laid down in secondary school. It is diagnostic and encourages the development of study skills which will be useful throughout your life. The Advanced GNVQ builds on earlier skills and knowledge, preparing you for higher education or employment; it is broadly equivalent to A-levels, with the advantage of including more practical or process work.

Practical sessions

Art, craft and design have always encouraged student-centred learning. They are also process-based: you have an idea, you do the research, you make the outcome. Your tutors act as catalysts rather than teachers, helping you to make the most of your own ideas and pointing to historical and contemporary practitioners who may be relevant to your work.

Don't be resistant to working in a team: much professional work is done in this way. Your fellow students will be important contributors towards your education, as will you to theirs.

Theoretical sessions

The *context* of art and design is important too; communications, history and professional or commercial practice all play their part. It is essential that you develop as an all-rounder. You will need to draw on your wit, intelligence and general knowledge, as well as your creative talent. Professionalism requires the interaction of theory and practice, of skills and knowledge – and great personal enthusiasm.

Creativity

Creativity is the secret ingredient. Hard to define in itself, it gives the sparkle, the brilliance and the uniqueness that are recognisable in the best solution to a design problem. Think about a recent film or TV commercial that excited you and has stayed in your mind. What made it special for you? Was it technique, special imagery, typography, colour? When you have analysed it, is there still something beyond all the analysis? That is the creative input.

Some people have the knack of selecting things that work well together. They can mix things with confidence and produce results that to other people are clearly out of the ordinary. Whether it is a ceramicist choosing a glaze that exactly complements a particular shape, or a TV director who makes a particularly successful series of advertisements, there is this common attribute: creativity.

Nurture yours. Keep your visual diary going. Keep your eyes and ears open to the world around you; think about what you notice. Try to draw every day, and keep your ideas flowing. There is a whole world of possibility in art, design and crafts. Enjoy it.

Start right! Good luck!

8.6 Glossary

attributes Qualities ascribed to a person or thing.

chronological Arranged according to date.

curriculum vitae (CV) A brief personal history, usually showing qualifications and achievements.

role-playing Acting out a situation in order to learn from doing it.

Appendices

A.1 Equipment list

You will already have much of this equipment, all of which you will need if you go to school or college.

- Putty rubber and plastic soft rubber.
- Gouache (14 mm tubes): white, black and the three primaries, red, blue and yellow.
- Chalk pastels: black and white.
- Pencils: H, HB, 2B, 4B and 6B.
- Bottles of fixative (or ozone-friendly hairspray to use as fixative).
- Scalpel.
- Steel-edged ruler.
- Plastic ruler: 40 cm.
- A3 ideas sketchbook (spiral-bound).
- Drawing board clips (4).
- Pointed brushes: points 2 and 5, nylon or sable mixture.
- Flat brush: 6 mm.
- Decorator's brush: 24 mm.
- Masking tape: roll.
- Watercolour pencils: 1 set of Caran d'Ache or Lakeland, soft.
- Black marker pen.
- Black fibre-tip pen.
- Paint-mixing palette.
- Lino-cutting set.
- T-square.
- Set square: adjustable, 20 cm.
- Protractor.
- Pair of compasses.
- Hole punch.
- Scissors.
- A4 ring file, with A4 plain and lined paper.
- A1 folder, with transparent sleeve inserts.
- Art box. (Sectioned plastic tool boxes, available at most supermarkets or DIY shops, are as good and cheaper.)
- A2 drawing board: approx. 45 cm × 65 cm. (A sheet of lightweight board such as plywood or MDF cut to this size is a reasonable and cheaper substitute – see DIY shops.)

As you work through the book, you will be introduced to a range of other materials. You can choose to buy some of those you enjoy working with, and your future birthday and Christmas gifts could be watercolours, poster colours or other general art equipment and materials!

A.2 Useful addresses

The Arts Council of England
14 Great Peter Street, London SW1P 3NQ
Telephone: 0171 333 0100

The Art & Design Directory
AVEC Designs Ltd, PO Box No. 1384, Long Ashton, Bristol BS18 9DF
Telephone: 01275 394639

Business & Technology Education Council (BTEC) Edexcel Foundation
Central House, Upper Woburn Place, London WC1H 0HH
Telephone: 0171 413 8400

The Chartered Society of Designers (CSD)
First Floor, 32–38 Saffron Hill, London EC1N 8FH
Telephone: 0171 831 9777

City & Guilds of London Institute
1 Giltspur Street, London EC1A 9DD
Telephone: 0171 294 2468

Crafts Council
44a Pentonville Road, Islington, London N1 9BY
Telephone: 0171 278 7700

The Design Council
Haymarket House, 1 Oxendon Street, London SW1Y 4EE
Telephone: 0171 208 2121

Design Dimension
Dean Clough, Halifax HX3 5AX
Telephone: 01422 344555

Royal Society of Arts
Examination Board, Westwood Way, Coventry CV4 8HS
Telephone: 01203 470033

National Council for Vocational Qualifications
222 Euston Road, London NW1 2BZ
Telephone: 0171 728 1957

Universities and Colleges Admissions Service (UCAS)
Fulton House, Jessop Avenue, Cheltenham, Gloucestershire GL50 3SH
Telephone: 01242 222444

Index

abstract 50, 54
accreditation 4, 9
amplification 2, 9
art and design 1–2, 5, 78, 91–2
Arts Council of England 86, 100
assessment 2, 9, 83, 85 *see also* self-assessment

BTEC 2, 100
basic design 27
brainstorming 12, 17, 79
brief 12 ,13, 17 ,50, 66, 68, 70, 86

calligraphy 74, 77
cameras 45, 49–51
careers 19, 79, 91–3
case studies 20, 22, 26
chiarascuro 50, 54,
City & Guilds 2
client 84, 90
collage 15, 17
college 4, 73, 91, 92, 94, 97
colour 27, 39–45
common skills 8, 9, 26
communication 4, 9, 19, 22, 63, 71, 82, 94, 97
complementary colours 40–1, 55
composition 63
computer 7, 11, 19, 21, 94
contextual study 19, 26, 82, 97
copying 20
craft 1, 15, 24, 78, 91, 92
creativity 27, 46, 61, 74, 97, 98
critiques 73, 77
cultural influences 74, 86, 92
curriculum vitae 93, 98

design 1, 12, 15, 25, 61, 66, 69, 70, 74, 78, 79, 83, 91, 92
drawing 4, 5, 12, 15, 27, 62, 63, 65, 66, 88, 98

ephemera 11, 17

evidence indicator 2, 9, 72
external testing 3, 9

Fimo 72, 89, 90
fine art drawing 63–4, 72
flow chart 12, 18
form 32, 33, 54, 62
formal elements 27, 54, 57
frottage 34, 55

grading 3, 4, 82
grey scale 41
ground 34, 55
gummed strip 80, 90

hue 42, 43

icon 4, 9
interpersonal skills 8, 9, 95, 96
ideas development 12, 18, 68, 71, 88
inspiration 10, 18, 20, 60

key skills 2, 9, 19, 22, 26

landscape (orientation) 52, 55
light 44, 50
line drawing 8, 15, 29, 30, 31
lino printing 34, 88
logo 52, 55

making techniques 64, 65, 72
maquettes 59, 72
marketing 52, 55
masking materials 53, 55
mechanics 74, 77
media 15, 28, 87
mobile 61, 72
model-making 58, 59
monochrome 43, 55
monoprint 52, 53, 55
mood-board 16, 18, 83

nets 74, 77

notebook   5, 11, 47, 52, 58

objets trouvés   58, 72
opaque   35, 55
outcomes   3, 9, 11, 54, 70, 81, 83, 88, 89

packaging   73–6
painting   80–1
palette   80, 90
paper stretching   80
pattern   30, 32–4
performance criteria   2, 9
personal log book   3, 9, 13, 51
personal reference material   11, 18
personal research   11, 18, 81, 83, 88, 92
perspective   85, 90
photography   45–8
pigment   39, 55
plane   58, 72
portfolio   3, 4, 9, 11, 81
presentation   53, 75, 80, 94, 95
primary colour   40, 43, 55
process   3, 53, 60, 88
professional practice   4, 9, 19, 46, 97
projects   13, 27, 38, 52, 68, 73, 78–90

RSA 2,   100
realisation   75, 77
registration marks   21, 26
relief printing   53, 55
resist   35, 55, 88
role-play   95, 98

scale   59, 72
scrapbook   4, 11, 28
sculpture   58
secondary colour   40, 43, 55
self assessment   13, 14, 17, 28, 39, 51, 54, 62, 69, 82
shape   31–5, 37–8, 55
sketch book   5, 11, 52, 62, 63
spatial   36, 55, 59
spot colour   84, 85, 90
study skills   6
surface pattern   49, 88

tactile   36, 55
talent   10
tertiary colour   40, 43, 55
testing   3
texture   36–9, 58
theoretical studies   see contextual study
thumbnail sketch   12, 18, 75
time management   7, 9
transferable skills   26
translucent   20, 26, 35
transparent   20, 35, 56

unit   2, 9, 78, 89

verifiers (external and internal)   3, 9
visual language   2, 27, 39, 57, 79, 82
visual literacy   51, 56
visual resource   11, 18, 53, 85
vocational units   2, 9

word association   12, 18, 64, 79